During the final years of the last century, there still stood a mansion in Limehouse, to the east of London, known as The House on the River.

Here men with bizarre tastes would meet once a month in order to terrify each other by means of true stories of horror and the supernatural. Those story-tellers who failed to impress the assembly were – it is said – never seen again. Those who succeeded were permitted to join:

THE CLUB OF THE DAMNED

Supernatural

Seven stories based on the
television series on BBC-1

Devised and Edited by Robert Muller

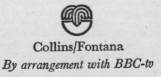

Collins/Fontana

By arrangement with BBC-tv

First published by Fontana Books 1977

© Robert Muller 1977

Made and printed in Great Britain by
William Collins Sons & Co Ltd Glasgow

Bmarte (handwritten)

CONTENTS

DORABELLA

or

IN LOVE WITH DEATH

adapted by Rosemary Timperley

It was called the Club of the Damned, that secret society to which Sir Dermot Flood introduced his young nephew Richard that night. The members held their hidden meetings in an old house of ruined splendour, near the river Thames to the east of Limehouse. Richard had often urged him to take him to one of the bizarre meetings, as a guest, but now that they were on their way there, he felt distinctly nervous.

His uncle had told him that to become a life member of the Club, one had to tell a story of terror, a true tale based on personal experience. If it sufficiently chilled the blood of the listeners, one was duly enrolled. If not, if there was even one black ball among the whites at voting time, then the applicant had failed. Not only that. Rumour had it that a failed applicant was never seen again. So Richard was thankful to be merely a visitor – sworn to secrecy but not this time required to make the macabre bid for membership.

And what an eerie night it was! Swirling mist blown by an icy wind. No sound except the lapping of water, the mournful hoot of distant vessels and the echo of footsteps. The friendly clip-clop of the horses of the hansom-cab which had brought Sir Dermot and his nephew to the House on the River had long since died away. All the elements combined to chill the blood . . .

Then suddenly the two men came upon the house – a Georgian building, unexpectedly splendid in the squalid surroundings. Lights shone from many of its windows.

'Is that it?' Richard whispered.

His uncle nodded. 'Yes, Richard. This is indeed the House on the River.'

Lackeys in eighteenth-century livery opened the doors to allow the men inside. They padded along a shadowy wine-red corridor with red curtains and carpets, and were ushered into a warm, crowded drawing-room.

This was attractive enough at first glance, with its bright log fire and blazing chandelier and friendly cigar-smoke. But on the walls hung pictures of horrors: vampires, werewolves, spectres, ghosts, all of them looking half-alive to young Richard as the firelight flickered.

Around the fire were easy chairs, tables set with glasses and delicacies to eat – and the assembled members of the Club. They were men of different types, old and young, handsome and deformed, well-dressed and shabby, but they all shared one characteristic: a certain look, *an expression in the eyes, as if they had seen more than men should ever wish to see – as if they had gazed into the very abyss of hell.*

Sir Dermot had already settled down in one of the soft deep velvet chairs; the other members were forming a closer group round the story-teller of the night.

From where young Richard sat, he couldn't see his face, only the silhouette of his head. Somehow that mysterious head added to the anticipatory fear that Richard felt as Philip Hambledon began his story . . .

When I was a young man, long, long ago, I knew a man called Walter von Lamont. He was born in a Scandinavian country, the only son of aristocratic landowners. When Walter was ten, the family estate burned down in mysterious circumstances and his parents perished in the flames. He was sent to England and brought up by childless relations in the country. When they, too, died, Walter inherited their wealth and set out to spend it freely. He took to travelling about Europe in search of adventure or, as he once confessed to me, to seek out and recapture his 'lost childhood'. I did not then know what he meant. Perhaps it was because of my own conventional upbringing, my predictable, moral steadfastness, as he called it, that Walter asked me to be his travelling companion, though it seemed to me that more often than not I was an encumbrance, even an obstacle, a censor to his wilder and more extravagant excursions . . .

All this happened a long time ago, before the railways began to spread like spiders' tentacles across the entire continent of Europe. We travelled by public coach, collectors of the unusual, the forbidden, the unique experience, but in truth searching, I now believe, for the instruments of our own destruction . . .

It is of the day that we first beheld the sharpest of these tools of fate that I speak now.

We were travelling by coach. Outside the rain swept down, and I observed that, probably to keep boredom away, Walter began to make secret signals to one of our fellow-passengers, a girl who sat primly between her parents. The hidden love-play embarrassed me and I looked forward to reaching our destination – an inn near the foothills of the Palatinate mountains.

We alighted and went into the inn's public room with its white walls, wooden tables, and candles lighting up the surrounding gloom. A few people were gathered there already and a couple of serving-girls dashed between kitchen and tables, carrying out customers' orders. Walter preferred what he called 'these common coaching inns' to more elegant premises. He clearly found 'disreputable' company more stimulating than the other sort.

The coach passengers sat down to eat and drink and chat among themselves, while their shadows danced on the walls. Across the tables Walter was still discreetly flirting with the girl-passenger, but it was obvious to me that he was growing bored already. Where was the promised excitement? It was then that Walter, with a glass of wine half-way to his lips, suddenly halted, staring over my shoulder at the bleak windows.

I turned to look. There was a new arrival. A private coach had drawn up outside the inn and a woman had alighted. She stood quite still for a second, an exquisite figure in voluminous beaver furs, then looked up at the inn sign. Her face was shadowed, but I could see that her eyes were exceptionally large and luminous. Ageless eyes. Haunting.

In her hand the girl was carrying a cage made of golden wire. I rose and opened the window slightly. What was it inside the golden cage? A black bird of some sort? Yes – a raven!

Walter, all lassitude departed, was already hurrying out

to offer to help with her luggage, but servants had by now carried her one trunk inside. I saw her smiling as she passed Walter the cage with the raven. He took it, then looked up at the sky – 'How extraordinary!' I could hear him remark. 'The rain has stopped. Quite suddenly.'

'But of course, sir,' said the young woman.

'Why "of course"? It's been pouring all day.'

She smiled. 'I *wished* it to stop. I abominate wet fur, don't you?' Laughing, she whispered something to him, then strode into the inn, Walter following with the caged raven. I stood by the window as if turned to stone, quite unable to move.

The landlord had come forward to greet her and to guide her towards the staircase leading to the upper floors. Walter, too, was standing quite still, gazing after her. With a dazed expression he handed the cage to the landlord and turned towards me.

As he passed by, the girl with whom he had been flirting before was trying to catch his eye. She even dropped her glove, hoping he would retrieve it. But Walter ignored her completely. It was as if she no longer existed for him. His whole frame was shaking with excitement as he reached for his glass.

'Do you know her?' I asked him. 'Who is that lovely creature?'

'Her name is – Dorabella,' Walter answered. And he made the name sound like a caress.

We sat down at our table again, finishing our drinks in silence. Waiting. Hoping. And not in vain. After an hour or so the apparition – Dorabella as I must henceforth call her – descended the stairs and sat down at one of the empty tables.

She was dressed in white and jewels glittered in her ears and about her neck. All this, added to the shimmering effect of candlelight, tended to obscure her face except for those remarkable shining eyes. Her beauty made my heart beat faster, but her effect on Walter was far more extreme. He looked consumed with desire. And more than desire: a terrible, unspeakable fear.

But someone else had arrived while we waited for

Dorabella: a young poet, apparently engaged to entertain the guests. He was now reciting a macabre poem of death, and as he recited he strummed a mandolin. Darkly handsome, with a pale hollow-eyed consumptive look about him, the young poet's performance was so intense that he seemed to be burning himself out before our very eyes. And all the time his coal-like eyes were fixed on Dorabella, while she returned his gaze as if her eyes were drawing the words from his mouth – and with them his very life-blood. We listened with ardour:

> The first that died was little Jane;
> In bed she moaning lay,
> Till God released her of her pain;
> And then she went away.
>
> So in the churchyard she was laid;
> And when the grass was dry,
> Together round her grave we played
> My Brother John and I.
>
> And when the ground was white with snow,
> And I could run and slide,
> My Brother John was forced to go,
> And he lies by her side.
>
> 'How many are you then?' said I,
> 'If they two are in Heaven?'
> The little maiden did reply,
> 'O Master! We are seven!'
>
> 'But they are dead; those two are dead!
> Their spirits are in Heaven!'
> 'Twas throwing words away:
> for still
>   the little maid would
> have her will
> And said
> 'Nay, we are seven!'

As soon as he had concluded the poem the poet bowed to the applause, then stood like a statue, staring first at Dorabella, then – with unmistakable hostility – at Walter.

Choosing to ignore the poet's dark glances, Walter leaned across to Dorabella. 'So now who else will entertain us? Did you not tell me, madam, that you can perform magic tricks?'

'Tricks, sir?' A touch of mockery. 'Only if the fancy so takes me.'

'Then let it take you now! Enchant me! A little artificial snow perhaps as a change from the beastly rain – or a duet with my young friend Philip. He sings surpassing well.'

I felt deeply embarrassed.

'Walter,' I interjected, 'our new friend may wish to rest.'

'I shall sing for your young friend,' Dorabella said suddenly. 'He demands much less more courteously!'

'Magnificent!' cried Walter. 'Ladies and gentlemen, silence pray! My supper guest has graciously consented to entertain you. Make way, give her passage.' Already rather drunk, he bowed Dorabella into the centre of the room.

The poet retreated into the background, but there he stood his ground, staring . . . I watched Dorabella picking up his discarded mandolin, and handing it to Walter.

'We will start. Play for me,' she commanded.

Walter began to play, tentatively at first, then gaining confidence as the woman sang. Her voice was sweet and delicate as a snowdrop.

I sat enchanted – yet suddenly, to my shivering disquiet, I thought I could hear, behind the singer's voice and the notes of the mandolin, some shrill and unearthly music being played by an invisible violin – painful, nagging music reminding me of an aching tooth. Had anyone else, I wondered, heard the high-pitched hum? The poet perhaps? Walter? Or was I taking leave of my senses?

Dorabella's voice grew softer, softer, until she seemed to be singing with a silent voice – than which nothing could be sweeter – and as her lips closed at the end of the song, the sound of the ethereal violin, too, ceased to assail my ears.

There was sincere applause for Dorabella's song. Two local youths approached her with a basket of fruit, and smiling her thanks, Dorabella picked out two shining red apples. Then – to our astonishment – she began to juggle with them – like the most expert of performers. Then, suddenly, she stopped, pointing imperiously to the raven in its golden cage. Walter, who was still clutching the mandolin, hurried across the room to the cage, thrusting the mandolin into my own hands as he went. Then I saw him picking up the cage to carry it back to Dorabella.

The moment she placed it on the table I could hear the mysterious violin music begin again . . . shrill, painful music – a tooth aching . . .

Now Dorabella bent over the cage and pressed her lips against it.

And – had my eyes deceived me? – the raven – *disappeared!*

'A magician!' cried the two youths. 'Wonderful!'

Now Dorabella turned once more to Walter and held out her hand. A diamond ring glistened on one finger. Walter, with rapt admiration, leaned over to kiss her hand, and as he did so – *Dorabella faded away entirely.*

Silence gripped the room. Then came the first gasps of wonderment. Where was she? I felt a sudden icy fear around my heart. This was surely more than conjuring – it was witchcraft! And then – a moment later – there she sat again at another table, laughing and applauding, as if someone other than herself had been responsible for the entire performance.

Before I could stop him, Walter had raced across the room, scattering chairs and crockery in his wake. I watched him take the laughing girl in his arms, joyously shouting over and over again: 'Magic! Magic!' So, I told myself – not without grim foreboding – he has found her – Walter has found the woman of his dreams at last – a creature of beauty, wit, intelligence – with a dash of mystery – indeed of sorcery.

From this moment, I realized he was hers to command . . .

But now the young poet, who had been so eerily still, sprang forward, clutching a small dagger in his hand.

Tonelessly, he kept reiterating: '*And-now-give-me-back-what-does-not-belong-to-you.*'

Walter, startled, picked up the mandolin and held it out to him. But the pale young man did not take it. He stood quite still, his eyes staring . . . then he raised the dagger and pointed it at Walter's chest. The other jumped to his feet, firmly seized the poet's wrist and without much difficulty managed to change the direction of the blade. With a crazed, joyous shout, the poet stabbed wildly, again and again, plunging the knife not into Walter's chest, but into his own.

Screams broke out. A few people fled the room. The poet held his hand against his wounded breast then withdrew it, gazing numbly at the blood on his fingers. He turned to Dorabella, opening his lips to speak, but Walter quickly stepped between her and the sick, wounded poet. And as – like some sick animal – he lurched sideways from the room, he left a trail of tiny drops of blood . . .

Dorabella had watched it all without apparent emotion. When at last she spoke, it was in a quiet, cool voice. 'I must see to him,' she announced. 'Don't follow me.'

'No – ' Walter tried to stop her, but she brushed him aside, swiftly following the trail of blood. Then she was gone.

'She will be back,' Walter murmured.

But we waited many hours that night and Dorabella did not return.

Finally we retired to our separate rooms.

Walter – so he told me later – did not undress at all. He lay on his bed, his eyes wide open, listening, listening . . . to the eerie sounds of the small hours: a dog barking, the wind whistling down the chimneys – and then . . . then a flapping of something against the small barred window. Leaves? Insects? Bats' wings? Then, quickly, came another sound: footsteps – a woman's – coming closer and closer, and – yes! – stopping outside the door. In the sudden silence, Walter gazed, petrified, at the door-handle. Earlier that night, it had seemed ordinary enough. Now – or were his eyes deceiving him? – it appeared to have altered its shape – it looked like a wolf's head – and it seemed to turn –

and creakingly the door seemed to open – and though Walter realized that he must be imagining all this (had someone drugged his wine?) . . . a terrible doubt remained in his heart. The night was suffused with – *magic*.

A distant scream outside made him leap up from his bed – a cry of anguish and terror. Walter looked towards the window, and stared at – a face, a human face, but what kind of a face? It was the visage of a hideous old crone, eyes staring, lips parted, grinning and gibbering.

Walter let out a croak of sheer terror, dived down under the bedclothes and wrapped them round him. He shuddered under this mound until dawn came and birds sang, dispelling the night – but not the nightmare.

Haunted still, he got up and went downstairs. There he found me – his friend and companion – standing in the doorway of the inn, looking out at the cobbled courtyard. An old cart stood at the far end and two stable lads were pushing a wheelbarrow towards it. The barrow was not empty. Something lay inert under a death-black cloth. Walter hurried across the yard and lifted the cloth.

Over his shoulder I could see the body of the passionate young poet; his face and throat were chalk-white, as if all the blood had been drained from his veins.

Somebody, *something* had killed him during the night. *A wild beast – a wolf?* Walter and I looked at each other with shame and terror . . .

Then he replaced the black cloth: 'Where's Dorabella?' he asked.

We went to find the landlord, who at first proved to be incoherent. Dorabella had gone, using – or so the landlord claimed – the public stage-coach. She had left a note for Walter, in which she asked us to be good enough to convey her own carriage and her luggage to a town some twenty kilometres to the north, where she would meet us once again for supper.

I naturally imagined that Walter would share my own forebodings. Yet, despite all the extraordinary events and terrors of the previous night, he was quite determined to continue with our adventure.

'But we intended to go south,' I protested. 'Why must we

do as she asks?'

'We must,' Walter said simply. 'There's no choice.'

I could see that Walter was a man possessed. It seemed extraordinary to me that he could not even then see the simple truth – that Dorabella had lost one friend and was now eager to supplant him with another. Clearly his infatuation had so intoxicated him that he was blind to the dangers of his new situation.

That first morning, as I looked upon his features, contorted with desire and dread, I thought I detected the pallid sheen I had first seen on the face of the young poet . . .

And so the second coach journey began, very different from the first. Dorabella's private carriage, far more elegant than any public coach we'd used before, was drawn by four black horses. And there were no fellow-passengers this time. Just Walter and myself – and Dorabella's trunk.

That trunk . . . it was scarlet, encrusted with jewels, and unbelievably heavy . . . We had gasped and panted as we had lifted it into the carriage.

And then there was the raven in its golden cage, physically lightweight, yet its very presence seemed to crush our spirits.

While I sat inside the coach, left to watch over our strange luggage, Walter sat on the coachman's seat, driving like a madman. He yelled at the horses and lashed them with whips. He was almost foaming at the mouth with impatience to reach the promised rendezvous with his strange beloved . . .

My own fear and unease increased with every second. Dorabella *was* beautiful . . . I could understand Walter's desperation . . . and yet . . . and yet . . . here we were, impelled to go north, when we had planned to go south.

Then another thought struck me – the horses seemed a little too familiar with the route. I could see that they were only pretending to be driven. How many others had come along this road before – in this luxurious coach – with its black horses, scarlet trunk and magic raven? And what happened to them in the end? And what end precisely awaited us at our destination?

Night had come when we arrived at the second inn. We took, as Dorabella had instructed us in her letter, three rooms. The first for Walter, the second for me. Into the third room we carried the scarlet, jewel-encrusted trunk. Candles were lit. Then the room was left empty to await Dorabella's arrival.

Walter and I went to our own rooms. I could hear Walter order wine, then listlessly pace up and down. As for me, I sat alone, seized by a grim sense of fatigue and foreboding.

Instead of looking forward with happy anticipation to the adventures and sport that a first evening in an unknown town might bring I felt deeply uneasy, suspecting that what my poor friend needed were neither the laughter of a friend nor the attentions of a new mistress, but the speedy ministrations of a doctor. Yet I did nothing . . .

The sound of Walter's pacing finally wore me down and I went to his room.

'What's the matter?' I asked.

Walter turned away, then in a distant voice he said to me: 'I think I'm going mad, my friend.'

'You've drunk too much wine,' I said consolingly, 'and you drove those poor horses beyond all reason. Try to rest now.'

'Rest!' Walter shouted, with sudden violence. 'So that *you* can inherit?'

'Inherit?'

'You can't deny it – I see it in your eyes – you want her too.'

'Walter, have we ever quarrelled over a woman, or ever desired the same – '

'But she *can't* be resisted! That's beyond dispute! Don't deny it!'

I had to turn away from Walter's rage-distorted face. 'Shall we meet for dinner?'

'Ah,' Walter shrieked. 'Then you do not deny it! Can you swear you are not drawn to her?'

'I *can*, but I *will* not,' I told him coldly. 'I shall order my dinner.'

'Listen!' he called after me. 'I must tell you! I have to! There's simply no one else to tell!' With some distaste I found that he was clutching my sleeve now like some demented beggar. 'There's one thing I crave more even than Dorabella – and that is to find out what is inside that scarlet trunk. I must see inside it, Philip! And I will.'

I shrugged my shoulders coldly and walked out, fleeing from my poor friend's demented cries. 'I will – I will – '

And with the decision came the deed.

After he thought I had left him to go to dinner, Walter took a lighted candle and crept with stealth along the passage to the 'third room', where the scarlet trunk waited, by candlelight.

The wind was howling outside like banshees on the prowl, but Walter did not heed its warning. He reached the door of the room, opened it, ignored the creaking of the hinges.

And I saw through the keyhole:

There he crouched, setting down his candle; kneeling in a state of crazed excitement before the mysterious red trunk. His hands rested limply on the lid. All the strength seemed to have drained from him. He had to open it – he wanted to – but how? Who or what had sapped his proud strength?

The violet-coloured curtains quivered. He glanced up, staring at the trembling material. He had begun to feel faint. Violets blurred together – a mass of flowers – a total blur – too much violet – then darkness –

And then the opening of his eyes and light again. And a beautiful figure in green velvet standing before him.

'Dorabella – ' He stretched out his arms jerkily.

Her strong arms came round him, embracing him tightly – 'You were impatient,' she reprimanded him softly.

'I think I fainted – forgive me,' Walter murmured, gazing at the shadowed face of her beauty, haloed by candlelight. Her face, I realized, always seemed obscured in some way. Neither of us had ever seen it by day.

Lightly she told him: 'You must learn to be more obedient to your lady's wishes.'

'Forgive me.' He tried to kiss her, but she drew away.

'No,' she said. 'Do you wish to stay with me? If so, there will be all the time in the world for kisses.'

'When?'

'Soon. When you and I are among those who love me.'

'It's I who love you, Dorabella.'

'I have a father whose blessing we must obtain before – well – ' She came close to him again and pressed her face against his shoulder, as if overcome by shyness.

'Yes, I see,' he said tenderly.

'Then I shall be yours, and you mine. But first I must make two conditions.' Her voice hardened. 'I've been ill. My father sent me to the south to get better, but I'm still fragile. That's why I must sleep during the day, and why you and Philip must continue to travel without me, bringing my luggage with you.'

'And the other condition?'

'You will be tempted to open my trunk, just as you were tempted tonight. You must resist that temptation . . . my love. Will you swear to resist it? Will you?'

She cupped his chin with her hands and held his eyes with hers. Then they kissed, and in the frame of that keyhole I could see that Walter was now totally caught up in a dark whirlwind of ecstasy.

So we began to travel northwards again, further north even than the land of Walter's 'lost childhood'.

Walter acted as coachman, whipping the black horses along roads glazed with frost, across lifeless valleys, through sombre pine-forests, while I crouched inside the carriage with only the red trunk and the caged raven for company. I became increasingly aware not only of the frightening alteration in Walter, but of a profound change in our relationship. He, whom I had known since childhood, became almost a stranger to me. He lost the precious gift of laughter, and became haunted by daylight dreads, phantoms and intimations of the nearness of death – a death personified, as if someone from across a dark river was beckoning to him, commanding him to follow.

His inner loneliness was complete. One day he got out of the carriage and I watched him as he stood in a high wind on a stretch of bleak moorland. He held his body strangely, as if he were not a living man at all but a scarecrow. And I feared for his sanity – and my own.

Only at night, after reaching some inn in a village or small town, did Walter's spirits revive. For it was then that Dorabella would mysteriously reappear, never explaining her absence or her mode of travel, instantly captivating Walter, and – yes, I must confess it – myself too, with her beauty, her vitality and good humour. When she was like that, there seemed to be nothing to fear at all. Dorabella's radiance lit up even the gloomiest of our resting places.

Yet throughout those cold nights and days, I could not help becoming more and more aware of my friend's strange deterioration. It was as if his entire being was slowly being sapped of its strength, its individuality and purpose, and sometimes of its self-control.

One night, after we reached an inn, we found Dorabella there already, ravishingly lovely in a red cloak. Walter ran to embrace her in the dark, and I stayed a few paces behind watching as they kissed passionately, suppressing my own feeling of desire.

Later, we dined in a private dining-room. A serving-girl waited on us, a pretty wench. Walter began to eat voraciously, like a greedy animal. Dorabella's eyes met mine across the table. I felt as if my heart had been pierced. Then she pushed her plate away, her food untouched, whispered a reproof to Walter and held a glass of wine to his lips: an amorous invitation. And amorousness is catching. The young serving-girl winked at me, and I grabbed her bare arm playfully. The girl enthusiastically kissed me full on the lips, and I was about to respond when – when I saw that Dorabella, who had seemed to be so absorbed in Walter only a few seconds before, was glaring at me with wide-open eyes. There was an icy rage in that glare, and, shaken, I released the girl instantly. She laughed scornfully and left the room. Only then did Dorabella turn her cold eyes away from me, but not, I regret to say, before Walter had noticed the incident. Henceforth, he saw in me not the true friend that I was, but a rival . . .

Next morning a further shock awaited us. As we passed through the courtyard of the inn on the way to the carriage, we noticed a wheelbarrow with something slung on top of a load of hay.

Something? It was the dead body of that poor serving-girl who had flirted so sweetly with me the night before. I could see that her face was drained of all colour; her eyes were fixed in a stare of horror.

Quickly, wordlessly, guiltily, we hurried away from the dreadful sight.

That day I climbed into the coachman's seat and it was Walter who crouched inside, half-asleep, his feet resting on the scarlet trunk. In the afternoon, as the sun came out briefly, we got out to sit and eat by the side of a lake. It was bitterly cold. Nearby we could see a narrow wooden jetty, a landing-stage for small boats. I watched my friend's crazed eyes staring at the horizon.

'My dear friend,' I said impulsively, 'even now it's not too late to – '

'One cannot undo one's actions, even if one so wished,' he interrupted.

'We could take the carriage on to the next village and then return by post-chaise.'

'Where we are going,' said Walter, a strange smile hovering around his lips, 'there is no post-chaise. You know that.'

'Walter – I beg of you – let us return home! This is no longer mere adventure. Wherever we follow *her* we meet with terror, disappearance and murder – '

'Then *you* return,' he muttered. 'I do not need you. *I* must go on.'

'Must I say it? Can't you feel the evil force that she radiates?'

'Evil force?' Walter jeered. 'Because she prefers me to you?'

It was then that I drew a cross from my pocket. 'At least carry this, close to your heart, for your protection – '

Walter stared at me. 'My poor Philip,' he said quietly. 'You love her too, and her indifference has unhinged your mind.' And he stumped away towards the carriage, entered it, and placed his hands, which had become oddly claw-like, upon the locks of the scarlet trunk. He struggled with them and even managed to raise the lid a few inches. But before he could look inside, he was half-stifled by the smell which came out. He let out a yell of anguish and staggered backwards against the carriage door.

'What is it?' I cried.

'Sulphur!' he said, slamming down the lid of the trunk.

And then we both heard – through the whine of the wind – the sound of Dorabella's echoing, disembodied laughter. Galvanized into action, Walter wrenched himself away from my protective arms and ran out towards the jetty, from where he imagined the sound had come. 'Dorabella!' he cried. 'Dorabella – ' He was wailing her name over and over again, as I hurried to his side.

And for a fleeting second, we both seemed actually to *see* her standing there at the end of the jetty – transparent and ghostly, wreathed in a flowing white shroud which quivered in the wind. There and yet not there, she seemed to be part of the earth and the air and the mist and the cold, cold greyness of everything. She was smiling and beckoning as, in the distance, a raven cawed. Then she vanished.

Had we really seen her?

And while we went off to search that jetty for signs of life, signs even of a phantom, something was happening in the empty carriage. *The lid of the scarlet trunk was being slowly raised, from the inside . . .*

'Walter!' A seductive voice floated across to the lake. And there – as we came hurrying back – was indeed Dorabella, standing by the carriage door, exquisite in her beaver furs, smiling a welcome. Behind her, the lid of the trunk was tightly shut.

Walter, demented with joy, took her in his arms. Then they settled down together, arms about each other, and I left them to climb up to the coachman's seat.

For a while they travelled on in silence, except for exchanges of whispers and lovers' kisses. Then I heard Dorabella coo into Walter's ear: 'I shall have made him so happy.'

'Him? Who?'

'My father of course. Haven't I brought home a bridegroom?'

'Oh, my dearest Dorabella, all day when I'm alone, there are a thousand questions I promise myself I'll ask you – '

'But why questions, my love? Why furrow your handsome brow? Our love must be simple. As simple as life and death itself. Look at me – watch me – laugh with me!'

He looked with love at her laughing face in the half-dark. He did not notice her hands. From her furs, she brought out two glasses which, by some magic unknown to man, filled themselves with wine. She offered one to him. He drank. Then he lay back against the black cushions, eyes closed. And for this little while my tormented friend looked almost happy.

But when night was over, and dawn broke, and light poured into the carriage, Dorabella had vanished . . .

When Walter woke, he accepted her disappearance as just one more of her 'magic tricks'. She was leading him a dance, but he loved the dance, even more than he feared it.

Even the brief joys did not last, for Walter now made a fatal error. One night, instead of following Dorabella's instructions about the inn at which we should stay, he determined to stop the carriage elsewhere. Guiltily, he waited for her to arrive. 'She's late,' he mused, 'so late again tonight.'

'Are you surprised?' I asked bluntly. 'This is not the inn of her choice.'

'But it is a much better one. She'll be happy at my decision.'

I doubted it. 'Shall we play cards while we wait?'

'No. I wouldn't be able to concentrate.'

'You're not well, my poor Walter.'

'On the contrary. I've never felt more vigorous,' he said defiantly. 'Oh, my friend, can't you see that I'm about to find true fulfilment at last? Every single moment with her is magic.'

'And if, in practising her magic, she were to make herself disappear forever?'

'What are you saying?'

'That even now there is time to turn back.'

'Now? When every day brings us closer home?'

'Home? Whose home? My friend, you must now hear the truth! Every day you're growing weaker and more deluded. I have watched it happen. Sometimes I no longer recognize you.'

Walter giggled feebly. 'But I'm enchanted! Don't you see? Enchanted!'

A sudden screech startled us. On the window-sill sat Dorabella's raven. At the same moment a gust of wind howled past us, and the door was blown open violently. Leaves swept into the room. And there, among the dead foliage stood Dorabella herself. Her eyes were angry and her voice icy as she said: 'This is not the inn.'

'Dearest, don't be angry,' Walter began. 'I thought – '

'You *thought*! I *know* this journey. I know every town, every village, every inn. Why have you chosen to defy me?' She turned to me. 'Or is this *your* doing?'

As I could only shake my head, she turned back to Walter. 'I dislike this room, and the one to which you have seen fit to consign my luggage is even worse. Don't you understand that your wilfulness could destroy us all?'

As Walter muttered apologies, I happened to glance at the mirror in the room. I could see myself; I could see Walter – *but where was the woman?*

For Dorabella cast no reflection.

The raven on the sill let out another screech – a warning of doom.

Dorabella was still scolding Walter: 'We shall not stay here. The inn whose name I gave you is farther up the hill. Our rooms for the night are prepared. Come.' She flounced out and Walter followed meekly. The wind caught the door and shut it heavily. Left alone, I felt trapped now. I looked at the window, but the raven had gone. Once more, I turned towards the revealing mirror. And something even more frightening happened then: I suddenly had a sensation of invisible fingers closing around my throat, trying to strangle the life out of me. I raised my own hands to fight off the deadly power, watched myself in the mirror gasping and squirming. Then, as suddenly as it had pounced, the murderous power released me, leaving me feeling limp and sick. And my ears were assailed once more by that eerily high-pitched violin sound that I had heard the first time I set eyes on Dorabella. Another sound broke in – short and sharp.

The mirror had cracked.

By the time daylight came, and we were once more proceeding on our journey, I had persuaded myself that my sole reason for going on was my desire to protect my poor, ailing friend . . . Yet – the onslaught the previous night by a force both powerful and invisible had strengthened all my forebodings. Sitting in my coachman's seat, the reins limply dangling in my hands, I observed bitterly that the strange lassitude that had overwhelmed poor Walter was also beginning to afflict me. However – as we approached our goal, Dorabella's home, I became aware that there was no longer any need to guide the horses. Travelling at great speed, without help from me they seemed to know their way . . .

And meanwhile, inside the rapidly-moving carriage, Walter was again overwhelmed by his curiosity. He was fumbling with the locks of the scarlet trunk, managed to lift the lid a little. Once more the sulphurous fumes blew into his face, but this time he was prepared for it. He wouldn't give in. He prised the lid further open, his eyes peering into the gap –

A flash of lightning instantly blazed from inside the trunk, and I could hear a clap of thunder. Struggling against the blinding light, Walter continued to open the lid . . .

And now a vision formed before his eyes: he could see a huge chandelier, burning with a hundred candles; then suddenly they were gutted, as if blown out by a gale. Beyond the smoking candles he saw the hall of a castle – a twisting staircase – a marble table – an open fire burning in the hearth – and a high-backed, nobly-carved wooden chair. Now weakness overcame him. His fingers lost their grip on the lid. It slammed down on his hand, making the blood spurt!

Walter screamed out with pain. Then, staring at his red-stained hand, he watched the blood begin to disappear, as if sucked away by magic.

The carriage jerked to a halt. I clambered down and came to the carriage window.

Walter tried to hide his hurt hand. 'It was nothing.'

I opened the carriage door. 'My God, Walter! Your eyes! What did you see?'

Shuddering, the other answered in a hushed whisper: 'I reached for the infinite, Philip, the unimaginable. I held hands – with death.'

And so on we travelled, past the point of no return. The horses had taken charge. When at last the animals deigned to stop, we found ourselves outside a great black castle, looming high over the twisting road. Few lights burned from its glowering windows. As lightning struck the sky, and thunder roared, Walter and I got out of the carriage. Like doomed men, we carried out Dorabella's trunk, to begin the slow trudge towards the castle gates.

A small wooden door set inside the gates opened, and four gnome-like, white-haired figures in black scurried out. Two of them carried the trunk inside. The other two bowed and begged the visitors to enter.

The door closed behind us.

We were inside Dorabella's castle.

When we entered the hall, Walter recognized the reality of that vision which he had seen in the forbidden trunk: here indeed was the huge chandelier with its hundred blazing candles, but this time the wind blew without extinguishing the flames. Here, too, was the twisting stair-case, the marble table, the open fire, and the nobly-carved wooden chair. The scene was set for the final agony.

And down the staircase came Dorabella, radiant in white, smiling and holding out her arms.

In a trice, the lovers were in a fond embrace. I watched Dorabella's eyes close in ecstasy, but when suddenly they opened it was not at Walter they gazed, but at me.

An aristocratic figure, white-haired and dressed in black, now came down the stairs. Though clearly old, he was as vigorous as a youth. His teeth were a dazzling white, his lips very red.

Dorabella's father came straight up to Walter and

gripped his hands in a firm double handshake. And Dorabella's face was aglow with triumph.

Later that night we dined in state at the marble table, under
the blazing chandelier. The father sat at the head of the
table, Dorabella opposite. I sat on the father's left, facing
Walter, whose eyes shone brightly.

'Are you happy, Papa?' Dorabella asked the old man.

He raised his glass to her.

'My search has come to an end!' she exulted.

Then Dorabella's father began to tell us his family
history, although, oddly, he gave that family no name.

'Ours is an old race,' he said, 'perhaps the oldest in the
world. Upon achieving maturity, our women are sent out
into the world to seek a bridegroom from another country.
Thus the race is rejuvenated and saved from decline.'

Again I could feel Dorabella's eyes on me, rather than
on her supposed bridegroom. I firmly averted my own eyes
to watch the four white-haired servants. For the first time I
realized that they were blind, but so swift and sure-footed
were they that they could easily do all the work of the house.
I also noticed that now the raven's cage, by Dorabella's
chair, was empty, as the father's voice went on:

'Many suitors have come forward to claim my daughter's
hand but, invariably, each one was found wanting in some
respect.' With lowered eyelids, he smiled dazzlingly at
Walter, who moved uneasily and glanced at Dorabella for
reassurance. Would he, too, be 'found wanting'?

She raised her glass, but it was difficult to see to whom
the gesture was made: to Walter, or to me.

Suddenly Walter's hand shook. He spilt his wine, which
flowed red like blood over the white marble surface . . .

When the macabre dinner-party was over, we retired to
our rooms. Walter, the bridegroom, was given the Black
Room, with its four-poster bed and white hangings, and
billowing white curtains over a half-open arched window.
He had lit a candle; the room remained full of sinister
shadows. Reclining fully-dressed on the bed, he found himself staring at the handle of the door – *shaped like the head of a
wolf.*

27

And from the window came an ominous 'Tap-tap-tap...'

Walter got up to close it, and saw the raven on the sill, screeching as if to mock his terror. Tentatively, Walter stretched out his arm to shut the window, when he heard the unearthly hum of a high-pitched violin, and at the window there now appeared again the face of the old crone, open-mouthed, cackling.

Fear now took possession of him. He stumbled back towards the bed, muttering. But someone had begun to follow. Someone? *Something*. An apparition? *Dorabella*.

She was wearing that same billowing white shroud in which he had seen her that day on the dusky jetty. Had that been real or a dream? Was this real or a dream? His mind was crumbling...

Now the apparition bent over him, enveloped him in her arms. He was sobbing like a terrified child. 'Hush,' she whispered. 'How pale you look. Rest, dearest. Tomorrow you will sleep, and the day after. You will use the day as I do, for sleep. You must do all the things that I do. Soon you will be as I am, forever young, *immortal* – '

Her whispering ceased. His candle went out.

Walter was alone – with the dark.

Next day Walter had to go through the engagement ceremony with Dorabella. He was in a state of near-collapse. I watched as the blind, white-haired servants gave him support throughout the strange ritual.

Though Dorabella's father himself officiated, I could not hear the words. For I was being treated like a prisoner in the castle. Doors were locked against me. Sometimes my own door was locked from the outside: I was trapped. The blind servants were uncanny gaolers, seeming to have the gift of sight in the tips of their fingers. They seemed to know exactly where I was; they made me come, go or stay as *they* pleased. Now all I was allowed to do was to stand at a discreet distance to watch Walter and Dorabella's wedding ceremony – no more, no less.

The ceremony reached its climax. Dorabella's father took a spiked ring from a small scarlet casket, a miniature replica of Dorabella's trunk. He placed it around the couple's little fingers. The spike was a golden thorn. Walter's face twisted with pain as it cut into his flesh. Then Dorabella removed her own finger from the thorn-ring-trap. She looked at Walter with a voluptuous expression, then kissed his injured finger.

They were betrothed.

And I could see my friend, and perhaps myself too, condemned for all eternity to exist in this grey limbo, somehow suspended between life and death – unless, even now, we could escape. Tomorrow, perhaps. After dark. But first I had to talk with Walter alone.

On the following day, the chance came more easily than I had expected. The servants had left me alone to walk with Walter along the corridors of the castle. Walter looked pallid – like a ghost.

'I have a plan,' I told him. 'We're going to escape from here. Soon. After dusk . . . When the servants are lighting the chandeliers, we'll creep down to the cellars and wait there till – '

'It's too late,' said Walter. 'And I'm too weak now. It's begun already, don't you see? The ecstasy. It's begun. Let it be. Let *me* be.'

That is when I became stronger than my friend. I succeeded in persuading him to come down to the cellars at dusk. As the sun set, I watched him descend, more ghost-like than ever, carrying a candelabrum. Together we felt our way like blind men down the stone steps of the castle.

We heard bats beating their wings; then the unearthly cries of night-birds. My poor friend clung to me like a child as we reached the foot of the steps. At first we could make out only each other's faces. Then shapes seemed to form in that vile darkness.

What were we seeing? Tombstones? Coffins? Trunks? We fell against a heavy object. 'It's all right,' I told Walter. 'Hold on to me.'

Then I saw what we had stumbled against: two trunks, a black one with gold locks, and a scarlet one encrusted with jewels – Dorabella's trunk.

'My God!' I gasped for, as we regarded it, the lid of the

trunk was rising slowly.

'Hold on to me,' Walter sobbed. 'I can't go on.'

The lid of the red trunk now opened wide. A few thin wisps of yellow smoke curled out. We had to hold handkerchiefs to our noses to keep out the hellish stench.

Walter drew further back; gearing up all my courage, it was I who stepped forward, lowered my face, and allowed my eyes to gaze down into that trunk . . .

And what I saw was . . .

Earth . . . !

Crawling with worms . . . !

This, then, this revolting mess was Dorabella's 'luggage' that we had conveyed over hundreds of miles of barren countryside.

This then was Dorabella!

Walter screamed, pointing to the cellar steps. There indeed stood the hideous old crone wearing Dorabella's magnificent white dress. She stepped forward, repulsive and vile but, in a flash, she had changed into Dorabella herself, *clad in her white shroud, smiling* . . .

'Quickly! Now!' I commanded, making a headlong dive for the stone steps. 'Follow me!' Walter followed, but not before he had gathered Dorabella up into his arms. Still his beloved – his adored, angelic Dorabella.

Then there was silence in the deserted cellar. Deserted? The black trunk with the golden locks had begun to open. And something came out of it. A black figure. It stood like a statue, its eyes closed. It was Dorabella's father.

His eyes opened wide.

And they had no pupils.

We fled from the castle, from the hellish nightmare. No one tried to stop us, as we stole away with two black horses from the stables. It was as if our gaolers connived at our 'escape', knowing that in reality we were already trapped by forces much stronger than castle walls. However far we fled, our fate was sealed, as we rode through the forest on Dorabella's black horses. Walter still held her shrouded figure in his arms. We reached a clearing.

Dawn rose. Sunlight filtered through the pine trees.

'Let's rest,' I told Walter. 'By noon we shall have put this ghastly horror behind us.' I turned to him. He was still mounted on his horse; A raven had perched on his shoulder; the burden of his love lay in his arms. A shaft of morning light fell upon him. He did not move.

'Come, old friend, let me help you,' I said. I reached up to relieve Walter of his burden. I touched it. It dropped to the ground like an empty sack. But where – ? On the ground I now beheld a mound of soil, crawling with thick, curling worms. This is what Walter had held wrapped in the shroud. This was Dorabella. And the air shrilled with the distant hum of the deadly violin.

Walter still sat motionless on his black horse. The raven left his shoulder and flew away. And I saw that Walter's face was chalk-white, drained of all blood, like that of the murdered young poet.

'The Pale Rider,' said Philip Hambleton. 'There he was. The Pale Rider, for ever more. And so my poor friend Walter von Lamont came safely home, not to the lost childhood he had sought – but to the eternal kingdom that awaits all of us . . .'

In the drawing-room of the Club of the Damned Philip was ending his tale.

Silence, then pleased murmurs and applause. But though he had been fascinated by the story as it was being told, Richard felt that somehow the tale had not been completed. Ignoring his uncle's disapproving face, he called out:

'But look here, sir, your story just can't be true, can it? It's quite obviously untrue!'

'Indeed?'

'Well, for a start, you have described all sorts of incidents and feelings which you couldn't possibly have witnessed unless you are some kind of supernatural creature yourself; and also, you're still young, yet you say this adventure happened before there were any railways! You couldn't possibly have been alive then. You don't look much older than I am.'

As the young man spoke, he became aware of a gathering silence about him. It was as if everyone was withdrawing in some strange way, except Philip Hambleton, who now turned his face fully towards Richard for the first time. He smiled, a dazzlingly white smile. His lips were very red. His eyes were closed.

Then he opened those eyes.

And they had no pupils.

'Then it's you who became — are — Dorabella's bridegroom!'
Richard gasped, and as he looked up, he suddenly saw not the
ceiling of a London drawing-room, but a chandelier with a hundred
candles all gutted as if by a gale from nowhere.

'My God, where am I?' Richard screamed, suddenly confronted
by a vision: the phantom of Dorabella herself — transparent,
shrouded, standing on a jetty over a lake. But this time she clasped
something in her bony hand — a scythe, symbol of darkness eternal . . .

'Where am I?' Richard groaned. 'Where am I? Where am I?
Where . . .'

Robert Muller

LADY SYBIL

or

THE PHANTOM OF BLACK GABLES

adapted by Mary Danby

Sir Francis Fell breathed heavily as he limped impatiently over the overgrown path that led up to the iron gates of the House on the River.

Anonymous hands opened a creaking door a few inches. Sir Francis – still out of breath – squeezed his spare frame through the gap.

'Am I late?' he whispered to no one in particular, certainly not to the bewigged and uniformed lackeys, who stood silently by the door to relieve Sir Francis of his cloak, a garment richly lined with purple silk.

A nervous, decadent-looking man in his sixties, Sir Francis could feel his eyes watering, his hands quivering with pleasurable anticipation as the lackey guided him along a dark corridor, covered with that dimly-lit, wine-red wallpaper that always held such promises of bizarre delights for Sir Francis and his ilk.

'Couldn't help it,' he was muttering to himself. 'That damn cabby lost his way completely . . .' He stopped briefly to raise his wet, doggy eyes up to the towering figure of the lackey, who was holding a candelabrum aloft. 'Started, have they? I was afraid they might have . . . Oh dear me, dear me . . .'

And with almost voluptuous alacrity Sir Francis thrust himself past the servant whilst dabbing his blubbering lips with a violet handkerchief.

Another door was opened to him – and Sir Francis now joined the group of men, who in that gaunt drawing-room of the Club of the Damned sat in their usual attitudes of pleasurable anticipation around a warming fire, listening to the evening's guest, who had clearly only just begun to speak.

To the left of the fire sat a clean-shaven, intense-looking man, whose smooth, pale face reflected the warmth of the glowing coals. 'I therefore hope, most sincerely, gentlemen,' he was saying, 'that my story will please and horrify your good selves sufficiently to enable you to favour me with the privilege of life membership of this establishment.'

Sir Francis raised one finger, and a waiter, poised in the shadows, came silently forward.

'Brandy, if you please,' whispered Sir Francis, not wanting to interrupt the proceedings. The fellow by the fire was rubbing his hands together, as if in anticipation of the gruesome feast he was to offer.

'Might one ask whom this story concerns?' enquired another member. 'Yourself, perhaps, Dr Manners?'

'Ah.' The man placed his fingertips together and sat back in the chair, so that his face was in shadow. Now it seemed less eager, clouded, perhaps, by such dark, dreadful thoughts as memory might care to summon. The fire flared briefly; smoke curled from cigars to the ornamental moulding on the ceiling; a clock in the hall chimed the half-hour; the waiter returned with the brandy, then left the room, clicking the door shut behind him.

There was silence. Then the doctor continued.

The tale I am about to relate is a true one. I can vouch for this, for it was my own father who first led me through the mists and labyrinths of its – well – its unspeakableness. You find my words dramatic, gentlemen? Then hear me out and see if you can find it in yourselves to resist the urge to bolt fast your doors when you take to your beds tonight.

My father, Dr Arnold Manners, a medical man like myself (though no longer able to practise his calling), was, as it were, on intimate terms with a family who lived on the outskirts of Dorking. Their house was not so very much unlike this one, standing as it did in its own parkland, with a deep, quiet stream running through the grounds. The mother, Lady Sybil, had been a widow for some fifteen years, and at the time of my story her two sons, Geoffrey and Edward, were in their forties, both still living in their childhood home. Geoffrey, too, was a doctor, and a room to the side of the house was set apart for use as his surgery. Although they were a moderately well-to-do family, since the death of Lady Sybil's husband they were not given much to entertaining. Lady Sybil, you understand, was much affected by the loss of her husband and had, over the years, tended to withdraw into herself, spending a great deal of time alone in her room. Be that as it may, though, she still held the reins, so to speak. Always something of a disciplinarian, she never relinquished her hold on the two sons, which was why Geoffrey remained unmarried, and Edward, who had been more ambitious in that direction, was now separated from a wife who had turned out to be as domineering as his mother.

Geoffrey, the elder, was a likeable man, solid, sober and careful in his ways, yet with an occasional touch of – how shall I put it? – petulance in his manner. He was an excellent, if uninspired doctor, admired by his patients more for painstaking attention to detail than brilliant diagnosis. Edward, on the other hand, some five years his brother's junior, demonstrated no such sobriety. A composer – by inclination rather than profession – his dress could best be described as flamboyant, and he gave the impression of being something of a ne'er-do-well. His mother would often castigate him for the hours he spent arranging his hair and combing his rich, brown beard, informing him that he looked less of a gentleman than a music-hall entertainer. Edward would look injured, then, and retire to his room, stammering words of self-justification. No, it was not a happy household, but how could it have been otherwise when Lady Sybil was locked in upon herself, with all the broodings and imaginings she would muster to cushion herself against the cold realities of modern life?

Every now and then, however, imagination tells the truth, and a flight of fancy takes tangible form. Coincidence? Possibly. But if you believe that in each and every one of us lies the power to communicate in some telepathic sense, then you might be ready to concede that the strength of our unspoken – even subconscious – desires is sometimes capable of promoting that very circumstance or action which is craved.

Let us suppose that Lady Sybil no longer wished to remain alive. I am not saying that this was something she admitted to herself, except, perhaps, in moments of extreme tiredness or despondency. No. For a woman of seventy she was decidedly healthy, though somewhat afflicted by arthritis, and her body was by no means nearing the end of its term. But the years of autocracy had taken their toll, and her spirit was fatigued. And if that spirit, once so fiery and strong, yearned now for release, what more natural than that her subconscious mind should seek ways to procure that very freedom?

Yet she was afraid of death. On the nights when there was no moon, and the wind moaned among the poplars by the stream, she saw shadows. And she was in great fear. What was it outside that seemed to move from tree to tree, watching her window? She would draw the curtains close and turn her back, resting on her ebony stick while she caught her breath, shuddering as the gaslight flickered. Her room, her old familiar room. On the mantelpiece, china figures seemed to dance at the command of the flames in the grate, leaping suddenly as a rush of wind caught the orange coals. A card table stood in readiness, with patience cards neatly stacked; brushes and bottles at attention on the dressing-table, beneath a large looking-glass. A book lay open on the bedside table, beside the framed photograph of her husband. Slop water cooled in the bucket below the wash-stand. So ordinary. So familiar. And now, suddenly, so menacing.

Picture the scene. Lady Sybil takes a faltering step forward and sees herself in the glass. Her eyes are wide in a pale, hard face. Wisps of fine grey hair disturb the outline of her otherwise neat head. She puts up a quivering hand and touches them lightly, not smoothing them, more as if in bewilderment at her own dishevelled state.

Then all of a sudden her eyes narrow. She listens. Anguish distorts her features as she turns to look at the door. Is the handle moving, or is the firelight playing some evil trickery on her?

'Geoffrey! Edward!' she cries out in a choked voice. 'Who is it? It has to be somebody . . . somebody . . . Oh, please!'

And with a loud cry she falls sideways on to the bed.

It is a cry of despair, the cry of someone who has suffered countless nights of terror and who can see no end to it. The cry, if you like, of someone doomed.

'I had another greatly troubled night,' Lady Sybil confided to her sons at luncheon the next day.

'Really, mother?' said Edward, winking at the maid, Arabella, who was handing round the mint sauce. She was a fine-looking, well-built girl, who replied to his wink with a pretty blush.

Geoffrey carved another slice from the leg of lamb and, without looking up, said: 'Arabella, would you ask Cook for a little more redcurrant jelly?'

The girl gave a suggestion of a bob and left the room.

'Surely,' began Lady Sybil, 'there is plenty – ' but Geoffrey interrupted her.

'It might be more prudent, Mama,' he said, 'were you not to discuss these – er – matters in front of the servants . . .'

His mother straightened her shoulders and glared across the table at him. 'It hardly befits you, Geoffrey,' she said scathingly, 'to instruct me on my choice of conversation where the servants are concerned. And,' she added righteously, 'you omitted to say Grace. *Again!*'

Geoffrey, chastened, lowered his eyes. 'Forgive me, Mama. I seem to be becoming forgetful in my middle age.'

Lady Sybil gave a little grunt. 'Maturity can never justify disrespect, Geoffrey,' she told him, folding her hands and bowing her head in preparation for Grace.

'For what we are about to receive, may the Lord make us truly thankful,' said Geoffrey. What the Grace lacked in punctuality it made up for in the sincerity of its tone, though its dignity was more than slightly marred by Edward's 'Amen', delivered from a mouth already full of roast potato.

'Edward! Really!' admonished his mother.

'Sorry, M-Mama,' he mumbled, a forty-year-old schoolboy caught out in a misdemeanour.

'You are, I regret to say,' she went on, 'becoming more like your late father every day. Now then, this prowler . . .'

'Oh, Mama,' said Edward, tutting into his napkin as he removed a speck of gravy from his beard.

'Exactly. Since no one in this house seems in the least bit

37

concerned, I have been forced to take appropriate action myself to – '

'You haven't – ' interrupted Geoffrey, 'you haven't been talking to that appalling fellow from the newspaper again!'

His brother chuckled. 'Oh dear me. "The Phantom of Black Gables." Oh dear me, Mama.'

Lady Sybil turned to him with an icy stare. 'Be silent, Edward! I never used the word "phantom". I spoke about a *prowler*. A prowler . . . It may cause you amusement, Edward – you never were noted for your sensitivity – but I assure you the police will not find it a matter to laugh at.'

'The police?' said Edward, barely concealing his mirth. 'I say, Mama, you haven't written to the *police*, surely . . . Oh dear, Mama. Oh dear me.' He rocked back and forth on his seat, shaking with merriment.

'Oh, do be quiet, Edward,' said his mother impatiently. Then she turned to Geoffrey. 'Night after night,' she said solemnly, 'I can hear someone lurching about outside my bedroom door . . .'

Geoffrey held up his knife in admonitory fashion. 'You mean you *imagine* that someone . . .' he contradicted.

'I imagine nothing, Geoffrey! Will you attend! Those strange, slimy footprints . . . from the stream, going along the path . . . to this house . . . inexplicable! And those footsteps in the hall . . .'

'Ah, "the Phantom"!' cried Edward, in the manner of the good Mr Holmes.

Lady Sybil half rose from her chair and stared at each of her sons in turn. '*Someone is trying to kill me!*'

Who – or even what – was suspected by the old lady of such fearful intent was not at that time vouchsafed, for at that moment Arabella reappeared with the redcurrant jelly and the conversation resumed its usual mealtime course of tedium.

Arabella, however, had not spent all this time in carrying out her errand, and, as she later observed to Johnson, the handyman-gardener: 'You'd be amazed what you can hear through doors.'

'Ain't nothing to do with us,' replied Johnson, contemplating his lunch. The leg of lamb was rather less attractive now, surrounded as it was by fast-congealing juices. 'Come here,' he told Arabella, reaching out to touch the back of her leg through the soft, dull fabric of her black dress.

'Let go, Matt,' she said half-heartedly, backing away from him. 'Cook'll be back in a tick. Anyway, I get enough of that in there.' She giggled a little, remembering the week before, when Edward had managed to reach right up her skirt without being noticed by either his mother or his brother. Really, the man was a terror . . .

'You're by far the best doctor in the district,' said Mrs Lowell that afternoon, replacing her feathered hat on her extravagantly coiffured head.

Geoffrey smiled gently and handed her a prescription.

'Three times a day, and try to avoid draughts. Do let me know if there is any recurrence of the symptoms.'

'You're so – so reassuring,' continued his patient, lingering by the door. 'It's your hands. They're so comforting, so warm . . .'

Geoffrey avoided her flirtatious look and opened the door. 'Glad to be of help to you, Mrs Lowell,' he said briskly, ushering her out. 'That's what I'm here for.'

He returned to his desk and rubbed his hands over his cheeks. Really, some of these women patients . . . And it was always the least attractive ones who . . . Now, if it had been the elder Miss Eavesleigh, or the curate's sister – the one so well-endowed with healthy feminine attributes . . .

'A different matter then, eh?' he muttered, addressing a glass case which stood on a table in the corner of the room. In the case squatted a creature, hideous to look at, lying inert along a twig, steadily contemplating its surroundings through saucer eyes. Geoffrey squatted in front of it, and the eyes didn't waver.

'I look at you, you look at me,' Geoffrey addressed the chameleon. 'How old are you, I wonder? You do not look happy. No freedom to roam? No friends? Does that count for so much? Are you, too, unwell? A household of patients . . .'

There were two raps at the door, a familiar signal, and

39

Geoffrey stood up. 'Come in, Edward.'

The door opened. 'Geoffrey, I say . . .'

'Is there anyone waiting?'

'No.'

Geoffrey shrugged and settled himself on a chaise-longue close to the chameleon's case. 'What is it, then?' he asked, leaning back and passing a hand over his forehead.

'You have one of your headaches,' said Edward, without sympathy.

Geoffrey turned his head towards the chameleon. 'Isn't the creature extraordinary? But fascinating, eh? Regard those vile eyes, Edward. Only the pupils can be seen through those lids. Shields! And each eye acting quite independently . . .'

Edward sat down in the patients' chair and stared at his feet. 'I am unhappy,' he said tonelessly.

But his brother was not to be distracted. 'If you will be patient,' he said, 'you may see one of nature's true miracles. A miraculous physiological change – expressing an alteration in his emotional condition. When he is like this – brown – he feels dull, lonely, fettered. But when the skin turns green, it is as if another being inside the creature had suddenly been released: young, adventurous, vicious . . .'

Dull, lonely, fettered . . . Oh yes, thought Edward. In this glass case of a house, this prison, where one must always be watched and commented on, like some biological specimen.

'But surely,' he said, 'it must be the other way round. It is *because* he is overcome by these feelings – the cravings – that he turns green . . .'

Geoffrey regarded him quizzically. 'Then you do understand, after all. But then why . . .'

Edward rose from his chair and began to pace up and down the room, his fists clenched and his shoulders bent as if to ward off criticism.

'Oh yes,' he said. 'Oh yes. You're so much like Mama. *"At your age, Edward, Mr Mozart had already composed forty-one quite excellent symphonies."* Oh yes. *"Try and work a little, Edward. Try and work . . ."* Well I *do* try. All day I hear melodies in my head, s-strange harmonies, fulfilling cadences, yet when I try to wr-write them down . . . Oh, there is too much coldness. Coldness round my heart.'

'And then you go out to play cards,' interposed Geoffrey, 'and you lose, because you really wish to lose . . .'

'No!'

'And then you begin to drink and the devil knows what else, and then you are depressed and angry with yourself, and so it begins all over again. You're like father was. No self-discipline. Only self-pity. Pathetic. Like a sickly child. Whining to have his sweets, and then, finally, drowning himself in a shallow stream. An accident, yes. But what adult drowns by accident in two feet of water, eh? And you will be the same, Edward, if you continue in this way.'

'But what can I do?' said Edward.

'Search within yourself, Edward. Search – and act!' Geoffrey swung his legs from the chaise-longue and slowly rose to his feet. You're free of Madge, are you not?'

Madge was Edward's wife, a cold, blonde, rather masculine lady, not unlike her mother-in-law. Indeed, they were far too similar to be able to live in compatibility under the same roof. If Edward had had means, had he not been so dependent on his mother for financial security, he and Madge might have been able to make some kind of life together, away from Lady Sybil. But it was not to be.

'Sh-she is willing to discuss terms for a divorce, yes.'

'So,' said Geoffrey, staring out of the window, 'that's something you may be grateful for, is it not?' His brother was silent. 'It's Mama, then, is it? You still feel – constrained . . .'

'C-constrained?' Edward was fighting the tight band of fear, clamped like a fetter around his brain.

'You must find your true self, Edward. Fiery, passionate, daring. Longing to dredge back the lost years, the wasted years . . .'

Edward put his hands over his eyes. 'No, Geoffrey . . .'

'. . . Following naked instinct,' his brother continued, growing slightly red in the face, 'regardless of where it will lead . . . *The green fellow!*'

Edward shuddered. He knew it was there, this other self,

41

this green fellow, but if it ever leapt from its bonds, if he were ever to release it . . .

'But I *know*, Edward,' Geoffrey was saying. 'I understand you. I also understand Mama . . .'

Edward looked up. 'Mama? Understand what?'

Geoffrey sat on the edge of his desk and peered into his brother's eyes. 'An obsessive dread of assault may actually conceal a desire for that assault,' he said heavily.

'Oh, but that's despicable!' exclaimed Edward.

Geoffrey gave a brief smile. '*You* believe someone is trying to kill our dear mama, is that it?'

Edward shook his head uncertainly.

'But you do feel happier for our little chat, don't you? Less *constrained*, perhaps? Less – ah!' He pounced on the chameleon's cage, then turned round excitedly. 'Look, Edward! Look! The *green* fellow . . .'

Edward stared at the grotesque little creature, which at that moment flicked out its tongue, as if to mock him. It was now a bright, emerald green, from its ugly, triangular head to the end of its coiled tail. 'It's unnatural,' he stated. 'Obscene. It makes me think . . . this awful image comes to mind . . . that thing – there – grown huge on its horrible appetites, emerging from the stream and walking upright on its hind legs, leaving those vile wet footprints . . .'

'That Mama claims to have seen.'

Edward gripped his brother's arm. 'I have seen them too, Geoffrey.'

'Ah, yes. "The Phantom." The most absurd of all Mama's hallucinations. Surely you realize what it all means? Mama believes – she *knows* that she drove our poor father to his death in that stream. Now her guilt conjures up this ghost, this phantom . . .' He frowned suddenly and closed his eyes. 'My head. I must have my rest.'

'Yes, yes of course.' Edward moved towards the door. 'Can I fetch you something for the pain?'

Geoffrey raised a hand. 'Thank you, no. I can deal with it.'

'There are times,' said Edward, lingering, 'when I wish so much I were more like you.'

'In that case,' replied Geoffrey, 'leave her alone.'

Edward flinched.

'The girl,' Geoffrey went on. 'Leave her alone, I tell you. It can only cause more trouble. If you need something like that, you must go outside for it.'

'Yes, Geoffrey,' said Edward.

That evening, as was their habit, the brothers dressed for dinner and joined Lady Sybil in the drawing-room for sherry. She was dressed entirely in black, except for the choker of pearls at her neck.

Nervous tonight, she tapped her stick on the floor beside her feet, her eyes darting every now and then to the windows. When they all went into dinner she turned and gave the curtains a nervous glance, as if afraid that they might conceal more than panes of glass and the feverish, moonlit night outside.

Arabella served fish in a light cheese sauce, taking care to swing her body away from the table as she offered the dish to Edward, but she felt the pressure of his foot against her ankle and, in stepping backwards, all but tipped the sauce down the back of his dinner jacket.

'Arabella!' snapped Lady Sybil, then gave her son a long, disapproving stare.

'Salt, Mama?' said Geoffrey.

They took their coffee in the drawing-room, and Edward seated himself at the piano, as he did on most evenings after dinner. They were thus not obliged to converse with one another – a fact which greatly contributed to what little harmony there was in the household. But tonight Lady Sybil was in no mood to listen to Beethoven's Waldstein Sonata, or, indeed, any other piece of music.

'It can't go on,' she muttered, interrupting the second movement.

Edward immediately stopped playing and said impatiently, 'Very well, Mama. Very well. What shall it be? Rossini, perhaps?'

'No, no, no.' She rose with difficulty from her chair and crossed to the curtains. Hesitantly, she pulled them aside.

'What is it, Mama?' asked Geoffrey.

She ran her hands over the catches on the windows. All

43

were secure. 'Nothing,' she said. 'I felt . . . it must have been a draught.'

Soon after that, she retired to her room, having first instructed her sons to be sure and check that all the doors were locked. 'Johnson is so forgetful,' she said.

When she had gone, the two men faced each other across the hearth.

'Well, Edward?' said Geoffrey.

Edward poked at a log with his toe. 'Well . . . well, what?'

'Going out? A little supper in town? A game of cards?'

The log fell to the back of the grate, and Edward bent to place the fireguard in position, ready for the night.

'No, no I'm not going out. But perhaps I should attend to the stables. As Mama says –' He straightened up, and found himself facing Geoffrey's somewhat severe gaze.

'Johnson attends to the stables,' Geoffrey said firmly. 'Good night, Edward.'

It was less a sentiment of benevolence than a dismissal. Edward cleared his throat, closed the lid of the piano and left the room.

The silence was disturbed only by the crackling in the grate as Geoffrey stood motionless for a while, lost in thought. Then, briskly, as if coming to a decision, he marched over to the curtains and drew them back. Outside, the wind sang through the poplars and sent clouds flying across the moon. Geoffrey opened a window and drank deep of the cold, turbulent air. In the moonlight, an observer – and who could say that such a being was not abroad in that rustling, chattering night – might have seen the trace of a smile upon his firm-set lips.

About one hour later, when all righteous men were abed and drifting gently into the arms of Morpheus, there were footsteps on the upper landing. Arabella, in the act of undressing, paused a moment and looked towards the door. It was merely a glance, and, seeing nothing untoward, she continued to disrobe. Had she been more sharp-sighted, she might have seen the shifting, squinting eye that studied her through the keyhole.

At the same moment Lady Sybil, her wrapper clutched tightly around her, was standing in the middle of her bedroom floor, listening. She made no movement, did nothing that might distract her ears from whatever fiendishness approached. The bedroom curtains were drawn. Open them, Lady Sybil. Open them. But no, she remains frozen, like some statue of an ageing Muse, while outside, beneath her window, a shadowy figure, unrecognizable in top hat and flowing opera cloak, emerges silently from the house.

A horse whinnies. The trees bend low in the gathering gale. The crack of a whip, and hooves pound over the gravel. In the wake of the traveller, borne high by the mettlesome wind, lingers the horrible echo of a wild, cackling laugh . . .

In the Club of the Damned, Dr Manners gazed around at his companions. Anticipation glowed on the face of each member.

'Surely there is more . . .?' said one of them, puzzled at the pause in the doctor's narrative. 'Who is the man in the opera cloak? It is Edward, surely?'

'No, no,' disagreed Sir Francis. 'It is the spirit of Lady Sybil's husband, returning to torment her. Or the gardener – Johnson, is it? He seems an individual who might be worthy of our suspicion.'

'Gentlemen,' said Dr Manners, 'I suggest that you ponder the matter while I order some more of this quite superb brandy. A prescription, shall we say, to aid the powers of deduction.'

A few minutes later, their goblets replenished, the members turned to him, eager for the continuation of the story. 'For,' said one of them, 'I shall not rest tonight until I know the answer to this horrendous riddle.'

'But the answer, dear sir,' warned Dr Manners, 'may prove to be even more disturbing than the riddle.'

There was no sleep to be had in the house that night. Even as Arabella, attired for the night and releasing from its cage of pins the tumble of her hair, heard a knock at her door and, with hesitant fingers, turned the handle – even as, recognizing her visitor, she backed shyly away, her hands to her breast – Lady Sybil was still far from sleep. In her demure lace nightgown she sat rigidly upright in her

45

bed, listening to the siren voice of the wind. 'Toni-ight . . .' it seemed to be saying. 'Toni-ight . . .' The wind lifted the branches of the poplars and whipped curls of froth on the surface of the stream. It spread cold tentacles to play with the little pools of water that collected in the soft, muddy footprints along the bank. And ahead of it, squelching its way towards a circle of bushes, was the dark phantom of the night, its cloak spread wide like the wings of a bat.

Lady Sybil reached out and turned the flame of the lamp higher. Then, trembling, and clasping her stick, she eased herself out of bed. She could hear footsteps along the corridor. Somebody – something – was coming for her, nearer and nearer.

'Who is it?' she cried out in a high voice, no longer able to restrain herself.

The footsteps came nearer.

'Who is it?' She pulled her dressing-gown around her shoulders and took a firm grasp on her stick. 'Geoffrey! Edward!' she shouted in anguish. 'Oh, why don't you come? Why doesn't somebody come?' She stared at the photograph of her late husband. It smiled complacently or, no – *malevolently* back. 'Oh–oh–oh . . .' She clung to the bedpost, whimpering a little. 'Oh please, oh please . . .'

The footsteps were louder now. They stopped outside her door.

'No-o-o.' Lady Sybil collapsed across the bed, her stick held aloft as a meagre shield.

There was a knock at the door. The handle began to turn.

'Mama? Mama, what is it? Let me in!'

Oh, dear Lord, Edward. It was only Edward. She hurried to unlock the door. Her son stood there in his night-clothes, his hair dishevelled.

'What is it, Mama?' he repeated nervously, then, seeing that she was on the point of collapse, he took her in his arms and stroked her head for a while, murmuring comforts. 'There, Mama. It's all over. You're quite safe.'

Suddenly, she lifted her head and fixed him with a hard, sceptical look.

'Where is Geoffrey?' she asked.

'Rest, Mama. You must rest now,' he said, guiding her to her bed, where she lay, pale and shaking, against the pillows. There seemed no vigour left in her, and he had to lean forward to hear what she was saying.

'All over again. Awful sounds . . . someone trying to get in . . . footsteps . . . far away . . .'

'The stream?' asked Edward.

'Trying to murder me in my bed.'

Edward sighed. 'But *who*, Mama? Surely nobody wants – '

He was interrupted by the arrival of Geoffrey, who swept in wearing a crimson dressing-gown, his hair neatly combed and his manner brusque.

'Yes!' he said. 'Who *does* want to murder you, Mama?'

'She called, Geoffrey,' explained Edward.

'You were so long in coming,' his mother moaned feebly. 'Why didn't you come?' She turned her head away from them. 'You still do not believe me – either of you.'

Geoffrey poured medicine into a glass. 'I believe only what I see,' he said evenly. 'Now, Mama, drink this. You'll feel much better in the morning.'

She took the glass and, without looking at him, drained it. Then she gazed at them through hooded eyes and said firmly: 'I do hear footsteps. And, don't forget, there are footprints by the stream. Believe me, if you were to go out there now, you would see them – dark, muddy, loathsome footprints . . .'

Geoffrey took the glass from her and returned it to the washstand, keeping his back to her as he said cruelly: 'What you mean is that poor Papa, drowned in the stream all those years ago, has risen from the dead to haunt you – to murder you – as *he* was . . . That's what you're saying, isn't it?' He turned accusingly.

'No!' cried his mother.

Edward held out his hands. 'Oh, Geoffrey – no . . .'

'Go to bed, Edward, your mother needs rest,' commanded his brother.

As Edward, shrugging, moved slowly towards the door, Geoffrey leant over Lady Sybil, his breath warm against her cold cheeks.

'Tell me, Mama,' he said, 'why do you lock the door?'
She looked up at him, puzzled.

'How can we help you,' he went on, 'if we cannot enter
when you call? Are you afraid of *Edward*, Mama? Is that
it? Or of me?'

Without waiting for an answer, he quickly left the room.
She lay still for a moment, gasping for breath, then reached
over to the bedside table and picked up the portrait of her
husband. 'I shall never,' she said to it, 'never . . . go where
you are.' Then she buried her head in the pillow and
waited quietly for the blessed relief of sleep.

Edward was standing in the doorway of his bedroom
when Geoffrey emerged on to the landing. He was clutching the doorpost, as if to steady himself.

'To bed, now,' said his brother. 'We will talk in the
morning.'

Edward lowered his head to his chest and muttered: 'I
can't . . . can't go on like this.'

'I know, Edward. I know,' said Geoffrey, laying a hand
on his shoulder.

'I'm far more terrified than she is.' Edward looked up,
imploring. 'I know it's insane, but . . .'

Geoffrey shook his head. 'No, Edward. You have every
reason. You cannot forget, can you.'

'Forget?' said Edward.

'Talk about it,' urged his brother. 'Exorcise those dreadful, grinning ghosts – those phantoms that are strangling
you as surely as they are strangling Mama.'

'But I don't . . .'

'Talk about that night,' went on Geoffrey, more softly,
'that night when father was still alive. You recall it as if it
were yesterday . . .'

Edward turned his face to the door. 'No, Geoffrey. It's
not right.'

'We both recall it, don't we,' said Geoffrey. 'Remember?
That bedroom?' He pointed to the room overhead, now
occupied by Arabella. 'The door was open. That young
girl, the maid – one among so many – she was screaming,
holding up her clothes in front of her. Remember, Edward?'

'No, no . . .' insisted Edward.

48

'And even now,' Geoffrey continued, 'Mama, poor dear Mama, is still making *you* pay for *his* sins. Worse than Madge, who imprisoned you, squeezed out all your joy, your talent, your youth from your body. Confront the truth, Edward. Do not shrink from it. The wildness is in you still. That is why you lust after that poor girl, is it not? But the wildness must be diverted, syphoned off, poured into something – someone else . . .'

Edward turned to him, wide-eyed. 'Who?' he asked. 'Who?'

'Aha!' said Geoffrey, smiling now. 'Why, the green fellow, of course.'

In vain did Edward remind Geoffrey of his own unhappy past, of the girl he had so loved – had wanted to marry – and how their mother had forbidden the liaison. Geoffrey had ridden off into the night, after her, with such inflamed passion that he had turned the horse too sharply on the road, so that it had fallen, and Geoffrey had been knocked senseless. How did he now manage to live his life on this plane of commonsense, unfettered by bitterness and fear?

'But Edward,' said Geoffrey, 'it is *you* we must talk about, *your* hope to free yourself . . . to live and enjoy all the golden things, the golden, inaccessible, forbidden things . . .' His face was alight with an unholy fire, as if he himself were partaking, inside his head, of these prohibited fruits.

Edward edged away from him, whimpering like a puppy.

'The green fellow,' Geoffrey insisted, 'the green fellow! Be who you want to be! Do what you will!' He leant towards his brother, whispering in his ear. 'It is not too late to save yourself – and do what you will!'

A flash of lightning lit the scene, then Geoffrey was gone, and Edward was alone in his room, hunched against the sound of booming thunder.

He sat there for some moments, trying to pull together his disordered senses. He needed – needed so desperately – to free himself, to loose his instincts from their tether of respectability. He stood up, clenching his fists. 'Do what you will,' Geoffrey had said. He would. Dear Lord, he would.

49

His face twitching with expectancy, he left the room, crept along the passage and mounted the stairs to the servants' floor. At the second door on the left he stopped and gently knocked. There was a rustling from within, as if bed sheets were being pushed aside.

'Please Arabella,' he said in an urgent whisper, 'please – it's me, Edward.'

There was more rustling, then Arabella's voice saying: 'No! Be off with you!'

Edward persisted. 'Oh please, Arabella. Let me in. Just this once, my dear. I only want to look at you . . .'

'Go away, sir.' She sounded tired, bored by his familiar request.

Edward sank to his knees, shaking, his forehead beaded with perspiration. 'Only like the last time, my dear,' he pleaded. 'I know you c-can be nice. Be nice to me, my dear. I only want to *look* . . .'

There was no answer. He tried the door-handle, but she had turned the key in the lock. Shaking with frustration, he made his way back to the stairs, shuddering as lightning flooded the sky outside the staircase window. He heard the rain, then, a slow pattering which swiftly gave way to a lashing downpour.

He had reached his own landing when a flash of lightning brought the shock revelation that he was no longer alone. His brother stood before him, leaning casually on the newel post.

'Geoff-Geoffrey . . .' he stammered. 'Wh-what are you doing?'

Geoffrey smiled and shook his head. 'What did I tell you, eh? What did I tell you?'

Edward leant back against the wall, his hand to his chest. 'You gave me such a – such a frightful shock,' he said.

'Go to bed,' said Geoffrey. 'Do you hear? You must do as you're told.'

Edward bit his lip. 'But you said just now . . . you told me I should . . .'

'Frighten that little trollop?' replied Geoffrey. 'Did I tell you that?'

'No, Geoffrey, but – '

'Then go to your room, now. There's a good lad.'

The fire, the passion of excitement, had died away. Edward dutifully retired, murmuring: 'Yes, yes, Geoffrey. Thank you.' And Geoffrey watched him go, and sadly shook his head at the follies of his younger brother.

The night wore on. The storm gradually abated. As the turmoil outside diminished to the regular thudding of rain on the gravel, anyone still awake would have noticed that the house was not as quiet as it should have been at this hour when all respectable people are lost in the slumber of the just. From Arabella's room could be heard the sound of two voices – one low and urgent, the other shrill, excited, demanding . . . The first was Arabella's, the second seemed to be that of a young man.

'No . . .' said Arabella. 'I don't want to . . . I've already told you. Let me be!'

The reply came like the yelping of a puppy for a bone. 'Come along now!' Then there was a wild, unnatural giggle. 'Come along! You know better, don't you? You know what to do . . .'

Arabella continued for a while to protest, then, as the giggles grew even more frantic and high-pitched, she became silent.

The giggle rose to a mad shriek of triumph.

The following day, a police officer called on Lady Sybil. She was in the drawing-room, discussing with Edward his hopes for divorce, when Arabella announced: 'It's the police – a Sergeant Cosley, Milady.'

'A *sergeant*? Are you sure?' said Lady Sybil. 'Edward,' she added, 'you may stay here with me.'

Sergeant Cosley was a local man, more used to investigating cases of stolen pigs than phantom prowlers. He was plainly ill-at-ease to find himself among gentry. The mere suggestion of a title sent his heart plummeting to the heels of his serviceable country boots.

He removed his hat and muttered a cautious: 'Lady Sybil . . . er, Milady . . . Sir.'

Lady Sybil did her best to make him feel even less comfortable by pointing out that not only had he called at a most inconvenient time, but a sergeant was hardly a satisfactory substitute for a Chief Inspector. 'Nevertheless,' she went on, 'since you are here, er, Officer, sit down.'

The sergeant remained standing and took out his notebook. He studied it for a moment.

'Someone making a nuisance of himself,' he read. 'At night. Footsteps . . . door-handles turning . . . fresh wet footprints near the stream . . .'

Lady Sybil tapped the floor with her stick. 'It's all rather more serious than that,' she said. 'Do sit *down*, Sergeant!' The policeman flushed slightly and obeyed.

'A prowler – ' he began.

Lady Sybil tut-tutted. 'I don't think you understand. As I told your Inspector, I have excellent reasons for believing that someone wishes to murder me.'

'What my mother means . . .' began Edward.

'Be quiet, Edward,' she remonstrated. 'I am perfectly capable of conducting this interview. Now then, Sergeant. My instincts tell me that the strange sounds I hear, the doors left open, someone trying to enter my room – all this points to a murderer. Not a burglar – after all, nothing is ever taken. No, my life is in deadly danger. Besides, my instincts never deceive me.'

Sergeant Cosley wrote laboriously in his notebook, then he looked up and said: 'While awaiting your Ladyship's attention, I took the liberty of speaking to your maid.'

'Arabella? By whose leave?'

The Sergeant shuffled his boots on the carpet. 'Well, you did ask for some enquiries to be made . . .'

'What did the girl have to say?' asked Lady Sybil. 'Has she seen anything?'

'Someone moving about in the hall. One night, it was. A gentleman.'

Lady Sybil was intrigued. 'A gentleman?'

Sergeant Cosley nodded. 'Wearing an opera cloak and top hat. That, if I may say so, would suggest a guest in the house, or – ' He turned to Edward. 'Or someone actually living in this house.'

Lady Sybil straightened her shoulders. 'You will remember, Sergeant,' she said, 'that the only gentlemen in this house are my two sons. Such a suggestion, therefore, is plainly ridiculous.'

Sergeant Cosley unbuttoned another pocket and withdrew a folded sheet of paper. 'Perhaps I should tell you,' he said, 'that we have also received a communication of a rather different nature.' He stood up and went to stand in front of her. 'I wonder if I could . . .'

She snatched it from him. 'Let me see.' She began to read, with Edward leaning over her shoulder. Her face grew dark and she began to splutter. 'But this – this is simply appalling! It's illiterate – a mad child . . .'

The Sergeant coughed. 'If your Ladyship would permit me to speak to the other servants . . .'

Lady Sybil screwed up the letter and pressed it into Edward's waiting palm. He immediately straightened it out and began to read it.

'It would not appear,' Lady Sybil said to the sergeant, 'that you need my permission. But since there is only Cook, who is deaf, and Johnson, and the two other maids who sleep out . . .'

Edward interrupted her. 'Mama! This is intolerable! The writer suggests that it must be Geoffrey or myself who . . .'

At that moment, Geoffrey, having completed the duties of morning surgery, entered the room. He was just in time to hear his mother say:

'He does not suggest. He *states*, Edward. In the crudest . . . possible . . . terms.'

Geoffrey was suffering another of his headaches. He lay on the surgery couch with his forehead creased and his eyes closed. After a while he opened them and gazed over to where the chameleon sat in its glass case, unmoving.

'Yes,' he told it. '*You* wouldn't put up with such a life. You would escape into your great greenness, your glorious, separate greenness.' He fingered the letter in his breast pocket, the childlike scribblings that had so upset them all. 'Amazing,' he mused. 'Quite fantastic. An insane, illiterate scrawl . . . different hand, different man.'

Arabella came in to tidy up, and he questioned her as to

the matter of the Sergeant's enquiries, but she told him she had said nothing, adding mysteriously: 'Don't you worry, sir.'

He frowned at her. Servant girls could become so familiar if one didn't keep them in check. Then he asked: 'Where is my mother?' It was time he had a long talk with her. This 'prowler' nonsense was getting out of hand.

'I believe she's in the garden,' said Arabella.

The garden, yes. A little fresh air might be good for his headache.

He found Lady Sybil down by the stream, perusing the banks for signs of footprints.

'They were there this morning,' she insisted when Geoffrey reached her. 'I know they were.'

He took her arm. 'Come, Mama, let's walk a little.'

She scowled, taking umbrage at his solicitous manner, but let herself be led away from the stream towards the rose garden, where the stark twigs of winter seemed to hold little promise of a colourful rebirth.

'You wouldn't think, would you, Geoffrey,' she said, 'that such drab, dead-looking objects could harbour so much fire – so much . . . so much *life*. Spring will come, and once again all will be green, then those yellow ones over there will be out – they are always the first. Not, of course,' she said testily, 'that I will be here to see them. Not unless somebody *does* something.'

'Oh, Mama . . .' sighed Geoffrey.

She turned on him, the sharp ridges of her cheeks flushed with annoyance. 'Don't treat me as if I were one of your patients!' she snapped. 'You know perfectly well that I speak the truth – that there *is* a prowler.'

'And that attempts have been made upon your life. No, Mama, I do *not* believe it.'

'*Someone* . . . *is* . . . *threatening* . . . *me*,' she insisted, under-lining her words by tapping with her stick upon the path.

Geoffrey led her to a stone seat, brushed curled, black leaves from it and invited her to sit down. 'I dare say we all suffer these feelings of oppression from time to time,' he said. 'Of being menaced . . . imprisoned . . . assaulted . . .' He stared out over the rose beds, the edge of his mouth twitching slightly.

Lady Sybil stared at him. 'But Geoffrey,' she began, 'you've always been so settled . . .'

He jumped up from the seat and began to pace to and fro in front of her. 'Have I?' he said evenly, as if the pacing helped him to keep control of himself. 'Resigned might be the more appropriate word.'

Lady Sybil reminded him that there had been an alternative – he could have married. Some nice girl. Some quiet-mannered, responsive, obedient girl.

'There *was* a nice girl – once,' said Geoffrey. But obedience – that was something else. Obedience meant giving way to his mother, and she had had too much spirit for that. He had not lacked spirit, then. He remembered his helter-skelter ride in pursuit of her, after his mother had ordered her out of the house. The fall. The headaches ever since. He put a hand to his head. The fresh air had not yet obliged with a cure.

'Anyway, Mama,' he went on, sitting beside her again, 'it's not me we have to worry about now, it's Edward.'

'What are you doing to help him?' she asked.

'I am treating him, of course, though I am bound to say his response is slow,' said Geoffrey. 'There are some fascinating new notions . . . experiments,' he went on, 'for treating hysterical symptoms.' He began to explain to her his theories regarding hypnosis and the power of suggestion.

'That sounds to me suspiciously like quackery,' said Lady Sybil.

Geoffrey smiled. 'Progress usually does in our profession. But, Mama, Edward *must* receive treatment. You see . . . a lack of – bodily restraint is often only an attempt to silence a more – a more deep-rooted sense of unfulfilment.'

'You're not – ' Lady Sybil clutched her heart. 'You're not trying to tell me that Edward . . . the letter . . .'

Geoffrey shook his head. 'One must never confuse an hysterical disturbance with – insanity, Mama.' He helped her to her feet, and they began slowly to walk around the garden. 'Edward thinks he does not remember. But he remembers very well. When certain childhood occurrences become intolerable to the adult mind, they have to be

55

exorcised. Like ghosts.'

'Ghosts, Geoffrey?' said his mother. 'Are you, a doctor, saying that someone – the dead – that they could actually reappear?'

'It's the *occurrences* that reappear. But in the disguised forms of "symptoms",' replied Geoffrey.

She clasped his arm and gazed up at his solemn face. 'Help me, Geoffrey!' she said urgently. 'Help me to understand what you are saying!'

Johnson came out of the stables and crossed the path in front of them, heading for the kitchen. He appeared to be in some haste. They followed him with their eyes, then Geoffrey said: 'Nature, Mama. Nature knows how. *The divided personality.* My little chameleon in the surgery – he knows, yet his secret is that he does *not* know. One moment he is brown and dull, the next a green fire of abandonment, but the two moods are quite separate. The green fellow is not even aware of the other one . . . refuses to recognize his existence, even.'

They had reached the french windows of the drawing-room now, and stopped to wipe their feet on the mat. Before going inside, Lady Sybil turned to Geoffrey, her face ashen, and said: 'You promised you would help me. I'd hoped . . . a holiday? A little quiet, a rest, away from all this – '

Geoffrey smiled. 'A holiday, Mama? Yes, why not? A very good idea. Tell me where you would like to go, and I will arrange it.'

'Oh, Geoffrey.' She clutched the edge of the door as she stepped through to the drawing-room. 'I need to lean on you a great deal.'

As he followed her, he put his hands on her shoulders and turned her to face him. 'And I on you,' he said, looking deep into her eyes. 'And I on you.'

In the kitchen, Arabella was sitting at the table, eating a slice of cake, when Johnson came in, having removed his muddy boots in the scullery. He sat in an armchair by the range and curled his stockinged toes before the smouldering coals.

'I've decided,' he said, nodding his head several times.

'We're leaving. The time is almost upon us. You'd best pack your bags, girl.'

Arabella looked up, and there was anxiety in her voice as she answered: 'No, Matt. We can't. We got no place to go.'

'We'll find somewhere,' said Johnson.

'We can't. Not without giving notice. Not without a reference from the master . . .'

Johnson snorted. 'The master! *He* won't give us no character. Remember, we've *seen* him.' He rose from the chair and went towards the door. 'Come on, girl. Get your things.'

'Matt!'

He sighed and turned back. 'What now?'

'They've found out. The letter . . .'

'What letter?' he asked impatiently.

'To the police. The letter to the police. I heard them talking about it.'

'*What* letter?' he asked again.

Arabella gazed at him, mystified. 'You mean . . . you mean you didn't write it?'

'Come on, girl,' he said urgently, clasping her arm. '*Pack your bags!*'

At four o'clock, Cook appeared in the kitchen, with her customary call: 'Kettle on to boil, Arabella! Her Ladyship will be wanting tea.' Seeing no sign of the maid, she set about the task herself, tutting over the preparations. When four-thirty came, and still no Arabella, she carried the tray up the stairs herself, and accompanied her entrance into the drawing-room with threats of notice. 'I can't serve meals, Milady,' she grumbled. 'Not up them stairs.'

'Where is Arabella?' asked Lady Sybil, pouring tea into bone china cups.

'What's that you say?' Cook was extremely hard of hearing.

'Arabella. Where is she?' shouted Lady Sybil.

'I can't find Arabella,' complained Cook.

At that moment, Edward arrived.

'See what has happened to that silly girl,' instructed his mother. 'We can't have Cook upset.'

57

Edward left the room, returning five minutes later to announce: 'She-she is gone, Mama. Her – her r-r-r-room is quite empty.' He was in a state of some agitation, and stood there rubbing his palms together, as if his hands were cold.

'Gone?' queried Lady Sybil.

'G-gone, Mama.'

But Johnson and Arabella had not gone far. For the last hour or so they had been hiding in the stables, awaiting the cover of nightfall, when they planned to slip away down the drive and begin the long walk to the nearest town, where they could find a bed for the night and a morning train to hurry them away to sweetness and sanity.

Dinner that night was a sombre affair. Cold mutton and potatoes, served by an aggressively tight-lipped Cook. Very little was eaten. Edward was still decidedly jumpy at the afternoon's turn of events, and his mother was evidently fearful of something.

'What is it, Mama?' Geoffrey was the only one of the three able to speak with any calmness. 'What are you afraid of now?'

'Arabella has gone,' she muttered, as if in a trance. 'Johnson too. Something will happen, now.'

'Yes,' agreed Geoffrey, smiling. 'I dare say Cook will give in her notice. Then we'll all be fending for ourselves, won't we.'

'Oooh, Go-o-d . . .' groaned Edward, unable to control his emotions.

His mother recovered her composure sufficiently to rebuke him. 'I will not have blasphemy, Edward,' she reminded him. 'And certainly not at the dinner table.'

Edward pushed out his bottom lip and rose from the table. 'Excuse me, please, Mama, Geoffrey,' he said. 'I must . . . I have to . . .'

'Really!' exclaimed Lady Sybil, but Geoffrey calmed her.

'Leave him, Mama. It is best he should be left alone to resolve matters in his own way.'

Later, he came upon Edward sitting on the stairway to the servants' floor. He was rocking from side to side in the moonlight and muttering to himself.

Geoffrey sat down beside him and held a lamp to his face. Edward was sweating slightly, and from time to time a muscle at the side of his mouth twitched convulsively.

'Are you ready?' asked Geoffrey. 'It has to be tonight.'

'Tonight?' echoed Edward dumbly.

Geoffrey gripped his arm. 'Afterwards you will be free . . . completely free at last. No more lurking about those awful places at night . . . no more shadows . . . no more shame . . . no more haunted, drunken nights . . . nobody left to stand in your way, Edward.'

'Nobody . . . nobody,' said Edward, as if trying the word for the first time.

'There are two separate men,' his brother went on. 'They must be made one. The green fellow, Edward. He's the *real* one, the *strong* one. Hurry now – go to your room and change. Your finest clothes – something fit for the occasion.'

He prodded his brother up from the step and watched him as he walked away in dream-like fashion to his bedroom. The time had come. At last the waiting was over.

A cloud crossed the moon, darkening the landing where Geoffrey still sat. After a while he stood up and, holding the lantern high, walked softly to his mother's bedroom door. From his waistcoat pocket he took a key, and, inserting it in the door, turned the lock quietly and firmly. There – nobody could enter the room now without his own knowledge and consent. His mother need fear no stranger crossing her threshold tonight.

'Geoffrey? Edward?' He heard her feeble call as she hurried to the door and tried the handle. 'Oh!' She frantically rattled the knob. 'Help! I am locked in!' she shouted. 'Someone has taken my key and locked me in!' There were sounds of furniture being pushed across the floor; a heavy, scraping sound – that must be the mahogany chest – towards the door; the crash of china; small, panicky noises from a tired old throat; the frantic tap of a stick against the bedpost. Silence.

Geoffrey turned away and made for the main staircase. Edward would be ready soon. It was nearly time. He chuckled to himself. Tonight the 'Phantom' would be on the prowl again.

As the grandfather clock in the hall struck midnight, a figure left the house and headed for the stream. Lady Sybil, imprisoned in her room, and by now almost rigid with fear, moved stiffly over to the window and, hesitantly, drew back the curtain. He was there, there in the garden, with the moonlight glinting on his top hat and the breeze lifting his cloak around him like the wings of a great bird of prey. He disappeared into the mist by the stream. Footprints . . . footprints . . . She could almost hear those black, prowling feet as they squelched through the mud. Why? Oh, why was she being made to suffer so? Where was Arabella? Johnson? What did they know? Why had they not stayed to support her in her hour of desperation?

She drew the curtain. There would be no more to see out there. The 'Phantom' would come inside now, as he always did, and mount the stairs, and stop outside her room. His gloved hand would be on the handle, turning . . .

She stumbled back across the room and leant against the bedpost, waiting. Tonight the prowler would not be staying outside the door . . .

'Geoffrey . . . is that you?' Edward stood uncertainly on the landing, listening. The clock in the hall ticked on in its slow march of dread. 'Now . . . now . . . now . . . now . . .' it seemed to say. There were sounds of footsteps outside the dining-room. 'Geoffrey . . . ?' repeated Edward, peering over the banisters. There was no reply, and he edged down the stairs, pausing every few steps to listen. 'Tock . . . tock . . . Now . . . Now . . .'

Someone was hiding just inside the dining-room. Edward could hear laboured breathing. He picked up a candlestick from the hall table and advanced.

As he did so, a white-gloved hand deposited on the front step a pair of muddy galoshes, then the front door silently opened and a black-cloaked figure swished across the hall and up the stairs. Edward, in the midst of attack, paused for a moment to contemplate this apparition. In those few seconds the dining-room intruder managed to disarm him and pin him against the wall.

Edward groaned. Even in such faint moonlight, it would

have been hard not to discern the homely, blunt, judicial features of Sergeant Cosley.

'Quick! Upstairs!' whispered Edward. 'Mama . . . he's going to kill her!'

They reached the landing and stopped short. Outside Lady Sybil's door stood the cloaked, top-hatted figure, familiar in build and bearing . . . but the voice – the voice! It teetered on the edge of madness, shrill and sharp with the lusts of a lifetime; the voice of nightmares, of witches, of the very Devil himself.

'Got key myself!' the figure was shrieking. 'Stupid old bitch! Open! Open! There! Die now! Die!'

'Go away!' breathed the faint voice of Lady Sybil. 'Whoever – whatever – you are, *go . . . away.*'

The door was being pushed now, pushed against the heavy chest that Lady Sybil had positioned to impede its progress. The chest was beginning to move.

'Come on!' Edward found his senses and pulled Sergeant Cosley with him along the landing. But as they reached the figure, the chest gave way, allowing the door to swing open.

'Where are you, bitch? Where are you hiding?' The figure advanced over the carpet, cane in hand. It stopped for a moment by the dressing-table mirror to admire its painted, pouting lips, the grotesquely rouged and powdered cheeks. It smiled foppishly and preened its eyebrows with a pink-tipped finger.

'Geoffrey! For pity's sake!' Edward's voice from the doorway made the creature turn from the mirror.

A sly giggle, then, in a high-pitched voice: 'No, it's not Geoffrey! It's me! *Me!*'

A moan of terror came from behind the curtains, and the cursing, swaggering monstrosity leapt towards Lady Sybil's hiding place, brandishing the cane.

'Geoffrey, no!' cried Edward.

The other's voice rose to a high shriek. 'Yes! Kill, coward! Kill her! Kill her, you fool! *The way I told you!* Kill the old bitch, before I *have* to!' He snatched back the curtain to reveal Lady Sybil cowering by the window in a state of wild, gibbering terror.

Edward stared dumbly, unable to move. Then, suddenly,

Sergeant Cosley leapt into action. He tackled from behind, and brought the assailant down.

As Edward comforted his weeping mother and led her to her bed, Sergeant Cosley, his truncheon ready to quash any further ideas of violence, knelt over the prostrate Geoffrey.

Geoffrey tried to sit up, his absurdly-powdered face creased with pain, his eyes staring, his ludicrous make-up smeared.

'My head,' he groaned with pain. 'Ah, there now, my head . . .'

'Very sorry I had to hurt you, Doctor. I had no choice.'

A smile crossed Geoffrey's face. 'Doctor? Why do you call me "Doctor"? The doctor is a much older man, surely – much older than me.' He chuckled gently. 'Dried-up old stick . . . Well past his prime – '

'But Doctor . . .' interrupted the sergeant.

Geoffrey moved his head so that he could see himself in the mirror. His red, cupid's-bow lips smiled grotesquely back at him as he said softly: 'I don't think I really know this 'Doctor' . . . do I? Eh?'

The fire burned low in the clubroom as the story-teller leant forward to conclude his tale.

'You see, gentlemen,' he explained, 'poor Edward would not – could not – kill against his own will. And he suffered for it. Madge, his wife, unable to achieve suitable terms for a settlement, returned to the fold, and to this day Lady Sybil rules them both, no longer fearing the retribution she has so long deserved. But, who knows? Perhaps one day the Phantom of Black Gables will strike again, eh? After all, Geoffrey has left the lunatic asylum now – he had little difficulty persuading the authorities that he was truly cured.'

'Dr Manners . . .' began Sir Francis, half-rising from his seat in his anxiety the better to study the face of the man by the fire. 'Dr Geoffrey Manners?'

The other inclined his head.

'Then it was you?' began one of the members. 'The Phantom . . .'

Geoffrey smiled, a malicious, sardonic grin. 'Oh no, gentlemen,' he said, chuckling at their horrified expressions. 'Not I, gentlemen. The green fellow . . .'

HEIRS

or

THE WORKSHOP OF FILTHY CREATION

adapted by BRIAN LEONARD HAYLES

What on earth was this?

The members of the Club of the Damned did not respond with enthusiasm to the idea of a writer joining their secret establishment. A writer liked to gossip. A writer invented things. A writer was unreliable.

Was he trying to hoodwink them, this scholarly, myopic gentleman who now stood by the fireplace waiting to begin his tale of horror? Was he possibly even a spy sent out by some unscrupulous publisher to discover new sources for gruesome tales of the supernatural?

It would never do to be careless about the choice of new members. What was said, what was done, at the Club of the Damned was not for the curious, the ordinary, the uninitiated.

Howard Lawrence, for that was the author's name, purported to be a writer of biography, though few members could ever remember having read a work by a person of that name. Sir Francis, as he watched the face of the speaker, fussed with his snuff-box and made a mental note to ask for a list of his works – if indeed there were any.

Sir Francis' rheumy eyes focused on the figure by the fireplace. Howard Lawrence had an ascetic face, narrow and bony, and there was a possibly deceptive mildness about his eyes. So mild indeed was his general demeanour that Sir Francis felt certain that the alleged author was under sedation.

'There is one story,' the speaker was saying, 'without doubt the most startling and the most original I have ever written, which will never be published . . .'

'Indeed?' Sir Francis exclaimed, 'and why not? Is it not a work of biography? Is it perhaps libellous?'

'It could be said to be both,' Howard Lawrence said, the crooked

smile around his mouth contradicting the spirituality behind his eyes . . .

In 1882, flushed with the critical success of my *Life of Shelley*, and accompanied by my wife and daughter, I sailed from England in an endeavour to follow as exactly as I could the footsteps of the poets Byron and Shelley in their tours abroad during the early years of this century. My purpose was a simple one: to gather and ascertain facts that would provide the material for further scholastic works, biographies of two men whose intellectual passions stood so closely to my own precise manner of thought. You may be familiar with some of my early writings, notably the biographies of Wordsworth and Coleridge, besides that of Percy Bysshe Shelley and his tragically charmed circle. Without undue modesty, I can safely assert that these works are not traditional learned monographs, sterile literary mausoleums founded solely on arid fact; for I insist that only a sensitive understanding of the creative spirit behind the master-works of genius can give us a true perspective of their aesthetic splendour. Though they are no longer with us, to me the vital essence of these men lives on – not only in the words and thoughts they have bequeathed us, but in the places they visited and the very dwellings they inhabited. It is as though the power of their remembered genius enables dead stones to live again.

Throughout my investigations into the hidden lives of these dead poets, the patience and solicitude of my dear wife Elsbeth had been of the utmost satisfaction to me; but on this latest expedition a further charming companion was to lighten my days of travel and study – our daughter Mary. Our only child, she was entranced at the prospect of celebrating her nineteenth birthday while actively journeying along the more secret literary byways of Europe. It was a delight to be shared by all of us, for not only would she be a tender companion to her mother, but also an eager vessel into which I could pour the distilled experiences of my continuing research. Shy, even stilted in the presence of strangers, my dear child almost glowed with bright curiosity behind her trim spectacles whenever the opportunity arose to discuss the discoveries of the day. I was pleasurably aware of her restless desire to grasp and appreciate new vistas of truth and knowledge that I gladly opened before her; if only she had been a son, what even greater affinities we might have shared! Even so, she was very dear to me; the blossoming of her mind, moulded by my discreet parental guidance, was an added and continuous delight.

By way of Belgium, then of France, we came at last to Switzerland and the environs of Geneva, where we were to remain for several weeks at the Villa Diodati. Does the sound of that darkly familiar name reverberate uneasily within your mind? The Villa Diodati . . . sinister, disquieting, a place haunted by the shadows of unanswered minds questioning the unknown. Here it was that Byron played host to his fellow fallen angel, Shelley, whose eighteen-year-old mistress Mary Godwin was soon to marry him after the suicide of his first wife, Harriet. Here, revolutions of the soul were born, shibboleths cast down by thunderbolts of intellect and passion, and new concepts of creation brought forth like dragons' teeth sown by vengeful cherubim. It was all there still, a grim miasma echoing that distant, dismal summer of 1816. Then, to pass the long rain-filled evenings, Byron and his mysterious secretary Polidori, Shelley, and the child he had liberated into womanhood, amused themselves by competing to invent a story based upon some supernatural occurrence. It was not to prove easy; long hours filled by discussing Erasmus Darwin had filled their minds with the grand theme of Man's challenge against the gods – the legend of Prometheus, no less. But out of those nights' amusement came a moment of nightmare imagination penned into literature by the girl soon to become Mary Shelley: its title – *Frankenstein*.

The strangely intense atmosphere at the Villa Diodati, added to the hours of long study that I undertook there, eventually took their toll; I was quite exhausted. It was at this point that my dear wife, ever concerned for my well-being and welfare, suggested that before proceeding along our chosen route to Italy, we should attempt to restore our health and calm our nerves by spending a few idle weeks in a friendly Alpine inn or guesthouse. The idea of a brief period of contemplation, exercise and rest appealed to me, and I agreed. As to why I chose the somewhat remote Gasthof Ritterhof, I can give no logical reason. Could it have been the inevitability of fate, or sheer chance? Or had the sinister spirit of the Villa Diodati mesmerized my subconscious into fortuitously selecting what appeared to be at first sight such an exceptionally tranquil and inviting establishment? Such questions are useless now; when we first saw that simple inn, nestling by the lonely mountain road, brightly picturesque amongst the serenity of sunlit snow we felt only an enormous sense of ease and imminent contentment. Here was a location so pleasant, so open, so unlike the brooding villa we had left behind us, that we each openly smiled in expectation of the homely welcome we were sure awaited us; in that, we were not to be disappointed.

Inside the inn, all was simplicity and rustic comfort. Although there seemed to be no windows, the plain white walls, punctuated by plain wooden doors and stairways leading to the upper and lower recesses of the house, imbued the atmosphere of the place with a soft light all their own. Through the open door leading to the 'Stube' stood a black stove, stark against yet more white walls, and rough wooden tables – scrubbed, like the floors, spotlessly clean. This limpid whiteness was brightened constantly by flowers set on tables and in alcoves. Heartening though this scene was, a moment of puzzlement crept into my mind: something was missing, something that should be there . . . and wasn't. In an instant, the thought had passed – we were confronted by our host, a person of remarkable friendliness waiting anxiously to attend to our every requirement.

'Our modest house is honoured, sir,' announced the innkeeper. His voice was kindly and courteous, his bow of welcome almost a parody, more suited to the theatre, perhaps. Mary, I could see, was as taken with our host's appearance just as much as I was, but she managed to control the smile that threatened to broaden into girlish laughter. As my wife addressed the innkeeper, I studied him more closely.

'We should like two rooms,' declared Elsbeth crisply. 'One for my husband and myself, and one for our daughter.' Our host listened as though hanging on each trivial word, his thin, arched eyebrows raised at the alert, and in stark contrast to the almost unnatural whiteness of his skin. His mouth, too, though thin, stood out boldly and surprisingly red, while the final touch of artificiality was supplied by his crop of hair – deep black, and obviously dyed. Vanity, perhaps? An unusual display for a venue so off the beaten track, I told myself. Not far behind our host stood a once-handsome but now emaciated Frau. Worn out by work, white-haired, she made no concessions to the passing of time over her ageing face. Like the innkeeper she smiled a gentle welcome, adding to this a simple, open-handed gesture that invited our trust and a warm response; but for a moment, when her eyes fell upon Mary, her anxious gaze flicked almost instantaneously away, troubled and furtive. The furs that Elsbeth and Mary wore made it quite clear that we were travellers of no little worth, a rare and welcome source of custom in this remote valley. It crossed my mind that the Frau was anxious that we might consider the inn not suited to our tastes, and I hastened to reassure her.

'Your situation here is both charming and secluded . . . just what we require . . .'

The woman curtsied slightly, obviously pleased, but it was her husband who replied. The near-perfection of his English added a quaintness to his dignified speech.

'We are simple people, but everything we have is placed at your disposal. Your rooms will be homely and warm, just as is our hospitality. Our name, sir, is Hubert . . .' A fond gesture drew his wife shyly to his side, and she half-curtsied again as he introduced her to us. 'Frau Minna . . . my good wife.' He smiled jovially at her, and she blushed as he spoke. 'You will never forget her cooking for as long as you live . . .'

These formalities concluded, our luggage was deftly collected to be taken upstairs, and we prepared to follow the sturdy fellow – Hans by name – who was to lead us to our rooms. We were still not free of Herr Hubert's hospitality, however.

'Some refreshments, sir?'

'Some tea, perhaps . . .' interjected Frau Minna, thoughtfully. 'Or some warm wine – it is cold now, even during the day . . .' The sleigh journey – we could still hear the departing jingle of bells – had been most invigorating, and the thought of a steaming beverage was to all our tastes.

'Tea . . .' cried Elsbeth happily, '. . . how splendid. In our room, please. I cannot wait to change my clothes . .'.

'Oh, please,' trilled Mary, 'but I should like some of your "warm wine" . . . if it is red, that is . . .'

The eagerness of her response both amused and disarmed any mild disapproval that Elsbeth or I might have voiced, had the occasion been less indulgent; accordingly, I confirmed our request for tea and a little Glühwein, and was thanked effusively by our host as he handed me the keys to our rooms. While Hans gathered up our various items of luggage, we looked about us; in the whole establishment, there was only one other guest – a cheery old peasant seated in the far corner of the Stube, drinking and watching all that went on with twinkling interest. We had barely started to follow Hans across to the stairs, with Mary chattering gaily to her mother, when the old peasant nimbly rose and intercepted us, glass in hand.

'Prost!'

I replied in kind, but without encouragement; I had no mind for this sort of confrontation, but the peasant was not to be put off.

'*Engländer?*' he beamed upon me. 'I am Otto! How-do-you-do! Button-my-shoe! Mixed-pickles-on-board! Ahoy!' Following which display of verbal dexterity, he cheerfully raised his glass, maintaining the bravado gesture until we were finally out of his sight upstairs. Elsbeth, ever prepared to admonish such impropriety, was about to put the fellow in his place, but I urged her on quickly. To have addressed the man would have meant running the danger of being perpetually buttonholed whenever we met again, and made to suffer the ordeal of Herr Otto's linguistic talents *ad nauseam*. Mary, less aware of the more regrettable aspects of such a person, made no attempt to hide her amusement.

'Papa – they are so quaint . . .! We shall be happy here,
I know it. It's so different from that dreadful Villa Diodati – '

'There are many strange things *here*, my pet . . .' observed her mother, pausing wearily on the stairs.

I glanced at Elsbeth, surprised that she too had noticed
that missing element that had nagged at the back of my
consciousness ever since we'd arrived. But as so often
before, I had miscalculated her powers of observation.

'Didn't you notice too, Howard? The innkeeper – Herr
Hubert – how badly his hair was dyed . . .!'

'Perhaps it's a wig . . .' suggested Mary, her eyes full of
mischief. 'Perhaps he comes from a long line of waiters . . .!'
Elsbeth, though tired, joined in Mary's girlish laughter.

'Switzerland is full of surprises!' she smiled.

We were on the landing now. Hans was well ahead, opening doors and depositing luggage in each room.

'The surprises are not only concerned with people,' I
remarked. 'Perhaps you will have observed that there are no
crucifixes to be seen – not anywhere. Nor even the small
portraits of saints, as is the usual custom . . .'

'How odd . . .' dutifully echoed Elsbeth. 'Could our innkeepers be extreme Protestants, do you think, Howard . . .?'

'Or even Israelites?' teased Mary.

'Swiss Israelites . . .?' Elsbeth half-stifled a giggle.
'Surely that's not so . . .?

'Oh, Mama – ' laughed Mary out loud, ' – what fun
we're going to have! Unleavened bread and Swiss cheese
for supper, even!' It was good to see them both so content
with our new surroundings. While my darling Mary
opened the window of her room and stared enchanted at the
dancing fall of snowflakes against the gathering darkness
outside, her mother solicitously unpacked the child's valise,
prior to dealing with her own.

I left them there, and entered the adjacent bedroom
alone. Suddenly I felt very weary, and laid myself upon the
massive double bed that shared domination of the room
with an ancient but efficient iron stove. My mind refused to
rest; for some reason, the shadowy figures I had hunted so

assiduously at the Villa Diodati insisted on peopling not only the deeper crannies of my consciousness, but almost, it seemed, corners of the room itself, despite all my attempts to turn my thoughts from them. That episode of our expedition was past, ended; for Elsbeth's sake, we were here to indulge in harmless relaxation, to free myself from the intense, secretive and irritable mood that had increasingly come to dominate my normal affability. I knew she dreaded the continuation of our journey onwards to Italy, with all the pressures it would bring, and I was determined that this brief sojourn at Gasthof Ritterhof should be an idyllic one. Yet the sensation of unease persisted. Without reason, unbidden questions began to form in my weary mind. Why did I feel such an instinctive bond between this simple inn and the sinister Villa Diodati? A homecoming . . . for whom? For Shelley – no, for Mary – but why? The confusion, far from clearing, intensified into a sharp, throbbing headache. My work is set aside, I told myself – I am free of them all: Shelley, Mary, his Lordship – all!

'My dear, you really mustn't talk to yourself like that. And remember what we agreed – no work!'

It was Elsbeth, returned from Mary's room; I could see she was upset. I should have shown concern, some sign of sympathy, I know – but for a few moments longer the only questions in my mind rejected all reality other than my dark obsession. I barely comprehended or acknowledged her tight-lipped complaints as, brusquely, she set about transferring our belongings throughout the room.

'I'm afraid Mary is a little over-tired. I have had to speak to her quite sharply . . .' She paused, waiting for me to question her about what had happened. But I was lost; in my mind's eye, I saw only the looming silhouette of the Villa Diodati, that treasury of dark knowledge. I had searched out everything of use there, picked every secret clean . . . and yet . . . could there be something more . . . ?

'Howard – ' my wife's brittle impatience invaded my mood at last. 'Did you know that Mary keeps a hidden diary? So secret that I am not permitted to have sight of what it holds?'

'Really, my dear . . . ?' She was in no mood to be reminded that such a personal confidant was virtually a romantic necessity in a girl of Mary's age; Elsbeth herself must have kept a similarly discreet journal when young – just as did Mary Godwin throughout her rootless wanderings with . . . him. Suddenly, I grew angry with myself; why did these ridiculous thoughts persist!

'It is no concern of mine – none at all!'

Elsbeth froze, shocked by the intensity of my outburst. Before I could even attempt to explain the impossible, Herr Hubert appeared silently at the door and announced that dinner was served.

The dining-room was at once picturesque and intimate, bright curtains drawn against the snow-filled night, bold red tablecloths, meticulously laid for our meal, soft shadows delineated by mellow candlelight. We sat and waited. I was uncomfortably aware of Herr Otto, seated as ever in his familiar corner, observing us shrewdly from behind the emissions of his ornate but to me noxious meerschaum pipe. Catching my glance, he waved – a small wriggle of his fingers, palm flat, a gesture I found intensely impudent. Inevitably, it was Elsbeth who ignored my muttered warning, and addressed the peasant eccentric.

'Do tell us,' she trilled, placing him firmly in the order of things crass, 'are we the only guests . . .?'

'Please?' came the guttural reply; his face showed a genuine surprise at her question.

'My mother was wondering,' explained Mary with innocent patience, 'if we were the only people staying here at the Gasthaus . . .?'

The surprise seemed to drain only slowly from Otto's face: such a question to be asked! 'No other people here, no – ' he affirmed, indicating the emptiness of the room with his meerschaum. 'No other people on board – only family Hubert. No guests, oh no – never . . .!'

'Never?' laughed Mary, certain that she was being teased and willing to enjoy such a game. Her mother looked no further than the immaculate tableware on which to base her own comment. 'Extraordinary. It's very well kept, for so little custom . . .'

I had to speak in spite of myself; naked curiosity steeled me to face Otto's rheumy blue eyes through the drift of pipe smoke.

'But how on earth do the Huberts manage?'

He looked towards me, old eyes squinting a shrewd appraisal of my purpose in asking, but with no reply. I was forced to explain, as to a dullard child. 'There appears to be no farm here – no livestock, even. How do they manage to exist on so little, the Hubert family . . .?'

His watery eyes grew huge with astonishment; here were such innocents, they did not *know*?

'*Die Marionetten* . . .!' he finally exclaimed in a whisper, as though this revelation would explain all. Then he slumped back in his seat, chuckling quietly and shaking his head incredulously at the ways of foreigners.

Before we could question Otto further, Herr Hubert had entered bearing the soup terrine and had begun to serve us with such style and dexterity that we were totally engrossed in his performance.

'You do that most wonderfully well, Herr Hubert . . .' complimented my wife.

'And with such panache,' Mary twinkled mischievously, 'just like a circus balancing trick . . .!'

Hubert acknowledged their remarks with a polite smile and the merest tilt of the head. 'I have served soup for many years,' he said, 'and before that, I was indeed part of the world of the circus. It is in the blood, you understand . . .'

I said nothing, but I could picture him in my mind's eye – that travesty of a face, those impossibly gauche movements, so deliberately artificial . . . and inhuman.

'Really?' bubbled Elsbeth. 'How fascinating!'

'A juggler?' Mary laughed, her eyes wild as she pushed her spectacles more firmly on to the bridge of her pert nose. 'I know – a lion-tamer!'

Hubert smiled, thinly, and I sensed his distaste at our clumsy hilarity. With an easy, almost comic movement, he drew back from the table and in that moment I knew what he had been, once.

'A clown!' I declared, flatly.

He bowed, smiled, and then was gone.

Made happy by this brief moment of serendipity, we turned to our soup – only to find that Herr Otto had scurried to the adjacent table and was leaning his ripe face towards us, eager with explanation.

'*Die Marionetten*' he blurted out, his pipe happily set aside. 'It is the Huberts who work the marionettes!' Intrigued, we had stopped eating, and the soup grew cold.

'They hold puppet shows *here?*' queried Elsbeth gently.

'Punch and Judy with alpenhorns!' teased Mary, her eyes wondering why I appeared so sober-faced. 'When does it happen?' It was to be this coming Saturday, Otto assured us, his face still showing surprise that we did not already know. Surely this was why we had come to Gasthof Ritterhof? Always people came – from far away, by horse and sled, great long journeys, just to see the Huberts give a performance.

A pause, as Otto looked at us slyly, convinced we were teasing an old man. 'Ach – I can see it in your eyes!' He chuckled, and poked his meerschaum at me, playfully. 'You *have* heard! It *is* for the *Marionetten* you have come...! Eh?'

Soberly, I assured him that our visit was purely accidental. His face grew shadowed, and he edged back as though aware that he had said too much. But Elsbeth had not yet finished.

'Truthfully – are you saying that nobody ever stays here at the inn except to see this ... puppet show? There must be other visitors, surely ...?'

If Otto had ever intended to reply, he had no further chance. Eva, the plump maid of all work who now advanced to clear our soup plates, observed that they had hardly been touched, and immediately knew the cause. With a flurry of skirts, she advanced fiercely on Otto and despatched him from the room with a volley of brisk, guttural yelps, none of them friendly.

'*Weg! Weg! Weg! Alter Trottel! Weg!*'

We sat in silence as, with Otto gone, Eva smiled rosily upon us, cleared away our dishes, and departed with the sweetest of smiles. It was Mary, her girlish sense of humour ever alert, who bravely broke the still moment.

'I do believe it really *is* a circus, Papa . . .!' She giggled, tossing her dark ringlets. 'Hubert the clown, followed by Eva and her dancing bear . . .! What next, I wonder?'

That night, sleep was impossible. A shifting kaleidoscope of sounds and images flowed through and over me as gently yet as insidiously oppressive as the snowfall settling outside the inn. Elsbeth slept, though uneasily, and for that I was thankful. I could neither succumb to her persistent solicitude and dismiss my imaginings, nor admit and explain them to her shallow mind. A map of Europe hovered before my eyes; lines crawled maggot-like across its frontiers, charting the progress of Shelley and Byron's restless, aimless journeyings. But there were gaps . . . many breaks in their itinerary that we knew nothing of – such as where, after the Villa Diodati, did they go? Could it be . . . why should it *not* be . . . here? There *was* a link, a bond, I knew it. Could I have come – by sheer chance, or by even a darker thread of fate – to the very wellspring of my quest, the heart of the labyrinth? Desperately I struggled to consider the logic of such an intuitive possibility – but the sounds, the sounds inside my head, the sounds all about me cobwebbed the clarity of my thought. A quietly mad but relentless orchestration of keening wind, clattering shutters, distant angry voices, countered by a vile percussion of banging, hammering, and stamping, choreographed a monstrous dance inside my head that ended only at dawn's first light. It was then at last, that I came to the truth. Not *after* their stay at the Villa Diodati . . . before they visited Byron – *before*! Shelley and Mary. Here, in this house. In a room just such as this . . . *before* . . .! And, as always, Mary writing up the day's events, her every thought, in that small, immaculately-kept diary. It would all be there . . . everything. Suddenly, all was peace. I *knew* . . . and now I could sleep. One last deceptively gentle vision drifted across my darkening eyelids: Mary, my own sweet child, writing in her treasured little book. The vision pleased me and I smiled, as I slipped into deep oblivion.

I cannot sleep. There are so many mysterious sights and sounds in

*this strange little inn. Poor father is greatly disturbed, I can sense it.
He is too obsessed by the bizarre occurrences that he investigated so
unflinchingly at the Villa Diodati, they haunt him. It is as if, far
from pursuing the ghosts of Byron and of Shelley, we have somehow
angered them, so that now they are pursuing us, in the mind if not in
the flesh . . .*

Next morning, I discovered Mary in the Stube, waiting
patiently for us to join her for breakfast. Elsbeth had woken
to find me already working at my notes, and had objected
bitterly; but I was not to be dissuaded from my task by a
woman and the ensuing quarrel had left her close to tears.
Knowing she would join us when she had sufficiently composed herself, I had gone downstairs, taking my precious
book with me. Greeting Mary, however, I found my
dream broken; she had not slept at all well, and with good
reason.

'Those dreadful sounds, Papa – !' she exclaimed. 'It was
as though we were lodging in a Yorkshire factory!' Carefully, I pointed out that since we were here out of season,
perhaps the Huberts were forced to carry out their annual
repairs in secret. Mary could hardly be expected to believe
such a lame explanation, and said so with bright candour.

'It sounded more like a drunken clog dance. Surely you
heard it too?'

'Dancing . . .' I agreed, about to sip my coffee – then, like
Mary, I froze, listening intently. The sound was there
again, furious and demented. But this time we could see
the perpetrator and his purpose; in the hallway, Hans was
nailing up a poster announcing details of the forthcoming
puppet show. At last he finished, and we laughed, just as
Elsbeth entered. She paused, puzzled and not a little put
out until we cheerfully explained, our dark imaginings of
the night quite swept away. The strange berserk hammer-
ings must have been nothing more than the Huberts preparing for the show – scenery, the stage itself – it was only
too obvious. Elsbeth was not amused, and complaining of a
headache, called for a jug of Glühwein instead of morning
tea. She cast a quick, disapproving glance at the book
beneath my hand, but said nothing. Mary noticed too, and

read the title aloud, mischievously.

'*Frankenstein* . . . by Mary Wollstonecraft Shelley . . .' She frowned, but her eyes showed interest, not disapproval. 'Really, Papa – you're supposed *not* to be working, you know . . .' I chose to say nothing, and her next words surprised me. Indeed, I felt a flicker of pleasure at so acute a question.

'How could she write such a strange story, Papa . . .? A girl of only eighteen years – my own age, in fact – '

'Nineteen, my dear,' Elsbeth corrected her. 'Tomorrow *is* your birthday, after all . . .'

'Dear Mama . . .' cooed Mary, and kissed her mother's brow; all the while her eyes were on mine – serious, questioning, demanding answers. But how could I even discuss with her the dark omens coursing through my mind? What strange secrets did that girl of eighteen comprehend nearly seventy years ago, that I could make clear to a child of today, my own daughter? Somehow, I knew the hideous answer was there to be grasped, but I could not speak it.

'Then I see I must find out for myself,' smiled Mary, as though she understood, perfectly. She took the book from me and I made no move to prevent her. The truth was, I wanted her to know, to understand . . . for herself . . .

Mary retired to bed early that night, giving the excuse that she needed adequate rest in order to face the imminent excitement of tomorrow's anniversary. Of course, I realized her true intent; the book which had been denied her all day long now lay waiting by her bedside, ready to feed her eager mind. Elsbeth, herself pleading indisposition and finding a genteel solace in increasingly frequent sips of aromatic Glühwein, also went to bed early and quickly fell into a fitful slumber. The opportunity that offered itself was not to be wasted. As night deepened, those sounds of nightmare issued forth again – the hammering, the stamping, the elusive, angry voices. My purpose was plain: to search them out, discover their fearful reason, and confront the terrible truth, face to face. Candle in hand, I advanced bravely through the shadows guarding the stairs and landing above; the sounds were louder now, yet without a precisely identifiable source. Door after door opened to my touch, only to reveal empty, uninhabited rooms. Then, just as I came to the final bedroom on that seemingly deserted floor, every sound ceased – utterly. I wheeled about, sensing some evil presence behind me in that terrible silence – and there, crooked and ancient as a fire-blasted tree, stood a wild-eyed, dishevelled creature reaching out its trembling, claw-like hand towards me! In the fragmentary moment before the candle flame guttered into darkness, I saw an incredibly old, deep-furrowed face framed by snake-like wisps of white, white hair, above a body enveloped in a long, greasy apron. Then the void swallowed us both, and I bolted for the stairs in ridiculous, mindless panic.

Stumbling and half-falling downwards to the safety of the landing below, I found Mary standing there, candle in hand, her eyes round and questioning behind her glinting spectacles. I gripped her, holding her fast, unable to say anything coherent. Her alarmed glance flicked past me towards the darkness of the landing above.

'The sounds, Papa – I had to come and see . . .'

'No!' I commanded hoarsely. 'Go back to your room at once, child . . . quickly!' I pulled her along with me, desperate to find sanctuary from I knew not what.

'But what is it?' she begged me. 'What did you see? Tell me. Is it the graveyard at the back of the inn?'

Only when I had shut the door firmly behind us did I realize that she had no fear; the terror was all mine. Our abrupt arrival had brought Elsbeth sitting up in bed, bemused and complaining.

'That dreadful banging . . .' She huddled the bedclothes about her, shivering. 'It really is too much to bear, Howard. How am I to get any rest . . .' Her voice slurred and faded as she fought against sleep and lost. Mary helped me settle her mother back on to the rumpled pillows. In the half-darkness, she probed my scattered defences with a tense, whispered excitement.

'It is so like the book, Papa. A waking nightmare . . .!'

She looked at me across the bed, and as she softly quoted that other Mary's words, I suddenly knew she was closer to understanding than I had dreamed possible in one so young.

'*My imagination, unbidden, possessed and guided me . . .!*' I ordered her to cease, but she would not. '*Was* it her imagination, Papa . . .? Or was it something more . . .?'

'For your mother's sake,' I managed to blurt out, 'we must leave this place – tomorrow!' I knew her answer even before she spoke; it was inevitable, and could not be denied.

'No, Papa – we have to stay. We have to find out the truth, you and I – together. Besides – ' her voice commanded me lightly but completely – ' – tomorrow *is* my birthday . . .!' And kissing me fondly, she slipped away to her own room, leaving me to face the night alone.

The next day was not only Mary's birthday, it was also to be the occasion of the marionette theatre, in the evening. The pleasure of celebrating our intimate family anniversary alleviated to some extent the unreasonable foreboding I felt at the prospect of the public show; but I had said nothing to Elsbeth or Mary about my eerie encounter of the night before. However, the coincidence of the two celebrations at least gave me an excuse to further my enquiries. Despite Mary's declared enthusiasm, I was determined not to involve her physically in my investigations. When I made my way to the inn's kitchen, I went alone. Frau Minna was there, preparing vegetables with Eva. They responded with sympathy and delight to my request that they might prepare a suitable cake for our birthday child – but when I tried to question them about the other subject on my mind, their attitude changed completely.

'The old man – ' I enquired pleasantly enough, ' – perhaps you can inform me of his whereabouts? I wish only to talk to him . . .'

'I know nothing of an old man,' replied Frau Minna, stonily. I turned to question Eva, but she had gone. 'I cook,' stated the innkeeper's wife, bluntly, 'and I will be pleased to bake the cake you ask for. That is all.'

There was nothing to be gained by defying this honest dismissal; I thanked her and left, but her very evasion intrigued and tortured me. What *was* the true mystery of this place?

In the afternoon I played Mary at chess, but I could not bring my mind to concentrate. Elsbeth, comfortably sipping wine against the chilling threat of the snow outside, smiled with benign vagueness as Mary deftly brought me into check again and again, happy in the belief that I was allowing her a birthday victory. My undoing was the distractions that I suffered – firstly the comings and goings of Eva and Hans, carrying benches into the room beyond, and more insidiously, by a growing sensation that I stood on the verge of a precipice. The others were blithely unaware of my secret apprehensions. Between moves, Mary took a girlish delight in slyly observing Hans clumsily manoeuvre items of scenery into the adjoining room, soon to be used as a miniature theatre.

'It is all so amateur and naive . . .' complained Elsbeth mildly. '*Must* we attend, Howard . . .? I simply cannot abide Punch and Judy shows . . .'

'We do not perform for children, madame . . .'

It was Herr Hubert who had answered. He advanced towards us, skilfully balancing Mary's candlelit cake, and presented it to her with a gauche flourish. Mary gasped with delight and applauded prettily, but my own gaze was fixed firmly on the bland white face of the innkeeper.

'This drama of yours, Herr Hubert – ' I indicated the poster in the hallway – 'I hope it is not too coarse or unsuitable . . .'

'It is perhaps a little primitive, sir,' he replied, quite unperturbed. 'But our audiences demand old favourites. Please see it as they do – a fairy tale for adults . . .' He gestured gallantly towards Mary. 'What could be better, to celebrate such a very special occasion . . .?'

'Charming . . .' cooed Elsbeth, sipping more wine. Mary spoke more to the point. 'These puppets,' she queried innocently, – 'do you work them yourselves? You – and your family?'

The innkeeper did not answer immediately, but watched

her unsmiling now, across the candle flames of the prettily decorated cake. 'We have not always been innkeepers,' he said carefully. 'Our little drama was first created . . . many years ago. By relatives . . . now deceased, you understand.'

'The old man,' I interjected quickly, 'the one who lives upstairs, your father perhaps – is *he* a puppetmaker also – ?'

'You must be mistaken, sir,' retorted Herr Hubert politely. 'It is our sincere hope that you will be adequately entertained this evening. Until then . . .' He bowed ingratiatingly, and was gone.

That evening, summoned by the clamour of an iron handbell, we entered the rustic, makeshift auditorium – somewhat gingerly, for the small crowd that bustled all about us was little better than a peasant rabble, poorly dressed, ribald and vociferous. The seats were rough wooden benches, the stage no more than a small raised platform fronted by simple curtains; the garish lighting came from red and green lanterns hung from wall brackets set all about the room. The almost childlike excitement of the audience subsided at last in response to 'the knocks' – two ominous raps of a stave on the wooden floor. The curtains were then pulled apart, clumsily . . . and the play began. But the first, unbelievable assault on our senses was the stench; sweetish, sickening, corrupting . . . something I knew, yet could not – dared not – identify. Elsbeth immediately complained of feeling faint, and I offered her my kerchief with which to cover her mouth and nose – a device used also by the ragged audience, casually, as though it was an accepted hazard, cheerfully undergone without complaint. Like them, Mary was too enthralled by the sights on stage, to overtly register that awful, enervating smell. I too watched, incredulous, appalled, yet fascinated. The settings, if that they could be called, were crudely painted in black and white and grey, punctuated violently by great daubs of lurid scarlet. The awkward-limbed marionettes, when they appeared, quite numbed my every sensation; not only were they extraordinarily lifelike, they were, startlingly, *life-size*. The total effect at once mimicked yet mocked reality; it was a nightmare come to life. *Her nightmare . . .!*

The story told by the play was as Herr Hubert claimed, primitive to the point of melodrama, and quickly stated.

Scene One: A Bedroom. A female marionette – The White Princess – struts on stage, and after taking in the audience, lies down upon the bed. At the window, the leering face of the marionette to be known as the Magician appears, made more hideous by the Japanese mask he wears. The curtain falls, to cries of frightened enthusiasm from the childlike audience.

Scene Two: A Cell. The third marionette – The Black Murderer – reclines, lifeless, in a coffin. The Magician enters, and with weird, expressive gestures, mesmerizes the Black Murderer into life. Rising from his tomb, the hideous zombie staggers, club-footed and with outstretched arms, first towards the shrieking audience, then offstage. Curtain.

Scene Three: The Bedroom. The White Princess is asleep, as the Black Murderer stares in at her from the window. She sits up as the Black Murderer enters, and is drawn by him into an obscene Dance of Death – for at its climax, the bride-like sacrifice is strangled and flung sprawling limply upon the bed. Just as the Black Murderer is about to stalk away, he is confronted by the Magician, who, enraged with grief, grapples with the vile destroyer and finally stabs him to death, urged on by the rabid cries of the now almost hysterical audience. Thus the play ended; but their rapture continued like the baying of wild beasts.

Elsbeth, Mary and I sat transfixed, petrified amongst that sickening pandemonium. For what we had witnessed, we dared not believe . . . the eyes, the very mouths and painted lips of those supposed wooden puppets – *had moved*. Not only that: when the Magician's knife struck home, *blood flowed*! Was this the unholy ritual that these crass, ravening animals had come to see: *marionettes that bled?* Whimpering, Elsbeth sought out a tiny concealed flask and raising it to her pallid lips, drained it. She shuddered, white-faced, her eyes shut tight against the dream that howled and stamped its feet all about us. Mary clung tightly to me, face averted, but her bright, feverish eyes still looked eagerly towards the stage. I could feel the mounting excitement of her tense body, the rapid flutter of her breath – and then, simultaneously, we both gasped aloud. The remaining puppet – The Magician – had stepped forward to acknowledge the orgiastic applause and with a flourish, removed his mask. The face revealed was not that of any puppet: *it was Hubert . . .*

Somehow, we left that amphitheatre of dread, and between us Mary and I brought Elsbeth to our room, where we laid her fully clothed upon the bed. Fatigue, shock, and the effects of the heady wine had brought her to a state of waking coma; she seemed almost totally unaware of who we were or where she was – a merciful though temporary amnesia. Leaving my wife safely at rest, I now escorted Mary to her room, bidding her to lock her door until morning. We had seen enough and I was determined we should leave as early as possible the next day. But the unquestioned silence that lay between us could not endure.

Regarding me with a brave, tremulous smile, Mary held out the book that we both knew now by heart.

'Everything is here, Papa . . .' she murmured. 'Enriched, embroidered . . . but only an echo of what we have seen tonight. Is it not so . . .?'

I could not deny it. The evil centre of those dark imaginings existed here in this simple, terrifying country inn. *This was the source!*

'Herr Hubert – the Magician, the Prometheus firemaker – he has to be the model for the Baron!' She spoke with growing excitement, each thought providing fuel for further speculation. I could only agree with her, our minds were so finely in accord.

'Some other family ancestor,' I corrected her. 'Who knows for how many tens of years this vile ritual has been performed . . .'

'And the White Princess – ' Mary continued keenly – 'is Elizabeth . . . Frankenstein's dear bride, destroyed on her wedding night by his own vengeful creation – '

'A creature without a name . . .' I shuddered at the memory of what we had seen, but looking into her face, I saw the feverish glow of excitement rising there again. I sensed that this child would dare anything to know the truth, and the challenge I expected, even hoped for, came.

'If the source is here . . . then so is a most terrible secret . . .' Mary insisted.

'Those sounds . . . ' I had not her courage; I dared only to whisper the thought. 'The making of those hideous puppets . . .'

'*The workshop of filthy creation . . .!*'

The words she uttered were from the book, Mary Shelley's own; and we had seen for ourselves the product of that nightmare. Still she continued quoting, relentlessly. '*I succeeded in discovering the cause of generation and life, nay — more: I became myself capable of bestowing animation upon lifeless matter . . .*'

The words came readily to me now, stirred by her eager prompting: '. . . *bodies deprived of life, which from being the seat of beauty and strength, had become food for worms . . .*' My throat choked with the memory of that first opening of the curtain and the wave of sickeningly sweet putrefaction that had greeted us.

'*Who shall conceive the horrors of my secret toil, as I dabbled among the unhallowed damps of the grave, or tortured the living animal to animate the lifeless clay . . .*' She paused, breathlessly, my shining angel of truth. 'Papa – what *is* it that they do? If *she* saw that, then surely so can we!' Her spirit consumed me, and I lost all fear. Taking her hand, I led the way on to the landing, and together we trod the shadowed stairway upwards.

Hubert was standing there, half-hidden by the eerie darkness, as though long awaiting our coming.

'Can I help you, Mr Lawrence . . .?' His arrogant civility took me aback, and tongue-tied, I could not frame a question. It was Mary who spoke, bravely.

'The poet Shelley – and his mistress, Mary Godwin – '

'I was never privileged to meet them, miss,' Hubert interrupted blandly.

'The old man – your father – ' I demanded hoarsely. 'He was the puppetmaster when they came here, just as he is now – admit it, man!' Such was my confidence that I would brook no more evasion. Hubert's face brooded, cruelly, before speaking – harshly now, without any trace of servility.

'My father does not merely work the marionettes, sir – he creates them! See for yourselves!' With a savage gesture, he wrenched open the door at his side, and Mary and I clung together, rendered dumb by what we saw in the room beyond. Standing there was the old man, grim, dignified and commanding. He said nothing, but stared out at us with eyes so old, so infinitely weary that even in my fear I felt compassion. All about him a thick, sulphur-yellow vaporous mist coiled and swirled like an aetherial snakepit. In his hand was a butcher's blade, bright with fresh blood; on the bench at his side was something that had once been made of flesh and bone, from which now arose that awful, familiar stench of corruption; and behind him, the hulking, inhuman figure of the Black Murderer, grotesquely erect. In that same split second, as its yellow, ghoulish eyes registered and fixed on Mary, Hubert slammed the door to, shutting out that hideous vision. Still we could not move, fixed by the malice of Hubert's thin, ghastly smile.

'Does it satisfy you, Mr Lawrence, now that you have seen our "workshop of filthy creation"?' His dry, strangely aristocratic voice commanded us grimly. 'You will ask no more questions. And you will leave early tomorrow, of course. For now . . . sleep well . . .' As he returned to the monstrous room from which he had come, the spell of fear was broken, and we fled.

We regained Mary's room, and there I would have stayed to guard her, but she was adamant: we should both rest before leaving the next morning. I left her fondly; yet as I went I observed again that bright flush of fever in her eyes and even as she closed and locked the door after me, her diary was already at hand, open for use. Sweet, brave girl – to be so composed that she could commit the night's bizarre experiences to paper! But she was never to delineate the final horror that concludes my tale.

I did not expect to sleep, but my mind was utterly drained. Oblivion washed over me almost as soon as my head touched the pillow, and I slipped into a velvet deep of sheer exhaustion. It was Elsbeth who woke me. She had cried out, only once, but in such deep and genuine alarm that I was fully alert to the unseen danger.

'Mary – my child!' She was sitting bolt upright. Flinging herself at our bedroom door in a fit of desperation, she cried out again. 'She is in terrible danger – I know it!' She struggled with the locked door, frantically. 'Howard – for pity's sake – *quickly*!'

I opened the door and we came to Mary's room. The rest was nightmare. Her bedroom door, smashed from its hinges, hung loosely open. Inside lumbered the vile form of the Black Murderer; held in his arms, swooning but not afraid, was Mary – her white nightgown clinging to her loose-limbed body, clasped tightly to that noxious creature in a bridal *danse macabre*. On the floor, crushed by those massive brute feet, were my child's delicate spectacles, alongside the open, unfinished diary. Elsbeth choked and fainted against me; my nerveless hands could not support her collapsing body, and she fell unconscious at my feet. I reached out, mute and helpless, knowing I was unable to prevent the ultimate act of horror. But suddenly I was thrust aside; I recall only the dark, urgent figures of Hubert and the Old Man mastering the monstrous creature, dragging him and his needless, trailing strings out of that ravaged room to I know not where. One final image forever haunts me – the living but mindless face of a doll that was once my own sweet child, delivered into damnation and madness by her father's corrupting ambition. For all the knowledge I had gained, I had lost my very soul: and will I ever find forgiveness . . .?

The speaker paused and asked for a glass of water.

'Are you saying,' Sir Francis mumbled, first clearing his throat noisily, 'my dear sir, are you saying that the Frankensteins really existed? That their heirs exist still?'

'For all I know,' the author replied with surprising blandness. 'the Huberts as they call themselves may even now be at work manipulating their puppets.'

'Manipulating? Do you mean there lives an inn-keeping family in Switzerland which fashions marionettes out of corpses,

the corpses of murdered guests, and imbues them with some kind of damned life?'

'I have no evidence that the Huberts have ever killed anyone at all,' Howard Lawrence said. 'There was . . . is no need . . .' He paused and sipped water. 'The proximity of the graveyard . . .'

There was silence then. Sir Francis looked about him. The members seemed duly impressed.

'I have one further question.' A member at the far end of the room raised a limp arm. 'What happened to your own family? How did mother and daughter survive their appalling ordeal?'

'As patients,' the author replied in a gentle voice, and for the first time that night Sir Francis registered the fact that the middle-aged writer's hair was white, totally white, and that his skin was that of an old man.

'Professor Lawrence,' came the voice from the back, and Sir Francis realized that it was that of the Chairman. 'In our opinion, your story is a pack of lies. The whole world knows that the book Frankenstein is an invention, a novel based on the nightmares of a wretched, over-imaginative young girl . . .'

Once again, the teller of the tale grinned.

'What my poor daughter and I have seen, we have seen,' he said in a hollow voice. 'What we have heard, we have heard.' He paused and his smile vanished.

'What we have dreamed, we have dreamed . . .'

ROBERT MULLER

COUNTESS ILONA
or
THE WEREWOLF REUNION

adapted by ROGER MALISSON

Mr Pettifer was late.

He hurried breathlessly down the corridor, a small, anxious, elderly man, followed rather more sedately by one of the Club servants who carried a candelabrum to light his way.

Grotesque shadows leapt and danced from the flickering, dripping candles as the slight scurrying figure reached the door at the end of the passage. It led to the room where the more punctual members were assembled for the evening's meeting.

He tried the handle; the door was locked. Kneeling, he peered eagerly through the keyhole. The members had already taken their seats and a tall stocky stranger was standing on the dais, his back to the door. Mr Pettifer turned desperately to the sombre lackey: 'I must get in. I'm one of the judges. Can't you . . .?'

The servant's face remained impassive, and his hand descended with finality on to Mr Pettifer's thin shoulder. Reluctantly, the little man dropped the handle and pressed his ear to the door. He could hear the new candidate begin his address:

'Gentlemen — my story, though it happened only a few years ago, will doubtless sound more appropriate to that pre-eminently superstitious era known as the Middle Ages, but I can guarantee its truth with my life; even with my honour, gentlemen, as a man whose very existence has been scarred — some would say, destroyed — by the horrendous facts I am about to relate.' The voice was pitched low and strong, with a faint mid-European accent . . .

An excellent example of Gothic architecture is Castle Tyrrh, which stands remote in the wild and rugged countryside of Eastern Hungary. It was built by the murderous robber-barons who infested that land long ago, and to them its grim aspect and inaccessibility, the danger to prying travellers from the wild beasts in the surrounding woods, were inestimable advantages.

The castle was – and is yet! – inhabited by the elegant Ilona, Countess Tyrrh. She presides over her estate as to the manner born, so that the most discerning observer might never guess her penurious origins; for Ilona was born the bastard daughter of a tradeswoman, and reared in the reeking slums of Budapest. From the first she was determined to rise from the slime of the streets, and being gifted with talent and beauty as well as intelligence, she managed to earn quite a reasonable living as a café entertainer. In this she was helped, as one might expect, by the numerous men she attracted, and eventually she entered an older and more lucrative profession. After all, such as she have little to lose.

During the course of her dubious career she shook off every trace of that squalid poverty to which she might have seemed destined from birth, and finally achieved respectable admission to the leisured class. For, following her childhood deprivation and ignominious success as the most desired and expensive courtesan of the city, came the unexpected arrangement of her calamitous marriage to the Count.

To Ilona, it seemed a fairy-tale climax in a life of hardship and struggle. At thirty she was not quite so attractive as before, and her future was uncertain. But now, thanks to a blessed quirk of fate, she could marry her prince and live happily ever after in peace and security. It was all she had ever wanted. Ask, and it shall be given – to your cost, usually, or too late.

Count Anton Tyrrh was a man whose evil nature made the worst reprobates in the land shudder. His peers shunned him, and despised him for a violent, uncivilized brute. As for the common folk, they regarded him with superstitious horror; in that unenlightened country myths and legends still cling in the popular imagination even as the new scientific theories fascinate modern minds here. The Count came from contaminated stock, and such tales were whispered of his bestial viciousness, of his unnatural, rabid cruelty, that his name became a byword in his province for all that was abhorrent and dreaded. This was the man

Ilona, in her ignorance of his true nature, married. But he did not long survive the union; within twelve months he was dead, and ambiguous, fearful rumours surrounded that death.

The same year which brought the marriage and demise of the Count also saw the birth of Ilona's son Bela, the sole heir. And exactly ten years afterwards – that is, on 13 March 1880 – the Countess Ilona chose to invite four old friends to the castle for a very special reunion party.

That morning began as usual. At dawn Ilona took her dog, a giant docile wolfhound, for a walk through the wooded grounds. As she re-entered the Castle her highly-trained servants bowed dutifully. She passed through the main hall, and only her little maid Magda, who regarded the Countess with awed devotion, glanced around to see that no one was looking and quickly crossed herself as her mistress swept up the staircase to her room.

Magda felt apprehensive about the arrival of the expected guests. Downstairs it was whispered that there was a man from the past whom the Countess hated with a vindictive and implacable hatred, and Magda knew from painful experience that it was not wise to arouse the Countess's wrath. Still, maybe the Lady had decided to forgive and forget, though she'd heard even more terrible rumours about –

'Magda! Stop gawking, girl, and fetch the Countess's tray.'

The stern voice belonged to the major-domo, Andras. Magda dropped a curtsey and shot off to the kitchens like a startled rabbit.

In her room, Ilona stretched luxuriously on her bed in the half-darkness, sleek and contented. Maturity suited her. Her slender figure in the thin white negligée was a little more rounded than formerly, perhaps; but the vicissitudes of her life were etched only faintly in the fine lines around her large expressive eyes, which grew impenetrable as a cat's when she dreamed her secret dreams.

Presently there was a knock at her door and Andras entered with her breakfast. Quietly and methodically he set down the tray and poured her coffee into a Meissen cup.

He broke a fresh egg on to the meal of steak tartare and sprinkled it with seasoning. Then he straightened. A tremor crossed his strong features; his gloved hands remained extended over the tray like a penitent's.

Languidly Ilona reached out and began to draw off the white gloves, finger by finger, in a half-playful, caressing gesture. It was the voluptuous, private ritual of two long-familiar lovers.

They did not hear the thunderous knocking on the main door, which Magda hastened to open. She admitted a tubby, buoyant teddy-bear of a man in a hairy overcoat who announced himself as Zoltan Vinzenz, grumbled good-naturedly over the discomfort of his journey and demanded the whereabouts of his hostess in a loud, wheezy, genial voice.

'The Countess is in her room, sir,' said Magda timidly, helping to relieve him of his hat and coat.

'What, not down yet? Shame on her! Ye gods, what a mausoleum.' He stopped short as he surveyed the great echoing hall which, in spite of its rich furnishings, still managed to sustain an atmosphere of medieval gloom. 'Poor Ilona, buried alive in such a place! Miles from any-where civilized! Ah well, fortunes of war as they say. Now then girl, I've travelled all night and I'm hungry as a wolf. What do you propose to do about it? Eh?'

'There is a buffet for the gentlemen.' Magda indicated a long table laden with delicacies at the side of the hall.

'Splendid! That's more like it, eh? This country air gives one an appetite, what?' This last remark was addressed to no one in particular. In the course of it he strode across to the table, grabbing cutlery and napkins from one of the silent servants in attendance, and began heaping a plate with salmon. Just for a second, with a forkful half-way to his mouth, he paused. Some prickling instinct seemed to warn him that he was being watched by eyes other than the servants'. He glanced quickly and uneasily towards the gallery which ran the length of the hall. Nothing there, of course. Creepy places, these moribund old castles.

Zoltan shrugged and applied himself avidly to his favourite occupation. He had known Ilona for years, for they had both been born in the same grimy district. When revolutions had broken out all over Europe thirty years before, few had raised the flag of protest more enthusiastically than that thin, ragged idealist, Zoltan Vinzenz. In fact he had spent a year in a sordid Prussian jail as punishment for his subversive activities. It was here that Zoltan had learned his first lesson in expediency. Later he had managed to accommodate himself to an important fact of politics; that no matter what radical changes are made in policy or personnel, government ultimately means the oppression of the miserable majority by the happy few who rule. Quieting his conscience with the logics of self-interest, therefore, Zoltan decided he didn't want to be a member of the downtrodden masses any more.

He became a sort of mercenary-by-proxy, that is to say, an arms merchant; a dubious profession no doubt, but a very remunerative one. For a number of years now he had been a confidential agent of Otto von Bismarck who, given his head at that time, would willingly have shot dead the likes of Herr Vinzenz for their attempted revolt in 1848. This irony was not lost on Zoltan, and he congratulated himself frequently on his shrewdness and success – witness the valuable masterpieces, mistresses and mansions he had almost carelessly accumulated on his way to the top of his profession; all due to living at peace with his idealistic and, happily, volatile fellow men! After all, people always appreciated the painstaking suppliers of their basic needs. Give them the means to murder each other, and they were grateful for his contribution to whatever cause they supported! And a happy, sympathetic chap like him got on terribly well with most of his important customers. With a proper understanding of mankind, life was really very simple.

Suddenly a familiar scent assailed his nostrils. He wrinkled his nose in a disgusted, anticipatory grimace, then turned with a hearty smile on his round face to welcome the newcomer.

'Why, Felix! I might have known!'

'Zoltan, my dear fellow!' If the second guest also felt a

qualm of repulsion at meeting his old acquaintance, it hardly showed. Dr Felix Kraus, a slim, well-preserved man, stepped forward eagerly and the two embraced with a convincing show of mutual enthusiasm.

'What a surprise! I had no idea you were invited!'

'You were an obvious choice,' said Zoltan, returning to his meal. 'Ilona's always adored you. But frankly, I'm surprised she asked me. D'you know what her last words to me were, when I saw her ten years ago? She said to me, she said, "Hell is too good for you, my dear Zoltan." She's planning something strange if you ask me.' He nodded wisely and spooned more caviare on to his plate.

Felix was hardly listening. He had just noticed the pretty Magda, who was standing demurely at the end of the table; his eyes gleamed for a moment with an expression of furtive lust. Zoltan noticed with distaste the subtle layer of make-up that the doctor had applied to his face, once handsome, but now bearing the marks of continual debauchery so plainly to experienced eyes. If there was one thing Zoltan detested more thoroughly than a prating moralist, it was a conceited and ageing fool.

Felix wrenched his attention back to Zoltan. 'Ah, yes, quite,' he said vaguely. 'Tell me, has our hostess put in an appearance yet? Who else is invited, do you know?'

'There's no guest list,' said Zoltan flatly. 'And it's too early for Ilona. She'll be making up or dressing I expect, you know what women are. None better, eh?' he spluttered, digging Felix clumsily in the ribs and spilling caviare on to his sleeve. 'But seriously, why don't you join me in some of this excellent food? You must be hungry after your journey.'

'No, thank you; my weight, you know,' said Felix, patting his taut stomach. He turned abruptly to Magda.

'My dear Fräulein, may I be shown to my room now?'

Magda glanced at Andras, who had entered the hall a few minutes before and was watching the guests with interest. He nodded to her curtly.

'Of course, sir.'

'How's the killing business?' was Felix's parting shot.

'It flourishes, my friend,' called Zoltan through a mouthful of fish. He glanced at the keen, intelligent face of the major-domo and chortled coarsely. 'Bread and murder!' he proclaimed. 'Two of mankind's indispensable commodities, son. Bakers and hangmen never starve. It's true, you needn't smile. Now then, is there any more of this delicious caviare?'

While Andras organized fresh supplies, Felix followed the maid up the wide staircase and along the gallery. The walls were adorned with the Tyrrh family portraits, and a haughty, sensual lot they looked, thought Felix. Some of the faces bore the unmistakable stamp of depravity or insanity. 'Anton, Count Tyrrh. 1820–1870', read the metal plate fixed beneath the last portrait. Felix paused and glanced up expectantly; the canvas was blank. Gazing at the empty frame, an unpleasant feeling of insecurity assailed him. Perhaps Ilona couldn't bear to look at her deplorable husband's likeness? Well, he could understand that.

A sudden crash from a nearby room made him start and turn, but all was still. Only Magda was present, waiting patiently outside his room. He followed her into the comfortable apartment, marvelling at her downcast serenity. She reminded him, as did all the servants here, of the kind of human still life Vermeer had painted. Too long in the atmosphere of this castle, he reflected, would have excoriated the nerves of lesser mortals. Maybe they were simply too stupid and otiose to notice.

Magda watched him with covert admiration as he flung down his travelling-case and reclined carelessly on the large bed. His self-assured charm struck her not as vain and dissolute, but exotic and exciting, just as Felix had intended.

'Now then, my dear, tell me your name and why we have been invited here.'

'It's Magda, sir, and I don't know, I haven't asked,' she answered shyly, flattered at his interest.

'You have a charming voice, Magda. It's sensual but not vulgar. Will you visit me in the afternoon, at about three-thirty?' He smiled at her astonished look. 'We haven't time to equivocate, have we? You see, my dear, I am an erotomane, that is, an indefatigable pursuer of lovely women. I used to be a doctor, a nerve specialist, but I gave that up after an old and ugly aunt of mine died and left me a lot of money, which I squander at will on my favourite hobby. I usually get what I want, and I want you.'

'Sir?' Magda stared vapidly, bewildered at his frank attack.

'Unless, of course, you have some squalid arrangement with that strapping fellow downstairs?'

'Oh no, sir,' said Magda guilelessly. 'Andras is more ambitious you see, sir.'

Felix turned away to hide a grin. So Ilona hadn't changed. She hadn't really changed at all.

The Countess did not appear for lunch. The meal passed quietly and afterwards the guests sought their rooms, one sleepy, the other hopeful.

Over the distant Transylvanian mountains grey clouds gathered and muttered, threatening storms. The beasts and birds of the forest fell silent, sensing thunder in the clammy atmosphere. The castle too was silent. Everybody seemed to be taking an afternoon rest.

In his nursery three doors away from Felix's room, the little Count Tyrrh moped and yawned over his book. He was tired of studying and bored with staying in. It was all the fault of those friends of Mama's; he wasn't to disturb them by playing or making a noise. Bela had peeked at the two men from the gallery when they were in the hall and found the one with the loud laugh rather vulgar and frightening, and he hadn't much cared for the other one either, the one who smiled and didn't mean it.

It was very stuffy in the nursery and he had pins and needles in his left foot. He wished Andras would come in and tell him a story or play a game; Andras was his friend. If it hadn't been for Nanny sitting there watching him he would have been tempted to go in search of Andras. She seemed to be asleep but you could never tell with Nanny, she was so old and clever she could see even with her eyes closed, a feat Bela regarded as enviable and rather awe-inspiring.

Sylva had nursed the young Tyrrhs for three generations. She sat ancient and upright in her hard wooden chair, fragile with age, her will unswervingly directed to the protection of her young charge. Suddenly her eyes opened wide.

'You must read your book, my child.'

Bela stared resentfully at the cadaverous, spindly figure. 'Why?' he muttered. 'I hate them! I hate all books, Nanny, this one most of all!' He flung the book angrily into the fire-place.

Sylva ignored the tantrum. 'You must read,' she insisted quietly, retrieving the book.

'But Nanny,' wailed the child, 'it makes me dream! Such awful dreams!'

The old woman softened. Bela had inherited his mother's classically perfect features and huge lustrous eyes; he was difficult to resist. Besides, his distress was genuine.

'Would you like a glass of milk, little one?'

Bela nodded, and Sylva went to fetch it. As soon as she was gone Bela scrambled up on to a high stool and took a colourful book of fairy-tales from the shelf. He started violently as the door swung open again – but it was only Andras.

'Come and look at this, Andras!' cried the child excitedly. Andras took the book from him. It fell open at the story of Little Red Riding Hood. There was a lurid illustration of the heroine on her way through the woods, with a huge and vicious-looking wolf skulking in the trees, its blood-red tongue hanging from jaws lined with jagged yellowish teeth. In the white spaces of the picture other wolves had been drawn by a childish hand.

Andras looked askance. 'What do you mean by this, Bela?'

'It's my dream,' explained the boy. 'Lots of wolves, with glowing eyes, hiding in the forest. But this story doesn't end how you tell it, Andras. The wolf became the grand-mother; why was that? And it says the hunter killed the wolf with his knife but you always say it was killed with a silver bullet.'

Andras smiled grimly at the child's chatter. 'The wolf only pretended to be the grandmother,' he said. 'And the silver bullet is our secret.'

Suddenly Sylva appeared at the door, pale and angry. She shuffled into the room and put her arms protectively round Bela, staring at Andras with a look of mingled fear and loathing.

'Go!' she cried shrilly.

Andras's handsome, saturnine features twisted in a scowl. 'The boy is ten years old – he ought to be told! You, his nurse,' he added contemptuously, 'you understand nothing!'

Sylva glanced involuntarily at a huge antique cutlass which hung on the wall. Andras followed her gaze and laughed tauntingly. 'That thing's no use. Remember: the bullet made of silver!' He flung the book of fairy-tales contemptuously into the fire and strode out.

The door slammed behind him, and Bela began to cry.

'Bela, my precious, I will never let it harm you, never,' crooned the old woman, and she rocked the frightened child in her arms until he grew calmer.

A major tragedy had occurred while Ilona's third guest was walking from the railway station to the castle. Hugo Hoffman, the great musician, had stepped into a puddle and mud had splattered on to his new and costly beige trousers. The scarcely-suppressed rage and sorrow he experienced as a result of this sad accident was aggravated by the inordinate length of time it took him to reach his destination. He had miscalculated the distance by several miles. Also, the village lad he had hired to carry his luggage was panting tiresomely with fatigue before they had come half-way, and the stupid creature would stop, with such a look of terrified distress, every time a branch cracked in the forest, or a timber-wolf howled from the mountains! Really, it was too bad. Hugo reached the doors of Castle Tyrrh in a grievous state of exhausted vexation. He would not have undertaken such a journey again for a kingdom.

Andras opened the doors and Hugo tottered inside.

'Tip him,' he snapped, and Andras tossed a coin to the lad, who dumped all of Hugo's suitcases in the hall and raced off home as if the Devil were after him.

Hugo refused refreshment and was shown immediately

to his room, where he threw himself on to the bed and endeavoured to rest and restore his ragged nerves. Instead he lay awake and fretted.

Why hadn't Ilona greeted him personally? Would these fools of provincial servants be able to understand that he must have his bath drawn at a temperature of 27° precisely? That he required white roses in his room because they soothed him? – In a word, were they capable of taking proper care of him? They looked a dumb and churlish lot, though the major-domo was rather attractive. Still, in general, he preferred women. Ilona had always appreciated that his genius must be protected and nurtured. She was the only person who had ever really understood him.

One day he would die, the flesh would fall from his bones with some frightful wasting disease, then they'd all be sorry, and serve them right, the philistines! No, artists simply must be given special consideration, for life treated them so cruelly. Heaven knew he did his best to preserve his talents for the world, but he did feel the need of a strong, sympathetic and loving personality to help him along his thorny path.

He'd never been robust. Geniuses seldom were. And what was it, two years now since he'd composed anything? Even his love life was on the wane. Maybe he was fading away already! He got off the bed to look, but as he reached the mirror a distant timber-wolf flung a long keening howl into the twilight. Hugo shuddered and drew the curtains. What kind of wilderness had he strayed into?

Returning to the mirror, he peered anxiously at his almost girlishly handsome face. Yes, he was showing signs of strain. Soon his youth would be gone. He sat on the bed disconsolately, his lip trembling.

Hugo had changed greatly from the lad of twenty-two Ilona had known, when he was striving for the recognition of his musical gifts in a harsh and indifferent world. Eventually he had found his fame, but success had proved catalytic to the vices and morbidities of his weak character.

Outside his door, Andras paused and listened. All was quiet. He made his way to Ilona's room and slipped inside. She was at the window, watching the rising moon.

'Only three of them have arrived so far.'

'There should be four,' answered Ilona regretfully. 'But it's too late for the other to come now. No coach will venture into this region after dusk.'

'There will be one to pay the price,' murmured Andras. Ilona smiled.

In the great hall a long table had been set for dinner. The crystal and silver glittered in the light from the blazing chandeliers. Zoltan was the first down, warming himself at the enormous roaring fire and devouring the champagne and canapés which Andras and Magda were serving. He was joined a few minutes later by his fellow-guests.

'Any ideas as to why we've been invited?' asked Zoltan.

'We are all ex-friends of the Countess,' said Hugo, sipping critically at his wine.

'Ex-lovers, you mean,' said Zoltan blandly. 'And rich. We could afford her. I bought her the Esterhazy diamond, you know.'

Hugo wrinkled his delicate nose in distaste at this vulgarity.

'What puzzles me is the occasion,' persisted Zoltan. 'I mean, are we meant to be celebrating the tenth anniversary of her marriage, or old Tyrrh's death, or the child's birthday, or what? Eh?'

'I should think her husband's death must be the chief cause for rejoicing,' said Felix with a grimace.

'I think she killed him,' said Hugo unexpectedly.

Felix shook his head and Zoltan roared with laughter. 'Ilona? Nonsense! She couldn't kill a rabbit! – And here she is! My dear . . .'

He broke off quickly as he spied Ilona descending the staircase, proud and magnificent in an exquisite white evening gown. In her hair she wore the legendary Esterhazy diamond, as a compliment to Zoltan, perhaps, or to tease him. They greeted her effusively. After a great deal of hand-kissing and flattery, Ilona seated herself at the table and her guests followed suit. Their sense of nostalgia was keen; ten years seemed to have slipped away like a night's rest.

'I must apologize for the absence of our fourth guest, my

friends,' said Ilona. 'Unfortunately the leader of His Majesty's unofficial opposition insists on travelling in his own coach, and I fear the heavy rains have delayed him.'

There was a general gasp.

'Von Haller? What, you and that – that devious rascal!'

'But Ilona, he's such a dreadful bore! All he ever talks about is politics!'

'How could you bear his company?'

Ilona laughed and changed the subject. 'It's good to see you all looking so prosperous!' She leaned back and raised her glass. 'What shall we all drink to? What do we hold most dear?'

'Why love, surely,' said Felix, with his charming smile.

'No, art,' exclaimed Hugo petulantly. 'It's the only thing that matters, ultimately.'

'Money,' contradicted Zoltan. 'People can provide both love and art, and people, thank God, can always be bought. Anyhow, here's to you, Ilona!'

'The great experience of all our lives,' supplied Felix hastily.

They raised their glasses and drank. The evening passed pleasantly enough with wine and laughter, and much reliving of old times.

Over coffee Zoltan, in his cups, began holding forth about his friend and hero, Bismarck.

'Say what you like,' he said dogmatically, waving his glass, 'democracies will never achieve the great feats despotism has produced. Blood and iron, that's what's needed today.'

'Yes, the Chancellor's managed to make a virtue out of ruthlessness,' yawned Felix. 'He seems to have bought peace and security with it. I can't see Germany ever embarking on another major war in Europe. But the bloodletting, my dear fellow! Atrocious!'

'The masses, what do they matter?' cried Zoltan heatedly. 'Most are born to die for the grand designs of tyrants, and they're happy to do so for a living wage!'

'All this must be very boring for our hostess. It's boring for me, at any rate,' Hugo interrupted truculently. 'Ilona, may I ask you about the late Count? Was he really as appalling as his reputation?'

Zoltan chuckled. 'He thinks you killed him.'

'Then Hugo is mistaken,' she replied calmly. 'The Count was killed in a hunting accident, attacked by wolves, you know. I'm afraid he suffered a great deal.'

The awkward pause this statement produced was broken by the appearance of Bela; the guests turned to the boy with relief, and Ilona introduced him.

'What an angel!' cried Felix.

Hugo, sensing competition, turned away. He did so hate to be out of the limelight.

'Here, little fellow!' shouted Zoltan boisterously, tossing the child a gold coin which he ignored, pressing close to his mother and regarding the strangers with round-eyed solemnity.

'Give him some candied fruit, Felix, he loves it,' suggested Ilona.

Felix assumed his best bedside manner. 'He will grow into a fine young man,' he pronounced, offering the sweets. Privately he thought that this oppressive, isolated old place was the worst possible environment for such a sensitive, intelligent-looking youngster. Still, it wasn't his problem . . . or was it?

When the child had accepted a candied pear and trotted obediently up to bed, Zoltan bluntly remarked that it was strange the boy had turned out so beautiful, the late Count having been quite the most hideous man he'd ever met.

'Really, you are so tactless, Zoltan,' Hugo snapped peevishly.

'It's true,' returned Ilona sweetly. 'Andras, Herr Hoffman's glass is empty. It seems unlikely, anyway, that my son was fathered by a man as repulsive as Anton.'

She paused while Hugo's glass was refilled, to let them absorb the implications of her remark. Andras handed her an old music-box with a little dancing couple on the lid. To the strains of a tinkling Strauss waltz she continued, smiling at no-one in particular.

'Do you remember that summer ten years ago, when we all behaved so . . . badly? The summer little Bela was conceived. And now, it is time to bid you all goodnight, and may I wish you a restful first night under my roof.'

She snapped shut the lid of the box and rose. The men followed suit, and bowed as she left the table. Felix lit a cigar with a thoughtful air.

'Strange that Ilona should mention the Count's death like that,' he remarked. 'The way I heard it, he did not die immediately from his accident, but a few months later, of lycanthropy.'

'What the Devil's that?' demanded Zoltan.

'Clinically speaking, it's a disease in which the patient, usually a lunatic, suffers delusions of transformation into a wolf during the hours of darkness.'

Hugo paled. 'A werewolf, you mean? But there are no such things!'

'Precisely,' answered Felix. 'It's a mental affliction. Our ancestors, in their superstitious ignorance, would have called the sickness atavism, that is, devil-dealing in order to produce a throwback to the nature of a beast. The subject was supposed to absorb and develop the more savage qualities of the brute in question, for example its strength, its sexual prowess – '

'But that's absurd!' protested Hugo, badly upset. He took a gulp of wine, made a face and turned on Andras in sudden fury. 'This is inferior wine! Filthy stuff! How dare you serve it?' He flung his glass into the grate and glared at Felix as if it was all his fault.

'What are they said to look like, these creatures?'

'Oh, enormous and very hairy, half-man, half-beast. Their strength and aggression are abnormal, and so is their craving for human flesh. They have claws for hands, and their eyes – '

'That's enough! I won't listen to any more!' Hugo stood up abruptly and marched off to bed.

'Well, he did ask,' murmured Felix. He wondered with professional interest how long it would be before young Hugo developed some crippling disorder to match his emotional hypochondria. That's what usually happened to that type of neurotic, in Felix's experience.

'He's a pathetic creature.' Zoltan took a swig of brandy. 'Well, I think I'll turn in, too.'

When she was sure everybody had retired, Magda left her bed and tiptoed along the gallery to Felix's room. Suddenly she sensed a movement in the shadows; she stifled a scream as Andras's tall figure loomed before her. He spoke caustically:

'There's no need to wait up, the fourth guest won't be arriving tonight. You slut!' he added viciously; for a moment she thought he would strike her, but he strode past her and down the staircase. Trembling and bewildered, Magda hurried to Felix's door and opened it quietly. Felix turned with a look of expectation, which dissolved into ill-concealed disappointment. Magda stopped short.

'You expected my mistress,' she said flatly.

Felix shrugged, then smiled, and drew her into the room.

'Not another word from you, my dear,' he whispered, 'Till dawn.'

In his room Hugo, about to undress, suddenly felt strange. He swayed alarmingly and clutched his throbbing forehead. It was as though he'd been poisoned . . . the wine!

With an effort he staggered to the door, calling for Andras in a hoarse whisper; his throat was dry and burning. He found the staircase and wandered down it, weaving like a drunken man, reeling against the wall. It was all so weird and misty; he was sick, all the proportions were distorted, somebody had drugged him, the dying fire and guttering candles throwing crazy red shadows in the dusky corners of the great hall, it was getting difficult to see, suddenly there was a door in front of him with a big brass handle, it was all getting senseless, any minute now he'd be on his knees asleep, no it couldn't be . . .

The organ case was Gothic, the gold embossed pipes extended to the high ceiling, there must be twenty steps leading up to the instrument and the whole vast room seemed like some unholy cathedral. Hugo stumbled and crawled towards the organ and half-fell upon the stool.

In his delirium he began to play wild discordant music, a requiem for a maniac. Then his sweating hands faltered over the cold white keys: something was behind him. Slowly, trembling, he turned.

It was Ilona, serene and beautiful in black, reclining gracefully upon the steps.

'My darling, I knew you would come!' he cried feverishly. 'You arranged all of this, didn't you? – This reunion, so that we could meet again! Ilona, I always loved you!'

'You loved so many things, Hugo,' she murmured. 'Wealth, fame, adulation, and now you have them all. Your musical genius is acknowledged; you're married to a rich princess. Strange that you cannot be content!'

'All my success is due to you, Ilona,' he said humbly. 'You sold yourself over and over again to keep me alive when I was starving in Budapest. You gave me your faith when nobody else believed. I had to leave you behind, my dearest friend, when I found acceptance in those exalted circles which would neither have understood nor welcomed you; such is the way of the world. And what has happened to me since? My genius, my zest for life, even my potency are diminishing with the years. My wife and I are separated; my fame withers. I am an artist, I have special needs, Ilona, and only you can supply them!' His voice rose to a childish wail, and tears of maudlin self-pity stood in his eyes. Covering her white hand with kisses, he begged,

'Come back to me, Ilona! Help me find peace!'

'Dear Hugo. For all you did for me, you shall have peace.' She rose and left him, and his eyes followed her with a kind of wondering adoration. To think he had once abandoned her to the streets, left her desolate and penniless while he wandered in the bright rich pastures of renown! And she had not uttered one word of blame; she would save him again! His fingers caressed the organ-keys, for only music could express his exuberance; his world was suddenly expanded, filled with elation and joy.

But what was that black hunched thing, looming out of the night to seek the lighted window? What kind of a creature was it that could stand upright to lunge its great bulk so savagely against the glass?

The night was very still. Hugo sat, frozen with shock, as the thick glass burst with a splintering crash and the beast scrambled like a dog into the room. It crouched, fixing him with burning yellow eyes, teeth bared in a venomous snarl;

then it crept towards him, silently, closing for the kill. Hugo screamed, and ran like a madman for the door, but the thing was after him; it tore him down with an easy spring, and he felt its teeth fasten on his shoulder while the great claws gouged at his flesh.

The death agonies of Hugo Hoffman rang through the stillness like a scream of torment from the very depths of hell, arousing the sleepers in that silent castle from dreams to a nightmare.

It was Zoltan who found the room leading off from the main hall and discovered the corpse. His digestion was none the better for it. Felix Kraus had seen nothing like it since wartime, but experience and professionalism sustained his composure. He made a clinical examination of the badly-mauled body and concluded that the cause of death was a wild-beast attack. He and Zoltan refused to let Ilona view the sickening sight, and so she quietened and dismissed the frightened servants and went to reassure her little boy, who was shrieking with nightmares of prowling, yellow-eyed wolves.

Zoltan, when he had recovered sufficiently, whispered to Felix through chattering teeth that Ilona's motives were now clear, for Hugo, who, she had implied, was the father of her son, had paid the penalty for his past misuse of her. Felix agreed, evincing the belief that he had been invited so as to issue the necessary death certificate. As for Zoltan, he was presumably needed as a witness.

Considerably relieved, the two surviving guests took themselves to their beds, and passed the rest of the night peacefully enough, confident that they had found out the reason, or pretext, for Ilona's reunion party.

At the Club of the Damned, the story-teller briefly paused in his narrative.

'And perhaps they were right, although some of you may be wondering why Ilona had chosen to invite four guests and not three, if three were all she required for her purposes. But, gentlemen, I see that the hour is come when you generally take some refreshment, and I confess my throat is quite dry. May I propose a short interval?'

There was a murmur of agreement and much pushing back of chairs, followed by subdued but intense discussion of the stranger's story.

Mr Pettifer turned impatiently to the patient lackey:

'Now will you open this door?'

A key was produced, the door was unlocked and Mr Pettifer was finally allowed to enter. He grabbed a glass of claret from a passing waiter and got as close as he could to the stranger, who was relaxing with his drink in a corner. He gazed earnestly at the man, and what he saw shocked him beyond measure. For sometimes the bereft of sight see clearer than their neighbours; Mr Pettifer, with only his two ears and his imagination to aid him, had built up certain mental images as he listened to the bizarre story. He shivered as he encountered the man's strange tawny-coloured eyes, and there was something odd about his mouth. Perversely, it was disfigured when he smiled, the front teeth were too long and somehow the grin gave a cold and menacing aspect to the otherwise handsome face, with its head of thick and prematurely-greying hair.

A terrifying suspicion gripped Mr Pettifer. Could this be the wolf, the werewolf? 'My life has been ... destroyed ...' The words bit into the old man's memory. What happened to that face when the moon was full?

Mr Pettifer glanced round frantically. He must warn the members of the monster in their midst; the creature must be stopped!

'To continue, gentlemen.' The candidate resumed his place on the dais and the room grew still. Mr Pettifer sank into a chair, watching him with horrified fascination.

'I have said that the Countess Ilona invited four guests to her castle. The fourth, delayed by heavy rains you will recall, completed his journey in a hired coach and arrived the morning after the slaughter of Hugo Hoffman.'

Josef, Baron von Haller, was a man driven solely by a will to power. Is it possible to climb the grimy ladder of political success and remain untainted by corruption? Not if Josef was typical. His enemies considered him a person of unrivalled deceit, but to the public and his supporters he was known as 'the man of principle'. He looked the part, which helped: blond, monocled, erect, even somewhat military in appearance; a real Siegfried, and evidently a man of uncommon common sense. He was horrified beyond words to be greeted at the castle with the news of Hugo's gruesome death, and repelled by its sinister implications. A wild beast attack? Nonsense! Who ever heard of an animal actually breaking into a building? Josef did not quite know what was going on, but he did know that a cool head and a firm hand were called for, and by Jove, he was the one to supply them! He was determined to conduct a proper investigation and get to the bottom of the whole affair. If there was a murderer loose, they might all be in danger!

He recoiled angrily from Zoltan's tales of werewolves. Such superstition was no more than one might expect from a newly-rich peasant like him. Equally repugnant were Dr Kraus's hints that he, or any of them, might be the father of Ilona's son.

'It's true,' insisted Felix, 'and she loved Hugo best, you know. He was more than a mere lover to her.'

'Do you think that's perhaps why . . .?' Josef ventured.

'Why he was murdered?' Felix continued. 'It seems likely. But the fact is, Baron, poor Hoffman was torn apart and partly devoured. Nothing human could have done that. He was barely recognizable when we found him.'

Josef was at a loss for an answer to this; it wasn't making any sense.

'I knew of Hoffman, of course,' he mused. 'Heard him play once or twice. A bit showy, I thought. Socially dead for years, of course.'

'He's literally dead now, in any case,' repeated Zoltan patiently. 'Attacked by wolves. Sure you won't have any lunch?'

'Really, Herr Vinzenz, how can you eat at a time like this?' said Josef primly.

'You'll have to address me differently soon,' chuckled Zoltan. 'I'm buying a title, as you bought yours, Baron, some years ago. And I believe it's the bane of Christianity, this denigration of the normal desires. Drink, and we are told our livers will rot; fornicate – eh, Felix? – paralysis and insanity loom. "Thirsty evils", both! But if a man has a healthy appetite, will good food kill him?' He patted his enormous paunch complacently. 'Of course not! It's all scientific mumbo-jumbo and religious hypocrisy, this prudish holier-than-thou attitude adopted by some of our revered politicians! Still, I expect it catches a few votes.'

Josef did not deign to reply, but Felix remarked, in a moment of unusual gloom, 'It's true though, my friend. We do die of our pleasures.'

Andras approached them from the shadows of the hall and addressed the Baron.

'I have informed the Countess of your arrival, sir. The Countess hopes you will understand that she is most distressed by Herr Hoffman's death and wishes to keep to her bed today. But she will be delighted to dine with you this evening.'

'Just a minute, fellow,' said Josef sharply. 'Tell me: has anything like last night's tragedy happened here before? I heard that the late Count was also attacked by wild beasts. Some kind of hunting accident, I believe?'

'We all entered service here after the Count's death,' replied Andras stolidly. 'Nothing untoward has occurred since, to my knowledge, sir.'

'Send for the police,' Josef ordered, and the ghost of a smile crossed the servant's features.

'The police would not come here, Baron. It is a tradition.'

'Why, then, summon a coach from the village! Or saddle me a horse! I will go myself to make a proper report!'

Polite and impassive, Andras met the Baron's gaze.

'The coachman from the village regrettably met with an accident last night, sir, and we keep no horses here.'

'I think Andras is telling us that the Countess does not wish us to leave yet,' interrupted Felix. 'Am I right?'

'The Countess wishes your every order to be carried out to the letter, gentlemen.' Was there a trace of a sneer in the man's voice? He turned and left.

Josef muttered and fumed, marching up and down the room, no longer attempting to conceal his agitation.

'It's rather entertaining to see you so frightened, Josef,' remarked Felix with a wicked grin. 'Strange that Ilona shows no sign of fear, don't you think?'

Josef was, in fact, very disturbed by the events of the past twenty-four hours. First the harrowing journey to this Godforsaken place, and then to be met with the news of last night's tragedy! He did not care two pins for the dead Hugo, though it seemed likely that he had not had fair play, but his politician's instinct warned him away immediately from the scent of scandal. Ilona could murder half the province for all he cared; the important thing was to get out of this or any kind of dubious situation without calumny.

Besides, those machine-like, blank-eyed servants got on his nerves; he'd taken particular exception to Andras, with his quiet insolence. Altogether, the claustrophobic atmosphere of the castle was depressing. He had expected a gay party, not a gathering in a morgue. No, there was only one thing for it: coach or no coach, he must leave as soon as he could and if that dreadful old roué Kraus and his food-slobbering companion had any sense, they'd join him.

In the afternoon the two other guests went to their rooms. Zoltan was sleepy after his enormous lunch, and Felix evidently had his eye on that plump maid. All comforts supplied, thought Josef wryly. He followed their example, tired after his journey. The air was close and clammy with the approaching storm, and he was soon asleep.

Bela left the nursery when all the guests had retired and went to stare at the blank frame which should have held his father's portrait. The sight of it always made him want to cry. He thrust his hands in his pockets and wandered back down the gallery, past the nursery where wizened old Sylva sat as if moulded to the furniture. She turned her head like a blind animal as he passed.

Ilona was still in bed when he entered her room. She took him in her arms and rocked him as if he had been ten months, and not ten years old, singing him lullabies and feeding him candied fruits from her own fingers.

'Mama, when shall we be alone again?' he asked wistfully. 'I don't like these visitors. I wish they'd go away!'

'Soon, very soon, my little love,' she murmured. 'But you mustn't worry about anything that happens. For you there is nothing to fear. Now, will you go back to the nursery? It's getting late and Mama must dress for dinner. Sylva will take good care of you.'

Her eyes followed the child with a kind of yearning despair as he left the room. She smiled bleakly at Magda, who had come to dress her:

'Never have a child!' she muttered, softly and intensely. 'Never have a child!'

The storm hung dry and brooding in the still air, until it burst in a fury as the guests were assembling for dinner. Ominous growls of thunder were preceded by vivid lightning flashes which lit the great hall with intermittent brilliance throughout the meal.

It was a gloomy enough occasion. Felix and Zoltan were experiencing an uneasy sensation of déjà-vu, though they tried to keep up some sort of social conversation. Josef, pre-occupied and tense, picked at the sumptuous food and said little. All of Ilona's gaiety, for she was very high-spirited that evening, could not arouse him.

'Well, Josef,' she sighed, settling back in her chair when dinner was over, 'It's wonderful to see you looking so prosperous, so noble and handsome! Success suits you!'

Josef smiled frigidly, and answered with his usual decorum:

'I'm delighted to see you again, Ilona, and in spite of the tragedy, looking more lovely than ever.'

It was true. Her eyes were sparkling with youthful joy; radiant and sensuous, she turned to Felix.

'As for you, my friend, you're incorrigible! Poor Magda, she couldn't resist you, could she?'

Felix shrugged vainly, rather pleased at this public tribute to his virility.

'Did you know she had bad blood?' Ilona continued impishly.

'Bad blood . . . ?' Felix paled in sudden horror.

Zoltan shouted with laughter; it was exactly the sort of joke he relished. 'More than one way of killing a cat you know, old man,' he grinned.

'If that's so, perhaps it would have been wise to bring a food-taster, Zoltan,' she suggested mockingly.

Zoltan stopped in mid-chew and stared at her blankly.

Josef frowned at this incongruous levity, and the mischief vanished from Ilona's eyes.

'Josef, you are not amused! We are not behaving conventionally, are we? You would prefer me to put on a show of grief for dear Hugo? Well, he was an extraordinary man, and he met an extraordinary death. But I will see to it personally that he has a proper burial, and his family are informed. Andras!'

The major-domo filled Josef's glass, then placed the music-box before her. Felix and Zoltan watched the miniature dancing couple on the lid with fascination as the tinkle of the waltz began, but Josef's sense of propriety was sadly affronted; he drained his glass and angrily pushed back his chair.

'Really Ilona, to countenance music, with poor Hoffman scarcely cold! It's intolerable!'

A sudden pain gripped his temples, and he rose unsteadily to his feet. Quietly Ilona closed the music-box.

'Why, Josef,' she said with concern, 'You are not well. I shall attend to you myself!'

She took his arm to support him as he staggered towards the staircase. Nervously Zoltan began to attack the chocolates. Felix shook his head and stared moodily into his glass.

Towards midnight, Josef was trying desperately to struggle out of his stupor. He was convinced that Ilona had tried to poison him. The sooner he was out of the place, the better. Hectic and clumsy, he was tossing his belongings haphazardly into a suitcase; he started violently at a quiet voice behind him.

'There are servants to pack for you, Josef. I never thought you a coward; but leave me, if that is your wish!'

Josef recovered his self-control with an effort. It didn't do to let things get out of proportion, and he might, of course, be misjudging her.

'Forgive me, Ilona, but something strange is happening here. If you are in any sort of danger, I will of course stay to protect you. But I . . .'

He stopped and rubbed his forehead. His vision was

blurred and concentration difficult.

'I only wish,' he continued carefully, 'that certain misunderstandings between us could have been clarified before you married that abominable man.'

'But our problems resolved themselves, did they not, Josef? I was married off, and you became leader of the Party.'

'I could not marry you, Ilona,' he burst out. 'I know I spoke of it, but such a marriage – I'm sorry, my dear – it could have ruined my career. Real power was within reach, Ilona! It would have been unthinkable to let it slide from my grasp! Yes, I was ruthless over the Gregor affair, but you know he was a dangerous liberal; by eliminating him we saved the Party's unity, and the country from the rule of the mob!' He paused again, confused and sweating with fever.

'And so you arranged a scandal,' Ilona prompted softly. 'I spent the night with Gregor, and the next day all the country knew of it.'

Josef's composure crumbled; he could not meet her eyes. 'We *had* to ruin his career,' he cried passionately. 'It was imperative to discredit him, Ilona! And nobody could foresee that he would commit suicide, having first murdered his wife and children! The man's brain was unhinged!' He was shouting now; the 'man of principle' was no more. 'Ilona,' he continued pleadingly, 'you found him attractive, did you not? Perhaps we should have told you what we had planned, but we kept your name secret! You suffered no defamation for this – this one small act of political expediency! Ilona – '

He turned, but she was gone. He called her name once more in hysterical despair, then sank abjectly on to the bed, spent and wretched, while the high winds screamed around the castle and his head felt as if it would split.

A sudden movement outside the window jerked him out of his torpor. He hurried to the door and called for Andras. He was taking no chances after what had happened to Hoffman.

'Is something wrong, sir?' Andras regarded the quivering Josef with calm surprise.

'The window, man! Go and look!'

Andras obeyed. 'It's only a broken shutter, sir. It will be attended to first thing in the morning. Good night, Baron, I hope you will sleep soundly.' He bowed courteously and closed the door.

Josef stared at his shaking hands. What was the matter with his eyes? Images were blurred . . . his heart pounding. If only the wretched storm would stop and let him sleep. But the storm was at the height of its fury. It blustered and shrieked relentlessly round the castle, lashing the old stone walls with pelting rain, dementedly rattling the doors; it found out Josef's window and tore about it madly, until the catch broke and the windows flew open, filling the room with squalling tempest.

Sullenly, the wind abated, the thunder ceased. There was only the patter of rain on the soaking carpet. Josef crouched on the bed as if mesmerized.

Was it a nightmare, the half-hazy familiar thing with the half-human face, whose huge shoulders filled nearly the whole of the window-frame? It flowed smoothly, silently over the sill, and skulked on all fours by his bed, gazing at him with preternatural yellow eyes.

'*You!* But it can't be – no – help! Help me, for pity's sake!' Josef flung himself, screaming, from the bed; but nothing in the world could have saved him as the slavering beast leapt swiftly and surely for his throat.

A rending crash of thunder drowned Josef's cries and the snarling, worrying sounds the creature made as it dragged its twitching prey into a corner and began, greedily, to feed.

Towards dawn Ilona rose and went for a walk with her wolfhound through the castle grounds. The storm-washed air was sweet and sparkling; the early sun dappled the trees and glittered in the dew. As she re-entered the castle, her servants were crossing the hall, bearing the body of Josef von Haller on a stretcher. Parts of the shroud were soaking red. Ilona smiled slightly and went to her bedroom, where she waited for Andras to bring her breakfast.

Zoltan rarely felt sick, but he could not touch his lunch that day. He kept pacing about, getting on Felix's nerves, muttering, 'Did you see his face, what was left of it? Did you see?' with obsessive stupidity.

'Look,' said Felix harshly. 'Hugo and Josef treated Ilona abominably; rejection, humiliation, betrayal, all the way. She may have arranged their deaths for revenge. But I will have to issue the death certificates, don't you see? And you are a witness. If she'd wanted to murder us she could have done it by now, and besides, why would she want to? I adored Ilona. Dogs and women,' he continued bitterly, 'Treat 'em properly and they'll never let you down. Give 'em affection and they'll respond with devotion. It never fails.'

'You still believe we're safe?' demanded Zoltan with a chattering laugh. 'You, of all people?' His voice rose hysterically. 'Don't you see yet, you vain fool, it's a plot to kill us all! She's got some kind of a wild animal chained up here, that madwoman – she's out to destroy us all!' In his agitation he grabbed a turkey-bone from the buffet and began to chew it furiously; spitting shreds of food as he cried, 'She's not getting rid of me! Not Zoltan Vinzenz! Why, I've survived everything, worse than this! Money, it can still buy life, my friend, you'll see!' He laid a trembling finger against his nose and resumed his caged-beast pacing.

'I doubt anyone in this house will take a bribe,' remarked Felix; he was considering his own form of bribery.

Zoltan wasn't listening. 'We'll pool our money,' he suggested eagerly. 'How much have you got?'

'Nothing, alas. I gave all I had to the delectable Magda.' Felix shut his ears to the uninhibited expression of Zoltan's opinion of him, and went in search of the delectable Magda.

In his room Felix carefully packed a special little case. He wasn't concerned about his clothes, but this case contained details of his female conquests; a lock of hair, a garter and a love letter from each, meticulously collated in a list with which he endeavoured to amuse his friends in Budapest. As he was adding Magda's name she came in to tidy the room, and Felix proposed that she secure him a horse so he could get to the station in the village, promising in return to send for her as soon as he reached home.

She listened to him very attentively, eyes downcast, as he

enumerated the delights of city life, half his attention still given to the contents of his case; he had a superstitious fear that if ever he lost it, his potency would vanish.

'You know how fond of you I am, my dear. Sometimes the briefest affair can be the most intense,' he told her; it was a formula that usually worked. 'But it's imperative I leave at once, and you will help me, my dear little Magda.'

He turned to face her – she was gone, the stupid little slut! But she'd be back. No woman had ever let him down. Fighting off an insidious feeling of apprehension, Felix sat down to await her return, clutching his case as if for security.

Zoltan seemed to have similar luck. He had approached Andras and offered to make him a rich man in return for a coach to take him to the village. Andras pretended not to hear; Zoltan had been reduced to following the apparently oblivious servant through the hall, stuffing bank-notes in his pockets and promising the earth. There was not a man alive who could resist the lure of wealth. Andras would come through, all right. Still, it was as well to be circumspect – it was impossible to tell what that crazy woman would be up to next. Zoltan hurried up to his room to make preparations for his departure. To hell with Felix! Let the optimistic fool look after himself! He tip-toed stealthily down the stairs and through the hall, intending to make his escape under cover of darkness.

No one was about. Quietly Zoltan reached for the handle of the great door.

'Must you leave us so soon, Zoltan?' The musical voice echoed clearly from the gallery. Holding her little son by the hand, Ilona began to walk down the staircase towards him. 'I am so sorry you're going! Bela, let us try and per-suade your uncle to stay. Andras, forward!'

The tall figure of the major-domo appeared out of the shadows. Zoltan turned to him in a panic. 'Where is the coach, you fool? I gave you all my money . . . Ilona, I did not want to disturb you with my departure.'

'You are too kind, dear Zoltan,' she replied, drawing near. 'And I see you are determined to go. Will you embrace me, for the last time? No? Why then, goodbye, my friend.'

Zoltan's eyes darted from Ilona to Andras like a trapped animal's.

'Come, Ilona,' he wheedled clumsily, 'have I ever harmed you? I bought you everything you ever wanted!' Ilona merely smiled, and fright turned his cajolery to bullying:

'Damnation, woman, do you take me for an idiot? I saw through your sordid little plan from the beginning! Hunt down your enemies by all means, but Ilona, I never willingly injured you! All I ever did was to introduce you to that scoundrel Felix – with the best intentions; I had no inkling . . .'

He broke off as Andras politely handed him a basket full of food, and proceeded to unlock the great door.

'Herr Vinzenz is ready?'

'Your coach is waiting, Zoltan,' said Ilona sweetly. 'Bela, you may kiss your uncle goodbye.'

Zoltan backed away from the child as if he had been venomous, and with a last wild glance at the sinister trio he turned and ran for the open. A gentle gust of wind ruffled Ilona's hair as she and her son waved farewell; then the great doors crashed shut.

There was no sign of the coach. Somehow, he'd known there wouldn't be. From the depths of the forest came the tremulous call of a wolf, rising and dying on the still night air, hypnotic and mournful in its lonely ferocity. Zoltan felt the hairs at the back of his neck begin to prickle. Wolves! Wide-eyed and terrified, Zoltan ran for his life. He dropped his basket and the food scattered in the undergrowth as he stumbled, panting painfully, along the woodland path.

But then something far behind him sensed his vulnerable presence. It chased in a circle, grunting and snuffling, seeking out his scent: now upright, its arms outflung like an ape's, now on all fours; it found his trail and loped unerringly after him. A fit man could not have outrun it; Zoltan, gasping and sweating, heard the heavy swift footsteps pounding behind him and turned at the moment it sprang upon him. The arms dealer's screams rose high above the wail of the wind as he was torn bloodily limb from limb.

The sounds of slaughter echoed through the night. Felix trembled, sick with horror; the killing of a pig was not comparable. The man who had sold death, grown fat on the profits of death, was now meeting his end as the food of a hungrier beast. The ghastly logic of it was more than Felix could stand. Nauseated, haggard, suddenly old, he rose and groped his way out of the room, grasping his case which was full of the keepsakes he prized above the women who had owned them, and which now represented his only link with the world he knew. Thank God, he could still be saved, he was not like the others! If only they had all resisted the frisson of the unexpected, if only vanity had not prevailed, and they had not accepted this invitation into the decaying jaws of hell! He would never get over the shock and the terror; he had aged ten years these last few hours.

Wearily, Felix walked down the great staircase, crossed the hall and plodded towards the doors of the castle. And then Ilona appeared before him, smiling her sweet and ready smile. He shrank from her, whimpering, clutching the handles of the huge doors. Outside he could hear shuffling, groping noises; something was trying to get in.

'You never used to be afraid of my husband, Felix,' said Ilona silkily.

'Anton is dead!' his voice was a muted scream. 'You buried him!'

Ilona shook her head.

'But, in the name of Christ, Ilona! Why did you not destroy him? Why did you let him live?' His eyes strayed fearfully to the door, and he grasped the handle convulsively.

The growling and snarling outside the door were getting louder. Ilona shook back her hair and gazed at him steadily.

'When the Count was alive, Felix, I was his creature. Do you understand? Look at me, don't wander! Do you know what I'm saying? – And I was his because you arranged it thus, knowing what he was, Felix. Hugo and Josef abandoned me; what did I matter, so long as their careers were assured? Zoltan introduced me to you, like a good friend, and you arranged my splendid marriage. Think of it, to be discarded and passed on like a pair of slightly-soiled shoes! And I, so excited at the prospect of being wedded to a Count – and a rich one at that. What an innocent I was! But you knew, didn't you, Felix? You knew how far the Count's depravity extended – his bad blood, as the peasants call it. So far, so bad; the Count died some months afterwards, so why did I lust for revenge upon you all? I will tell you.'

She paused, smiling fixedly; Felix, realizing her purpose, shook with terror.

'I endured the Count's brutalities. No doubt you thought my upbringing sufficient preparation for that. But then I was pregnant with Anton's son. Sylva, his nanny, had only to touch the child to know that he was congenitally infected with his father's disease. She knew, and she told me, that it is only a matter of time before my lovely child develops his father's symptoms. There is nothing any living being can do to prevent my son being condemned, through his father's evil, to hell.' Her eyes burned.

'That is your legacy to me, Felix, yours and your friends'. You are about to experience my gratitude. The years I have spent, planning and dreaming this moment! It is more than revenge to me.'

'But the Count *is* dead,' mumbled Felix stupidly; his wits were failing under the strain. 'You cannot mean that all of us – that we were all brought here to die!'

'Just so,' said Ilona quietly. 'I have said the Count died, and so he did, in a sense; his hunting accident was convenient, and averted popular suspicion. In fact, it was the beginning of his final state, which never ends. His humanity is lost, dissolved in the propensities of the beast; he is one of the Undead. Ever since he has been mine to command. I control him, as he once controlled me. And now I am sick of this discussion. Andras, open the doors!'

'*No!* Ilona, have pity!'

Andras appeared and brushed aside the gibbering Felix. He flung the doors wide open, then he and the Countess vanished into the shadows of the hall. Felix staggered backwards, stumbled and tried to crawl for the safety of the stairs, but it was too late. His dilated eyes were riveted to the gaping doorway as he cowered, shivering, at the sound of a shrill lingering wolf-howl outside the moonlit castle.

Silently it entered, his last enemy. The Wolf was bigger than he. Dark matted hair covered it all over, and the long claws scratched upon the polished floor as it advanced across the hall to the terrified doctor. But the brutish face was still recognizable; yes, even though the eyes were staring and mad, and the pendant tongue licked hungrily over the slavering jaws.

'I beg your mercy, Count Tyrrh!' Felix pleaded in a hoarse whisper.

The werewolf growled and skulked in the shadows, weaving before him like a nightmare-image. Felix grovelled before the evil and the power of the demoniacal beast.

'Remember,' he whimpered, 'I gave that woman to you! I gave you that whore – '

The werewolf rounded on him in a sudden hellish fury, rearing upright; the slimy black lips curled in snarling savagery, the gleaming canine teeth snapping viciously as it struck, tearing, rending its helpless victim into oblivion with maniacal strength. The kill was over in seconds, and then the beast hunched jealously over its prey like some obscene living fungus, settling to gorge itself upon the bloody, half-dismembered corpse.

'You see, my darling, I said it would soon be over,' said Ilona to her little son. They were relaxing with Andras in front of a blazing fire. All traces of the guests were removed, and Magda had brought them some supper on a tray.

'It's good to be alone again,' said Andras, smiling at her fondly. He took a candied peach from the tray and offered it to Bela, who accepted it happily; Ilona sipped at a glass of wine, and sighed with contentment.

'Yes, just the three of us, dearest Andras – our little family!'

'Such is my tale, gentlemen.' The new candidate stretched his long

arms and smiled at the gathering. 'I hope as a result of it you will see fit to favour me with membership of your renowned institution – '

'No! Impossible!' Trembling, Mr Pettifer rose to his feet. He glanced wildly round at his fellow-members. 'Can't you see what this man is?'

The shocked silence which greeted his outburst was broken by the stranger:

'Oh no, sir,' he said quietly. 'You are mistaken in your assumption; I am not that dreadful husband of the Countess Ilona. He was despatched some time ago by a silver bullet, a somewhat brutal but entirely effective method, I assure you. Now, gentlemen, if I could – '

'Then in God's name, what – who are you?' cried Mr Pettifer, ignoring caution and the disapproving frowns of his colleagues.

The man gazed at him with a cold, yellow-eyed stare, as if he were fixing the face and form of Mr Pettifer indelibly on his momory. Suddenly his stern features relaxed in a wolfish grin, and he turned to the room at large:

'May I be so bold as to ask you, gentlemen,' he enquired politely, 'for a glass of water and . . . a little candied fruit?'

VIKTORIA
or
THE HUNGARIAN DOLL

adapted by the author

It was customary for applicants for membership to the Club of the Damned to wait to be announced. But tonight's visitor did not wait. Impeccably dressed in evening clothes – white tie, tails, a modishly-cut cummerbund – he strode confidently into the room and faced the assembly.

But faced is not perhaps the mot juste*; for the visitor had no face.*

His entire head under the brilliantly shining top ·hat, was covered by a soft white silk scarf, neatly tied like a bandage around his face, leaving only a tiny aperture behind which – or so the members assumed – was a mouth.

The visitor stood by the fireplace, upright and faceless. With consummate authority he summoned the senior member of the Club, that venerable blackguard and murderer, Sir Francis Fell, and handed him a large envelope.

Lips trembling with almost childlike anticipation, the old man's quivering hands broke the seal and extracted some sheets of paper from the envelope.

'Gentlemen,' Sir Francis announced, 'for reasons of his own – er – indisposition, our applicant has requested that I – as the senior member present – should read this tale of supernatural terror, with which he hopes to gain admission to our establishment. Do you object?

The members leant forward eagerly. They had no objection. Might not the story reveal how the visitor came to lose his face?

It would make capital entertainment.

The story that Sir Francis had begun to read, starts seventeen years previously – in the year 1873 – in a bleak house in Budapest ...

It was a blank, empty face with powder-white cheeks and

huge, glazed eyes. It flopped obscenely when the old crone moved it in the tiny, cramped room. The incense curled to the ceiling, stifling the air, making her work more difficult and strenuous.

For the doll was the size of a small child.

The old woman muttered and muttered to herself, calling upon a world that no longer existed.

The doll sat waiting. It had waited a long time – almost two generations – holding a tapestry frame in one hand and a blunt needle in the other.

The old woman's quavering voice rose and fell; the smoke thickened the air and slowly, imperceptibly, the doll's cheeks seemed to redden.

Viktoria had spent the day throwing stones at the rats in the back yard. She was a child and her aim was not good. The kitchen cat, she observed, had a much better eye.

She had wished her parents good night, speaking Hungarian to her mother and English to her father because she knew it would annoy them.

It was not yet dark as she drew back the curtain and opened the window. It was a warm, heavy evening. The sound of rumbling carts going into the town reached Viktoria's ears. Someone laughed in a near-by house and the laughter stopped abruptly.

Grown-ups! Viktoria sighed and closed the window.

When *she* grew up, she would change the world, of that she was absolutely sure. But how was it to be done?

'I shall be a remarkable young lady, that's how it must be done,' Viktoria decided.

In the warmth of her bed, Viktoria touched her unformed breasts.

'These will eventually grow,' she whispered, 'and they'll help me be that remarkable young lady.'

Then she slept as only a ten-year-old child can sleep.

Paul Strickland was by nature a silent man. His desire to survive within society outweighed his desire to be sociable to that society and it had made him lonely but self-contained.

When he brought his wife – a Hungarian peasant girl –

into his rich social sphere, his fellow-members at the Consulate admired him even more. There, they said, was a man who knew what he wanted and – for all his moods and silences – he was not afraid to take it.

A daughter was born and it seemed Paul's life was complete and happy. But a well-suppressed secret within him would rise up and choke the man of silence until he wanted to scream for a very long time.

Elizabeth Strickland woke suddenly from her sleep. The darkness lay heavily around her and she could hear no sound.

The candle by her bedside had burnt down and there was a strong smell of wax in the air.

Instinctively, her hand reached to touch the soft sheets beside her, but she knew already Paul would not be there.

Elizabeth turned her head away. She had been crippled for so long, she could guess when the nightmare would begin again and she would wake, trembling and alone, waiting for the torment to pass.

The dream had once been a reality. Again she could hear the creaking leather, the jangle of spurs, the scream of the horse. Paul had been there.

Elizabeth closed her eyes in an effort to blot out the memory – that look of pure hatred she had seen on her husband's face.

She remembered the pain in her back as she fell, like flames spreading from her neck to somewhere deep in her bowels.

Paul was attentive, polite and distant during the convalescence, much as he had always been during their marriage.

The doctors prescribed medicine for the pain in her chest, medicine for her sadness, medicine for everything except what she really needed.

Elizabeth's hands flew like birds across her own body, unwilling and unable to settle anywhere. Nothing would help now.

She closed her eyes wearily and tried to sleep.

*

Margaret Graham yawned, closed her book and slipped it carefully under the mattress. It was an interesting edition, but not one she could let Viktoria see, precocious as the child was.

The candle flickered slightly. Tunbridge Wells seemed a lifetime ago and Margaret felt oddly content. She had escaped from malicious, evil tongues and a stern, suffocating family. It was enough!

If people had known the truth about what really happened between her and . . .

Margaret smiled. People would have been shocked if they had known the truth. She had lived too long surrounded by other people's horrified disbelief – she had escaped to Budapest and now she knew when to keep her mouth shut.

She also knew she was an attractive woman, and that was a hindrance. She smiled into the darkness as the candle flame grew dimmer. She always seemed to attract – the wrong kind of people.

They would be horrified, too, if they knew the truth.

There were roses everywhere. On the table, the mantelpiece, the book-case, the sideboard – they overpowered the room, greedy for the light and air.

Paul glanced up briefly from his book as his wife threw open the doors and wheeled herself into the room. She was competent, strong, something Paul thought he was incapable of being. The accident had given Elizabeth an inner strength which he admired.

He turned the pages of his book slowly. Elizabeth opened her sewing-box. She sewed as a therapy, to end the long, monotonous, dull days with a cushion cover here, a patterned cloth there. Now she was repairing the clothes of her old, precious doll that sat in a nearby chair.

Paul cleared his throat and crossed his legs carefully to prevent creases forming in his beautifully-cut trousers.

Elizabeth put down her sewing.

'Why do you do that?' she enquired.

Paul tensed. They had been together too long for idle curiosity to raise its head now.

'I beg your pardon?' He preferred to be studiously polite to women.

'Hitch your trousers in that manner?' Although she always spoke English to her husband, Elizabeth's Hungarian accent was still strong.

'I do not wish them to be creased, my dear.' Really, his wife was still a child.

'Does it matter?' She played nervously with the sewing needle but Paul did not fear for her safety.

'Some people at the Consulate might think it matters,' he replied.

'It is of world shaking importance,' she enquired sweetly, 'that your trousers are not creased?'

Paul suddenly felt very tired. No one really cared. He wondered if he needed a tonic. No, he knew exactly what he needed but he hurriedly put *that* thought from his mind.

'It matters to me.' He spoke quietly. 'As filling this room to suffocation with roses matters to you – my dear!'

She was capable of bringing out the hardness within him. He hated her for that.

Elizabeth's face paled.

'I like roses, Paul. I need to be surrounded by them. Where there are roses, there is life.'

'Exactly. The country girl.'

She wished he had left her that hot summer's day so many years ago and not brought her into the rich, exciting society she knew too well.

The silence in that room grew louder in Elizabeth's ears. She wanted to scream.

It was Paul who eventually spoke.

'The soirée in the Consulate grounds tomorrow night. Have you decided? Do you wish to attend?'

A bitter smile played around Elizabeth's mouth, but she hid it from him.

'Yes! I wish to attend!'

Once she had enjoyed the parties, the dinners, the celebrations. She had dared people to think what they liked about her then.

'Good!' Paul's complete attention returned to his book. He could now relax.

'I would be an embarrassment to you. As always! Of course I shall not come.'

Paul was once captivated by Elizabeth's cleverness. Now he walked blindly into her emotional traps. He wished for peace and knew it was impossible with her.

He took a deep breath and, with masterly control, did not look up.

'What a pity!'

The doll in the chair seemed to watch the two people, judging neither of them.

Paul tried to remember how he had once loved Elizabeth, but it was impossible. They had both been different people then, strangers to themselves . . . He had thought it would be all right, that she would make those other feelings go away; but they grew stronger instead, devouring him from inside.

'Did you see Viktoria today? Is she all right?'

Viktoria would always be 'all right'.

'I dare say, my dear.'

' "I dare say, my dear".'

The room had become unbearably stuffy. Elizabeth did not like windows to be opened. They reminded her there was a world outside where people could walk.

Paul's hand fell on the brass door-knob. It was beginning to turn black. He would have to speak to the servants.

Elizabeth's voice halted him.

'Will you look at the child . . . before you go out?'

'Gladly!'

He often looked at Viktoria. It disturbed him that she had become as much a stranger to him as her mother.

Elizabeth felt guilty. Her husband irritated her too easily, but she never lost her temper and flew into one of her old rages. She wheeled herself to the doll, anxious for an affection she could not find.

The dead eyes stared at her.

Death stared at her.

'You don't know what it's like, do you? Your eyes! Pitying! Patronizing! Wishing me dead!' She stretched out her arms. 'No, I didn't mean that. I didn't mean that!'

Paul watched his wife's madness dispassionately. He, too,

longed for a kind of innocence, but men were not allowed the luxury of a doll.

'Good night, Elizabeth.' He closed the door quietly.

Elizabeth held the doll to her and thought about Ferenc, the man who had awakened passion in her. He had been her one indiscretion and she had heard vile things about him. People were so jealous! They made things ugly with their jealousies. But Ferenc Toth remained untouched by them. He continued to charm and delight with his beauty and youthfulness. He did not even know that Viktoria . . .

'So much love. So much waste.' Elizabeth stroked the doll's hair and did not hear the old woman enter the room.

'Do not tease her!' Kati said.

Startled, Elizabeth turned to her old Nanny.

'What?'

'People may think . . .'

'Let them! Let them!' What did Elizabeth care what people thought. She was getting old, and one day the pain in her chest would probably kill her.

Kati peered short-sightedly at her beloved mistress.

'Have you a temperature?'

She had known Elizabeth since she was a child and had nursed her for many years.

Elizabeth became that child again.

'I shall embroider roses on the tapestry. Red roses!' She pointed to the doll's frame.

Kati could smell the farm-yard again and see Elizabeth playing in the dust. That was where she belonged, in the soil of the country, not by the side of some Englishman in a rich house.

'You make everything more beautiful. She will be grateful to you – always. I *know*!' She touched the doll and Elizabeth could smell incense in the air.

'Fetch me my attar of roses, Kati.'

Elizabeth applied the scent to her wrists, conscious of the load that lifted from her brain.

'Keep Viktoria away from . . . from her father, Kati. That is most important.'

The old woman nodded and shuffled out of the room.

The lamps spluttered. Elizabeth shivered and the sewing needle sank into her finger.

The blood blossomed like a rose as the doll watched over the room.

Margaret had heard Paul's footsteps passing her door.

She sat up in bed and removed her nightdress. It was another warm evening and she wanted to feel the sheets next to her skin.

How she could despise that man, her employer, and yet how he fascinated her. She admired him because he existed in such a shambles of a life. She needed order, routine, peace.

That peace was shattered when Elizabeth threw open the bedroom door.

Margaret sat up quickly and pulled the sheet to her chin. How silly, she thought.

'Mrs Strickland . . .'

Elizabeth's knuckles whitened as she gripped her chair.

'People seem to think, Miss Graham, that because I'm confined to a wheel-chair, I have become mentally deficient in some way.'

'I'm sorry . . .?'

'You are an attractive lady in a foreign country – *my* country . . . I don't want to be treated like a child who is slow at learning, Miss Graham. You may own half the world, Miss Graham, but you do not own my husband or my child!'

Margaret feared, momentarily, for Elizabeth's heart. She saw a trickle of blood seep down the woman's finger. What had she been doing?

'No, Mrs Strickland.'

Elizabeth felt sure Margaret was laughing. Even in the semi-darkness, she could feel waves of laughter rising in that still figure on the bed. Tomorrow it would be different. Tomorrow they would be ice-cold in the daylight and avoid looking at each other's eyes.

Elizabeth wheeled herself out.

Margaret shut the door and, as she padded back to bed, she caught a glimpse of herself in the full-length mirror.

Shadows danced across her still slim figure; a pool of darkness here, a sweep and dip there. For a moment it became a mysterious, unexplored territory.

Margaret recognized the body again. Was it possible that Mrs Strickland believed she and Paul . . .? Margaret laughed aloud at the thought.

She placed her hands on her hips and faced the mirror squarely.

In that darkened room, she liked what she saw.

The pain in Elizabeth's chest decreased. She swallowed her acrid, chalky medicine and reached in the drawer for her pills. Beside them lay a photograph of a young man in uniform. Ferenc!

How she could have allowed herself to keep that picture! But without it, she found it impossible to remember what he looked like. He no longer called at the house and she rarely went into town. Even when she closed her eyes and thought very hard, she could not remember his face. The curl of his hair, yes, the colour of his eyes, too – but his whole face eluded her totally.

Elizabeth's head ached. The darkness still frightened her as it did when she was a child. The house seemed unnaturally quiet and the lamps were beginning to fade.

Her limbs felt heavy and numb – the medicine always had that effect – and the pain in her head throbbed and throbbed, beating, pounding rhythmically like horses' hooves.

Elizabeth swept aimlessly around the room, her body like the butterfly that never settles anywhere for very long.

When she picked up the tortoise-shell hand mirror and looked at herself, she saw many people; and yet she was still the same. Memory was a fearful thing. She knew how the child had felt, the girl, the woman. She had not really changed. It had culminated here in a chair, with a bitter, angry woman growing old before her time. She would never resign herself and stop wanting so much. Even now . . .

The figure appeared suddenly in the mirror, just over her shoulder.

It was in uniform.

Headless!

A claw gripped at Elizabeth's chest again and her blood froze.

She spun her chair.

There was nothing!

A slight breeze from nowhere whispered across the roses. The thumping of her heart merged with the beating of hooves, getting louder, coming closer, filling the room and her head.

Elizabeth's hands covered her ears, trying to block out the noise, the memory of her nightmare that came to her when she did not sleep.

The noise eventually died and her heart stilled.

She sat for a moment, trying to piece the shattered fragments together.

A sharp pain flashed across her eyes and she turned when the hand lightly touched her shoulder.

Ferenc would do that!

She turned to smile at him, as he would stand and wait for her.

She retched.

It was Paul's face that watched her, soundless words escaping his twisted lips.

The drumming hooves filled Elizabeth's ears and she lost consciousness.

The doctor ordered complete rest and a hush fell over the household.

Kati scurried from the kitchen to the bedroom and back, bearing trays of fragrant, secret liquids that slowly gathered Elizabeth's strength.

Paul continued to go out at night, unwillingly drawn to a circle of men who only seemed to exist when dusk fell over the town. He avoided the governess and consulted old Kati regularly on the health of his wife, providing money and attention for her well-being.

Viktoria banged her toy drum and watched the doll. She wondered if her mother would die.

'One day, Mama will be well again — soon!'

Kati tucked the little girl into bed.

'That is not true, Kati, is it? It is her heart, isn't it? Her sick heart!'

Faced with such directness from a child, Kati used her adult's privilege to make light of it and change the subject.

'It's all a question of rest, you see!'

Viktoria had her mother's eyes. One day she would have her passions too.

Kati's lips touched the child's forehead and the doll's skirts rustled. If power had any visual form, it would have created a triangle between the child, the old woman – and the waiting doll.

Slowly Elizabeth recovered from her collapse. She lay in the white bed, sometimes her head turned one way, sometimes the other. When Paul paid her a rare visit, she stared straight ahead and hardly spoke.

She listened to the sounds of the house; the creaking of old furniture, the discreet opening and closing of doors, the quiet tread of people determined at all costs not to disturb her, the invalid. Their reverence for sickness made her want to cry aloud, for her spirit had never been ill.

She ordered the doll to be brought to her bedside and behind the closed door her voice could be heard rising and falling.

When the doctor eventually pronounced her fit, Elizabeth returned to the drawing-room. The doll was never far from her side.

An uneasy peace reigned. Paul never questioned his wife and she provided no explanations. He did not go out every evening and seemed content to sit with Elizabeth and read a book. He wondered if he was getting old. He began to feel more and more irritated with his wife. What had attracted him once, her strength, her hidden passions, now repelled and angered him. She had the strength of a man and it disgusted him.

So the days and the nights passed, and the doll watched the married couple grow steadily from boredom to hatred.

Sunlight streamed through the windows. It was Sunday

afternoon and everything was still. Even the doll had its eyes closed, as though sleeping off the effects of a large lunch.

Elizabeth put down her sewing and rubbed her shoulder. The pain seemed worse than it had been before. Paul looked up from his book.

'My dear – shall I call Kati?' Despite the heat of the day, Paul had been feeling extraordinarily cold.

'No!' Elizabeth snapped at him. She hated him to draw attention to her illness, unless it was on her terms.

But the pain got worse and Paul tried again.

'The Doctor . . .'

'That old fool! It's only a strained muscle. Just give me the tablets . . .'

Paul stared at her.

'Of course. How many?'

It had become Paul's unofficial responsibility to hand Elizabeth the tablets with a glass of water. Elizabeth's anger increased her pain.

'You know how many. Please . . .'

The chill struck through to Paul's bones. That's all we are eventually . . . old bones! he thought. Now he would release that pent-up volcano within him – anything to be warm again.

'By the way, my dear . . . young what's-his-name – Baron Toth's youngest – you know – the hussar – '

'Ferenc Toth!' Elizabeth's voice was almost a whisper.

'That's it! Ferenc! Fancy forgetting!'

Paul brushed an invisible speck of dust from his arm.

'Ran into old Baron Toth at the Black Cat yesterday. Ferenc is off on his honeymoon tomorrow. To Venice. Awfully conventional. But the young lady insisted . . .'

Elizabeth grew paler.

'Young lady!' She stared at Paul's face. She knew what was to come and wished dearly that she could be wrong.

'Not all that young, actually. Young scamp's got himself a rich widow from Vienna. Showed me her picture. Incredibly beautiful, too . . .'

Paul addressed himself to a corner of the ceiling, his fingertips pressed firmly together. He was the scientist, quietly excited and willing to discuss his latest theory, preparing himself to dissect a dead animal and show its guts to the world.

'They're very much in love, I believe . . .'

It was done! Their years together ended here, in a mutual trap.

Elizabeth did not care any more. She knew now that all this time Paul had known about Ferenc.

'Tablets . . .'

Paul seemed surprised.

'What? Your tablets! Of course! What can I be thinking of?'

He rose and walked slowly to the table. He seemed preoccupied and thoughtful.

The pills flew across the floor, white as snowdrops in the grass.

'Damn!' Paul said softly.

As he bent down to pick them up, one by one, he was very aware of his neat clothes. He wanted this suit to be perfect for his evening assignation.

'Kati! A glass of water, Kati! Quickly!' Paul felt cheerful and firm. He was, at last, in charge of a situation.

But by the time Kati arrived, it was too late.

Elizabeth was dead.

The anguish of the first days dulled to a vague, distant pain. Viktoria, who had cried hot, sobbing tears, then seemed to forget.

Paul drank more brandy than usual, wore very becoming black and hardly moved from his chair, building some private retreat within himself.

Margaret brushed her hair vigorously and tried not to think about dying. She quietly looked after the child and wondered how things could continue. Death was such a final thing.

Paul continued to avoid her. They had called a silent, mutual truce years ago to battle against some unknown enemy, but Paul's battle was greater. Margaret, at least, had accepted.

Carrying a lighted candle, she made her way to old

Kati's room, her shadow looming large and grotesque before her.

The door was slightly open and she could hear voices coming from within.

'They won't forget her. We will both make sure, won't we?' Margaret recognized the old woman's voice and was curious to know who else was with her at that time of night.

She pushed the door and it creaked open slowly.

'Kati?'

The room was dimly lit. The wheel-chair – newly polished – claimed the centre and was covered in fresh roses.

Margaret turned away, her stomach lurching against the thick smell in the room.

She came face to face with the doll, propped against the wall, its arms bent awkwardly.

It seemed to leer at her.

Margaret turned and fled; and Kati, alone, began to chuckle.

Paul stood among the packing cases musing on his good fortune. His second marriage – once more to a Hungarian woman – had occurred so swiftly he scarcely had time to catch his breath.

But Theresa, serious, young, attentive and – though he would not admit it – strangely resembling Elizabeth, had gravely acquiesced to his proposal of marriage. Now they were returning to England, to a fine country estate Paul had inherited. He had grown bored with the Consulate and with his night friends and the summer had given him blinding headaches. The doctor had advised a cooler climate.

Theresa was grateful to Margaret who organized all the packing and arranged to send Viktoria on ahead to England.

The governess had congratulated the married couple coolly. It was no concern of hers if Paul married again – he seemed sheepish, almost apologetic when first he broke the news to her. He might read scorn in her eyes but when she met Theresa she understood how he could feel about this young woman – for Margaret herself was attracted too. Her supervision of the packing brought her closer to the new Mrs Strickland, and Margaret could not sleep at night for thinking about her.

Theresa hugged Paul very hard. She had entered the room noiselessly, wondering for a second what he, her husband, could be thinking of, standing there so alone. His stillness disturbed her. They had shared a great deal in the last few months but she had not seen him like this before – waiting, poised to spring like an animal. She wanted to break his sinister silence and smash it for she suddenly felt very cold and alone.

'Oh Paul! I'm looking forward so much . . . England must be beautiful.'

He turned to look at her.

'Yes, my dear – like you!'

He touched her face. It seemed happiness could be this.

As they drew closer together, Theresa trembled. She had looked into Paul's eyes and seen her own face reflected there. I am becoming another person, she thought. She closed her eyes, unable to look at herself. Paul's face bent closer to hers. She wants me to kiss her, he thought.

Margaret dropped the boxes on the floor as she entered the room. Her bags were packed. She was ready for a new life.

Paul and Theresa sprang apart, the kiss half formed in the air between their lips. What can she see in him, Margaret wondered.

'Kati has come to say goodbye, Mrs Strickland.'

As Theresa turned to her, Margaret felt an urgent need to touch her, to protect her from some hidden power shimmering around them in that room. Too young for this, she thought. Too vulnerable.

Kati shuffled into the room and Paul, feeling deserted, made his own escape.

'I'll be in the study. My papers . . .'

He nodded to Kati. The old woman made his flesh creep and he had been secretly delighted when she had left his employ. His past was gradually shedding from him, skin by skin.

'I've come to say good-bye to Viktoria,' the old woman mumbled. She was carrying the doll and put it down carefully.

'She isn't here, Kati dear. We sent her on ahead to England.'

Kati was deeply upset.

'But I wanted so much to see her face when she unwrapped her present . . .'

Then the paper fell away, exposing the doll's head.

Theresa felt sorry for the old woman. 'I shall give it to her.'

'I made it for her, you know. It belonged to her mother. It wasn't finished.'

Theresa smoothed the empty cloth in the tapestry frame. She felt a sudden chill on her neck and smelt a strange scent. Roses? Incense?

'You are a dear, Kati.' She looked up.

The old woman watched her through half-closed eyes; she seemed to be smiling grimly.

It was then that Theresa shivered.

The house in England, set in the heart of Gloucestershire, was old and full of dark nooks and crannies which Viktoria explored thoroughly.

She was thirteen now, full of smouldering complexities and did not miss her mother nearly as much as she had thought she would.

Her father's marriage amazed her; his attempts at parental concern made her smile. He instructed her to do everything Theresa said. Viktoria was somewhat doubtful at this and would retire to her room and to her doll. She had christened her Rosa.

Margaret entered the bedroom. Viktoria was mumbling and rocking the doll back and forth.

'Were you calling me?'

The child looked up at the woman and smiled.

'No, Miss Graham. I was talking to her . . . to Rosa.'

There was a sudden cool breeze and Margaret shivered.

'I think it's time we did some work, don't you?'

Viktoria sighed. Adults!

That night she blew Rosa a kiss in the darkness.

Concerned about the child, Margaret elected to speak to Theresa.

'Has she a temperature?' Theresa felt very disagreeable. Paul had just received a letter from a friend who had decided he was coming to stay.

'No, Mrs Strickland. Viktoria talks to her doll.'

Theresa noticed that Margaret was very attractive. That, too, irritated her enormously.

She told the governess she would speak to the child. Margaret seemed unwilling to leave the room, hesitating over something she might say.

'Miss Graham . . .?'

The governess turned and almost ran from the room.

Theresa felt alienated and shouted at the cook, who threatened to leave. She was aware it was hardly fitting behaviour for a married woman but then marriage, she had soon discovered, was not as she had once imagined it. When Paul had suggested they had separate bedrooms, Theresa was secretly relieved.

She went upstairs to see Viktoria, who reassured her stepmother that she was perfectly well. The doll watched, its arm resting on the chair and its head thrown back. Was she mocking the woman who dared interrupt a little girl's private world?

What Theresa did not notice was that a blood-red rose had been exquisitely sewn on to the doll's tapestry frame.

Paul was becoming increasingly quiet and moody with her. The leisurely life of a country squire, at first so appealing, had become sedentary and dull. He looked forward with almost hysterical glee to Edward's arrival, making plans and arranging everything.

Margaret smiled as Paul instructed the bemused servants. She was now unable to go through a day without seeing Theresa at least once. She slept badly at night and was hardly ever hungry, seemingly living off some deeply-rooted neurotic tension which both exhausted and exhilarated her.

Margaret was young and therefore still believed that anything was possible . . .

The best silver had been laid out for dinner and Edward sat, elegant and impressive in his Army uniform, regaling his audience with stories about India. Young as he was, Edward had travelled widely and was an amusing and witty raconteur.

Paul listened attentively, a perpetual grin on his face, as though only he knew a secret joke which he would never share.

Theresa was vaguely aware that the stories were a little rude, but she did not really understand them. She intended asking Miss Graham later, that is, if ever they had a chance of being alone together.

She needed someone to confide in and wished desperately that person would be the silent, enigmatic woman who gazed so seriously at the wine glasses.

Viktoria glowered at her father. She had asked that Rosa attend the dinner too and Paul had only laughed at her and told her not to be silly.

Edward turned his smooth attention to the morose child.

'And what are you going to be when you grow up, Viktoria?'

His eyes, at first so animated and sparkling when he was telling his stories, now dulled over and became bland, empty and indifferent.

'A surgeon.' Viktoria looked straight into his face, daring him to speak to her.

'You mean you wouldn't like to be a governess, like Miss Graham – or married, like your mother?'

'My mother wasn't married – she was in a wheel-chair.'

In the shocked silence that followed, Margaret tried not to laugh. That child, she thought, will grow into a remarkable woman.

Paul was full of plans. He wanted to take Edward riding, to visit the tenants. Edward warmed to the subject.

'What of the land to the west of your estate? Any room

for improvement?'

Theresa cleared her throat gently and Edward was immediately repentant.

'Sorry, Theresa. Mustn't talk business, must we? It's simply that I'm – well – thinking of my future: farming, land-owning. So different from Army life.'

Theresa looked from her husband to his friend. Their faces were keen, expectant.

'Edward means he is thinking of retiring, you see.'

He spoke carefully, patiently, as though addressing an idiot child.

Theresa felt cold and sick. She wanted to strike out at their secret enthusiasms. Instead, she did nothing.

'Yes, I see.' Her husband was a complete stranger to her now.

Margaret rose and excused herself, suppressing an overwhelming desire to put her arms around Theresa and comfort her.

'It's Viktoria's bed-time. And mine.'

Edward stood up slowly.

'Must you really leave us too, Miss Graham?'

'Surely the child is capable of putting herself to bed.' Paul was tired of fuss and femininity. And besides – he wanted to be alone with Edward.

The chair fell over as Viktoria, white with rage, stood up.

'Surely!'

She ran from the room to the comfort of Rosa.

That evening, the doll watched over the child, its china eyes staring . . .

When Theresa had retired to bed, pleading a headache, Paul and Edward settled themselves comfortably in front of the fire. Wordlessly, Margaret had reappeared and followed them into the room. Paul nodded to her and she poured brandy for them both. Then she ceased to exist for the two men.

Edward looked at Paul.

'Bit temperamental, I should imagine. Your wife!'

Paul shrugged his shoulders. He had forgotten her already.

Edward leaned forward, lowering his voice so only his cousin would hear.

'Do you . . . do you *like* her, Paul?' He seemed genuinely puzzled and worried by the thought.

Paul wanted to lean across and touch the young man and reassure him. Instead he said.

'Tomorrow we go riding, eh?'

Edward smiled.

'Yes, old chap. I'll look forward to it.'

It was a low giggle coming from within that halted Theresa outside Viktoria's bedroom. It was not a humorous, childish giggle – it was a malicious, ruthless noise.

'Viktoria? Viktoria?'

The giggling stopped abruptly.

Theresa drew in her breath, then turned the door handle, but it was locked.

Quickly she backed away from the door and away from the choked sounds of giggling . . .

Paul wished Edward a good night.

'Sleep well, old chap!' Edward touched his shoulder. They had both drunk too much brandy and were feeling better for it.

As Paul lurched to his own room, Theresa stepped out of the shadows.

'Paul, I must talk to you.'

She had waited for him, jealous of the two men's enjoyment and comfortable chuckles.

'Sorry – I'm not feeling awfully well . . .' Paul clutched a table to stop himself falling over.

'It's about Viktoria – your daughter, Paul. I think that doll . . . *There's something the matter with it.*'

Paul's head began to spin.

'Take it away from her, then.'

'You can't just – *take* it. The child loves the doll.'

'Kindly do not refer to my daughter as "the child".'

Paul attempted to stand up straight.

'Paul, please – please . . .' Theresa's hands reached out for him.

'Oh, please – do go away!'

Theresa backed away as though she had been hit across the face.

'I am not a child, Paul!' she whispered. 'Or an invalid!'

'Theresa – my dear – what's the matter? What have I done?' He seemed hurt and bewildered. 'You have everything here any woman could possibly want – I don't even make . . . demands on you . . .'

A vision of Theresa's naked body appeared before Paul's eyes. The last time he had touched her . . . she was soft, so revoltingly soft. Paul swallowed hard. Oh, God, he thought, how could I . . . ?

He pushed past Theresa and staggered to his room to be violently sick.

The low, vicious giggling continued. It still came from Viktoria's bedroom.

Theresa was still in bed when she summoned the governess.

She had slept very little – tossing and turning – her thoughts bouncing from Paul to Viktoria to Margaret and back to Paul again. Theresa was the stranger in a household that shut away its past, protecting its secrets from prying eyes. She sighed; this way of life was not enough for her.

'Miss Graham, this is difficult for me! I want to ask you . . . I *have* to . . .'

The governess drew breath imagining what could come next.

'Please don't misunderstand, but what exactly is your relationship to my husband?'

The question hung in the air for Margaret's hesitation was mere astonishment.

Was it Theresa who had spoken? *Or was it – Elizabeth?*

'He employs me as a governess, Mrs Strickland.' Margaret's eyes strayed over the woman's face. She was a mere child, a frightened, lonely child.

'Yes, Miss Graham? And?'

Frustration made Margaret impatient.

'If you're not happy with the work I do here . . .'

The tears came to Theresa's eyes. She wanted more than sympathy.

'Did you like her? His first wife? Elizabeth?'

Margaret did not move.

'Poor Mrs Strickland.'

Theresa's nightgown slipped off her shoulders.

'I look like her, don't I?'

And the quiet desperation in her face indeed heralded the bitterness that had dominated Elizabeth's eyes.

Not this way, Margaret thought. Not like this! Don't let it happen to you, too!

'Did you call *me* "poor Mrs Strickland" just now?' She was surprised. Had the governess even noticed her before?

'Forgive me – I feel profoundly sorry for you and, if I may say so, I like you very much, too . . .'

'You like me? But I thought . . .'

It seemed so odd that this woman should be saying these things. She could not help but smile, realizing that what she had heard was what she most wanted to hear.

'As far as *Mr* Strickland is concerned, I have never been anything but an employee for him.' She paused, and the two women's eyes met for a second. 'Obviously . . .'

Theresa's eyes widened.

'*Obviously?*'

Margaret walked slowly towards the bed, crossing that invisible, dangerous line. She touched Theresa's hand, her arm, her bare shoulder.

Theresa watched Margaret's face, waiting for the governess to join her across that line where she – Theresa – had waited so long alone . . .

It was Elizabeth who came to sit in the chair opposite Paul.

He cowered away, spilling brandy across his shirt. She had come to him before, when the house was dark and Edward had retired to bed and Paul had finally drunk himself into merciful sleep to escape those staring eyes. But she returned again and again, sitting in the black leather chair, reproving him, reminding him that he had once hated her.

The echoes of whispering and hissing rose and fell in the

gloomy corridors. Paul realized he was not merely watched, but forever haunted . . .

And the doll knew then it was time to wake from its ancient sleep. Its mistress had returned at last. Rosa stood on the end of Viktoria's bed.

'If that is what Mama wishes. Yes!' The child's trance-like whisper responded to the doll's age-old instructions. 'If he must be punished, then punished he must be.'

Margaret walked slowly down the passage, carrying a decanter. She smiled, remembering the scent of Theresa's body in the darkness.

And Elizabeth was there, overpowering Paul as she had always done.

He backed away, the glass falling from his hand. His hatred for her, for all women, crashed into a thousand pieces.

There was a creaking noise and the sound of wood splintering somewhere.

Then the door swung open. And there, on the threshold, still and upright, stood Rosa, the doll. Its head turned this way and that, searching for him. Paul experienced a sudden paralysis of voice and limb. He felt suffocated by the overwhelming smell of roses.

Now the doll stepped into the room, walking stiffly and slowly across the floor, towards him . . .

It came closer and closer, its deathless eyes boring into his skull. It stopped within a few feet of him. An arm creaked as it lifted to point an accusing finger at the man.

His mouth opened in a silent scream.

The object in front of him said one word – 'Megtorlás'.

As Paul fell, he dimly recognized Kati's voice. His head hit the coal scuttle with a terrible sharp crack and the doll repeated the word as it turned away.

'Megtorlás.' The Hungarian word for revenge.

But Paul heard nothing more. The doll turned back towards the door. Its task was done.

Elizabeth's revenge was complete.

*

Viktoria looked up.

'He shouldn't have done it! He shouldn't have married again! He *knew*!'

Margaret poured the contents of the decanter into the flower-pot and turned towards the child with the vaguest of smiles.

The Coroner muttered something about alcoholic poisoning, but the verdict was accidental death.

Edward took Theresa's hand when the inquest was over. They both wore black.

'If there is anything, anything at all . . .' he said.

Theresa removed her hand from his and felt nothing but an enormous relief.

Edward bowed to Margaret, who held the door open for him and she caught a whiff of perfume as he passed her.

Theresa wandered aimlessly around the room. She had not seen the child who had locked herself in the bedroom with the doll.

'First her mother, now her father. It doesn't seem fair – on any of us!' Theresa wanted to weep.

Margaret looked at her.

'Viktoria is not his child! I thought you knew!'

Theresa stopped still, her eyes widening.

'Elizabeth had this affair – a young Hungarian officer. Ferenc Toth – dreadful fop. She thought herself to be very much in love with him. It suited Mr Strickland to tolerate the situation,' the governess added.

After the strain of coping with recent days, Theresa trembled again on the verge of tears. She really had not known the man she married – indeed, she had not really known herself either.

'We must never tell her – Viktoria! But why doesn't she come out of her room. I hear her – *them* – whispering . . . giggling!'

Margaret prepared a sedative, but Theresa would not relax.

'I've heard it! And now they watch everything. Perhaps they're watching now! She talks to the doll, you said. What else are they planning?'

Margaret moved towards her, then stopped. It was too soon! She spoke gently instead, wishing Theresa to be calm.

'It's all right! Viktoria has two doting mothers to look after her. There's nothing to be afraid of!'

'But what if she . . . what if they . . .' She became painfully inarticulate and Margaret put her arms around the woman. The time had come at last.

'Be still! Everything's going to be all right.' She soothed the woman. 'We must see to it that Viktoria grows into a remarkable woman!'

Theresa was calm.

'We're strong,' Margaret whispered. 'We're strong . . . together!'

And she was smiling when Theresa looked up into her face . . .

Sir Francis cleared his throat and stuffed the sheet of paper back into the voluminous envelope.

'I must say . . .' he muttered feebly. He felt a sense of outrage. Murder and mutilation were one thing, but there were some *things that really could not be spoken of without a blush.*

He turned to reprimand the elegant visitor, who suddenly stepped forward from his place in front of the fireplace and, after taking off his top hat and handing it to one of the liveried servants, deftly began to untie the silk scarf that concealed his face.

What would the members see under that scarf, what horror of malformed hideousness and disease?

They were not prepared for what was finally revealed to them, and one or two of them gasped out loud.

For as he threw the bandage on the floor, the visitor stood unmasked — as an exceedingly handsome, independent-looking woman.

'Well, gentlemen,' Viktoria asked simply, shaking out her long raven hair, 'am I accepted?'

'Well, really,' Sir Francis grumbled, 'surely this is a case of false pretences . . .'

'Really? Is membership of the Club of the Damned then restricted to men?'

'To gentlemen,' Sir Francis corrected her.

'I am not that,' Viktoria Strickland said and smiled. 'But there

is even worse to come. For I have not come to you without a companion . . .'

And the expression on Sir Francis's face froze, for the door had opened. The members could hear strange, clattering footsteps . . . and into the drawing-room of the Club of the Damned, there tripped, gently but confidently, first the silhouette, and then the sweet, child-like, monstrous outline of the creature herself . . . of Rosa . . . Viktoria Strickland's doll . . .

ROBERT MULLER

MR NIGHTINGALE
or
BURNING MASTS

adapted by the author

The fires burned low at the Club that night. Little could be expected of the visitor who had presented himself – or so the members thought, accustomed as they were to monsters of vice and haunted creatures of the night who came to the Club of the Damned to receive absolution or the final sentence of doom.

Mr Nightingale's hands shook feebly as he presented himself to the Membership. It took the efforts of two servants to guide him to the story-teller's place in front of the great fireplace.

They watched with some distaste as the wizened, rheumatic little man leant tentatively on his walking-stick, his watery eyes blinking briefly as one of the wigged servants handed him the traditional goblet of wine; they leant forward with curiosity as, after another moment's hesitation, Mr Nightingale suddenly grasped the goblet and drank its contents down in a series of noisy gulps of satisfaction, like a baby sucking at its mother's nipple. They had to cup their ears, as Mr Nightingale commenced his tale in a low, indistinct mumble . . .

'Gentlemen,' he began, 'I am in a manner of speaking not . . . or to be more precise . . .'

'Ask him to speak up,' came a sepulchral voice from the far end of the drawing-room. 'We cannot hear.'

The liveried servant leant forward to whisper something into his ear.

'What?' Mr Nightingale piped in a panic-stricken voice. 'Cannot hear me? You must forgive me, gentlemen, for you see before you someone who feels it necessary to hoard such pitiful remnants of bodily strength as he still possesses. Indeed, even as I begin, I am already overcome by anxiety lest I shall be unable to conclude . . .'

And the members watched with renewed interest as the wizened little man's frame was rent by spasms – as if an electric current was being shot through his body.

His mouth opened, lips parting in an unnatural smile, displaying degenerated teeth.

The grin was fearful, obscene.

One or two of the members gasped . . .

Let me say at once, let me admit it! Of course I am insane. And had you shared my experience, you too would now be – shall we say, unbalanced?

The events which changed my life began thirty years ago, during a visit to the Free City of Hamburg, then as now a town of great visual beauty and pulsating energy, even though its very heart and soul had been ravaged by the Great Fire of 1042.

I had been sent to the city by my father, a long-established East Anglian coachbuilder, who had inherited his business from his own father. We, that is, my widowed father, my elder brother and I lived in comfort and some style in Norwich, though it would be an exaggeration to say that I was happy. My brother, I am sorry to say, has always been a frightful bully, and my father a very strong character, and since there were no women in the family, I suppose it was only natural that all the members of the household should set upon me whenever their fancies so dictated. Indeed – to be truthful – I was treated more like an ill-fashioned daughter of the house than the idealistic though shy young man that I undoubtedly was.

My trip to Hamburg was the first task of any consequence with which my father had seen fit to entrust me. I was to negotiate the construction and sale of those canary-yellow carriages which the leading burghers of the city had found so ideally suited as public conveyances.

My host was one of the town's leading citizens, the venerable Senator Otto Steekebeck, an old friend of my father's, who had insisted that I should stay at the Steekebeck house during my stay in Hamburg, and live as a member of the family.

I was delighted by this decision – being somewhat anxious at the thought of having to stay at a strange inn during my first visit abroad. Moreover, all the members of the Senator's family proved to be as charming as they were hospitable. Their courtesy extended to their choice of language: they were determined to speak English in my presence. In all manner of other ways, too, they contrived to make the stranger feel welcome in their home.

Their house, an old, timbered one, with sloping red-tiled roofs, was one of a row of merchants' houses, set alongside a *Fleet*, or narrow canal, linking the beautiful Alster lake with the busy port on the river Elbe.

During the day, my hosts would show me the sights of the city, and I witnessed some magnificent new buildings rising from the ashes of the old.

Then in the evenings I would join the family in the salon, and there we would sit together around the warming, tiled stove, and by the glow of candle and fire beguile one another with eerie stories of ghosts and vampires and the like – all the while drinking Glühwein, or hot toddies – though, being a teetotaller, I myself naturally abstained from this additional enjoyment.

I noticed very soon after my arrival that the Steekebeck family appeared to collect gothic horror stories with quite exceptional assiduity – a strange hobby, very unlike the activities of my family in Norwich.

Nor had it escaped my observation that my father's intent in sending me to Hamburg may not have been solely in the interests of the family business. For – have I not mentioned it before? – I was thirty-five, and still a bachelor, and I suspect that my father and Herr Steekebeck had fashioned a plot, by which they hoped to bring together the unmarried English visitor with the other guest of the house, Frau Steekebeck's widowed cousin Elyse. Her wealthy husband, a shipbuilder by the name of Weissmar, had perished in the Great Fire before poor Elyse had even reached the tender age of twenty.

Ah, gentle reader, the passionate glances that would pass on those fire-flecked evenings, between the lady, herself so long deprived of conjugal pleasures, and the no-longer young bachelor, who had – yes, I admit it – never tasted them at all, nor indeed any of their vulgar and furtive counterfeits.

So picture, if you can, this shy, dutiful, possibly somewhat pedantic English bachelor in the midst of a happy, normal German merchant family: Herr Steekebeck himself – a solid businessman of evident substance; his wife, a friendly, always conscientious wife and mother; the old Steekebeck couple, Grosspapa and Grossmama, both enviably expert in telling the most gruesome of horror stories; the dreamy young daughter Felizitas (who or what could she have been dreaming of throughout those cosy, half-fearful evenings by the warm stove?); and Elyse herself, a lady of my own age with fine dark eyes, a well-presented complexion, and – if I may be permitted to say so – finely firm buttocks and breasts . . .

On the night of which I wish to speak now, it was the turn of old Herr Steekebeck, Grosspapa, to send shivers down our spines with a story which he claimed he had first read in a book by the English poet Edgar Poe. I had to correct this impression.

'The poet Edgar Allan Poe is not English,' I pointed out. 'He is an American.'

'Indeed!' Grosspapa said. 'American? How extraordinary. I thought all Americans were illiterate. Was he a Red Indian then?'

'No. Hardly. He was a gentleman.'

At that moment I looked away – for all literary conversations seemed to exhaust and embarrass me – and my gaze crossed with that of young Felizitas. I turned my eyes away sharply, for never in my life had I seen such – dare I say it? – such hunger in anyone's expression – it was really more than I could bear, and I felt instantly overcome by faintness.

I tried to make my excuses quickly. I had seen much of their beautiful city that day, I assured my hostess Frau Steekebeck, I had a right to feel fatigued.

'Then you must go to bed, Herr Nightingale,' I heard the brisk voice of Elyse Weissmar utter, and shuddered inwardly.

To pronounce the word 'bed' so openly, so utterly without – well – discretion . . .

I hastened out of the room, reiterating my wishes to the company for a restful good night.

*

The house was set on three floors, but only two were used by the family; the upper floor was used by Herr Steekebeck as an office.

Even so, I found that the walk from the salon on the ground floor to my own quarters upstairs required considerable and careful negotiation. The ground floor corridor was timbered and gloomy and, though I carried a candlestick, I was frightened by the slanting shadows I encountered everywhere, even – possibly especially – my own. And then that narrow wooden staircase, that creaked so ominously, by which I reached the bedroom floor – how dark, how fear-inspiring it seemed to be! Was it only because my head was still crawling with the monstrous and nameless horrors of Grosspapa's fireside tales?

As I reached the upper floor, searching for the door to my room – it was so easy to make a mistake – I felt an unreasoning anger rising within me. Once again, my hosts had amused themselves, unaware and probably uncaring that their hideous stories of vampires and werewolves chilled me to the bone.

Since my poor mother's untimely death, you see, I had become the victim of two obsessive fears – the fear of giving in to certain uncouth demands of the flesh – and the fear of death or dying. Indeed I often imagined that some day, some night like this one in my hosts' house, built on a canal in Hamburg, my spirit might succumb altogether, crushed between these two monstrous pillars of dread.

I also knew that I would never come to terms with the one fear, unless I succeeded in vanquishing the other. *Here*, I dimly perceived, as by dim candlelight I made my stealthy way along the wooden-boarded corridor of the upper floor, past the old people's bedroom, past the Steekebecks' room, past that chamber where I knew Felizitas would soon be sleeping, past the door where the buxom Frau Weissmar would shortly remove her clothing, piece by piece, yes, here was my last chance to conquer the dread once and for all – lest it were, finally, to conquer me . . .

Then I was back in my own bedchamber, a simple guest-room, low-ceilinged, timbered, with the windows that gave out on . . .

But, no, a servant had mercifully drawn the curtains, and I was spared the sight that I – so unreasonably – dreaded . . .

Oh, that the fear would cease! It was, in truth, a friendly room, I tried to reassure myself, a cosy room, a room built like a ship's cabin, a room promising not horror, but adventure . . . !

My eyes fastened on the bottle that dangled from the ceiling, a large shiny, green bottle which contained a skilfully assembled, detailed windjammer, beautiful but – in colour – grey . . .

A ghost-ship . . .

I put down the candlestick on the table with its hospitable red table-cloth. How they tried to please, my kindly hosts! There was, as always, fruit on the table. And a Bible.

I cast my glance towards the walls, with their framed etchings of merchant ships, all so painstakingly drawn, all filling the observer with promise of travel to far-away worlds across the wide-open seas. Only the last of the etchings disturbed me, for here again was the windjammer in the bottle, meticulously drawn and painted, the grey ship that went nowhere . . . *the ghost-ship.*

Almost mechanically, I turned away – to the window. The curtain stirred. I raised my hand, parted the soft, velvety material, and looked out across –

Oh, if only I could explain the fascination, the quivering *frisson* of horror of that inanimate view – the canal by moonlight, and facing me, across the canal, the massive warehouses – with its loading jetties and moored boats, its capstans, and ropes, all speaking of energy and industry . . .

Except for the one house . . . the house exactly opposite . . . !

The house that had been burned out by the Great Fire, so that it had become an empty shell, deserted, haunted, its black, charred windows looking implacably back at me – like dead eyes . . . *yes, dead eyes . . .*

Was it this – this view of a burned-out husk of a house – that somehow terrorized me every night from the moment

I crossed the threshold, or was it some other aspect of my room – the ship's cabin with its strange, flickering shadows?

In daylight there was nothing sinister about this white-washed nautical room, but at night, every long sleepless night as I heard the other occupants of the house walk along the creaking boards and enter their own bedrooms ... Oh, the dread, the inexplicable dread, the cunning of its devious terror!

I hid my eyes from the view, and pulled the curtain across the window, but not before ...

No, once again, I was not to be spared the sound and image that worked its horror most efficiently – the black seagulls, the shadows of black seagulls, swooping outside the room, swooping and mewing, like some monstrous harbingers of violent doom.

Quickly, I moved across the room to the curtained-off alcove, the bed-niche, where eventually, I knew, sleep would provide a brief respite, would overcome my fears, my consciousness.

My hand reached out for the alcove-curtains, but the blindly stretched-out fingers quivered in the air. I felt frozen in space, and knew I could not turn my head if I wanted to, if I needed to ...

For once again I recognized that I was being watched – perhaps guarded or protected – possibly even menaced – but by whom? Who – or what? – was it that seemed to hover above me in the atmosphere of that room, poised to strike – to seize me, as in the dead of night my dreaded fear of death seized me, clawing at my heart ...

Oh God! Seagulls swooping and diving outside my window ...

Black seagulls ...

That next morning as I made my way along the narrow polished wooden staircase from the bedroom floor, I encountered Fräulein Felizitas coming up, wishing me a polite good morning to which I replied equally courteously.

But as she passed me, for one brief second, the silk-like cloth of her dress, with her warm unbridled flesh pulsating beneath it, brushed against my naked hand and I felt as if an unnatural force were surging through my veins.

Did she smile? Had she, too, felt, even enjoyed the momentary contact? Had she – indeed, sought it?

Were others, other men, men of my age, so undone by such short-lived and possibly even imaginary contact with persons of the opposite gender?

My fears plagued and whipped each other as I fled round and round a ritual maypole of dread.

The table was laid for the lavish German second breakfast – an ample variety of cold meat and cheeses, smoked fish and fresh bread, served with coffee and the most delicately-flavoured Eastern teas.

The family met for this unusual repast at eleven every day – thus giving the old people enough time to dress, and Herr Steekebeck time to go up to his office to open his post and give the day's instructions to his staff.

Observing my anxious silence, my mere pecking and nibbling at the food, Herr Steekebeck tried to raise my sinking spirits with a paternal, almost tender smile.

'You do not have the second breakfast in England, Herr Nightingale?' he enquired, raising one eyebrow higher than the other.

'No, Senator, we do not,' I replied, making a pretence of dissecting a sliced sprat.

Grossmama leaned forward.

'No second breakfast?'

'No, we have luncheon.'

Frau Steekebeck appeared relieved that a subject had been found about which her English guest was willing to converse.

'But also,' she enquired, 'you have the afternoon tea, yes?'

'You have supper, too,' Elyse contributed.

She was wearing a very tight white blouse. I cast down my eyes. My hand shook.

'Yes,' Felizitas said, her mouth still full of buttered roll, 'I have read that in Mr Pepys' book. He is always supping.'

'Yes, indeed,' I managed to say.

Now Grosspapa entered the fray.

'But . . . that . . . that you have in the evening, no?'

'It is *dinner* in the evenings in England, Papa,' Frau Steekebeck instructed him.

'*Abendbrot*,' I heard Grossmama say from far away. 'Evening bread. Yes?'

Briefly I looked up again, just as Elyse Weissmar was folding her table-napkin, arching her back and pulling back her strong shoulders. God, why were they determined thus to torture me, even at the breakfast-table?

Felizitas was the most merciless of them all.

'You eat twice in the evenings in England? Dinner and then supper? Twice you have it? Every evening?'

I could feel hot flushes sweeping through my entire being. Was it all a trap? Which of their appetites were they really talking about?

'In that event you also dispense with tea?'

I looked open-mouthed at the old lady, but before I could reply, my hostess intervened.

'When you have no dinner, you drink tea in the afternoon. With cake, no?'

Felizitas laughed. Oh, how she laughed at my fiendish discomfort.

'You seem to – ' she paused to collect herself. '. . . to eat all day in England, Mr Nightingale!'

Her father reprimanded her with a cough, and this gave me time to rise to make my excuses, though I failed to find the correct words to make my intended and premature departure plausible.

Yet my gaze seemed still to be imprisoned by Elyse's eyes, her hair that seemed slightly bleached by the morning sun, the tormenting tremors beneath the starched white blouse.

She was cutting up an apple, and popping slices into her well-shaped, mature mouth, when her eyes looked up to meet my gaze steadfastly. Briefly but quite unmistakably I could read disappointment in those grey eyes. She had given me due consideration, and in some manner found me wanting. She had expected more. But what . . . ?

I sat down again – defeated, as the aimless conversation eddied around my consciousness once more.

'Do you care for fish, Herr Nightingale?'

'Fish?'

'We shall have it for lunch – plaice, fresh from the North Sea.'

'No, I am not overly fond of fish, Frau Steekebeck. Alas . . .'

'A pity. In this city we are famous for our plaice.'

'It is the best fish in the world.'

'An old fisherman brings them to me – the plaice – to the door – only a few hours after they have been happily swimming in the sea.'

'The North Sea, Mr Nightingale. The sea that is common to both of us.'

Would it never stop? I stood up again to speak, but though my mouth opened, I found I could not speak. My limbs had – for an instant – become frozen extensions of my body. My porcelain cup fell from my hand and crashed to the floor. I felt a murderous shudder surge through my body and my arm shook violently – like a branch in a storm.

There – by the wall – reflecting white morning sunshine – stood – for only a second – *a spectre* – formless but accusing, pointing a finger at me and laughing a grotesque maniacal laugh. The spectre laughed!

It was all over in a second, but afterwards nothing could ever be the same. For it was I who had laughed inanely, and now it was I who sat crouched forward across the table, exhausted by my inner struggle, and it was I who found my lolling head being cradled maternally by a woman's breast Elyse's? Felizitas's?

It was Elyse, and with her free hand she was offering me a glass of cold, fizzy beer – yes, *beer*!

I drank it gratefully.

'Are you better, Mr Nightingale?' Elyse asked solicitously. Her starched white blouse smelled of lilies of the valley.

Grosspapa's face loomed close.

'Someone walked over your grave, yes?'

I disengaged myself from the closeness of the woman and her enticing scent.

'You were saying,' I said, turning to my hostess, 'the fish comes to your front door – the plaice you speak of is brought by a fisherman? It is a pity that I am not more fond of fish. Yes indeed. A very great pity indeed.'

Later that day, I sat resting on a sofa in the salon, a book open on my knees but unread.

The room was full of bustling, humming, giggling women. Elyse, Frau Steekebeck, Grossmama, Felizitas were busy at the round table, cutting up cloth, using paper patterns, passing one another scissors and – from mouth to mouth – pins and needles.

I envied their great industry, their diligence, yet felt distinctly superfluous in their presence. This morning these greedy females had overpowered, undone me with their attentions. Now they were ignoring me. How typical of their sex, I thought, as I cleared my throat, and endeavoured to rise to my duties as guest of the house.

'You ladies, then, make all your own clothes, your own dresses?'

'These are not for us, Herr Nightingale,' Frau Steekebeck replied, cutting through a tinkling laugh from Felizitas. 'They are for the poor.'

I could hardly believe my ears.

All this work – this use of costly material – for the poor?

'Surely, your own unwanted clothes would be adequate for purposes of charity,' I ventured.

I was instructed that 'their' poor would not feel happy in cast-offs, that they, too, had their pride, that all the members of the family regarded their charity work as a privilege, that one could never know when one might, oneself, be a needy recipient of such good works. There had been the Great Fire; one could never ever be sure of anything in this life. Or, as Felizitas added, of anyone.

Suddenly I found myself warming to the ladies' chatter.

'Yes,' I said, rising and beginning to pace about the room. 'One cannot ever be sure of anything. Not even when one will die – not even that.' The ladies looked surprised, I thought, as I continued. 'Not even that, ladies, and I admit I have often wondered how incredible, how marvellous it would be to *know* when – *when* . . .'

Strangely enough, my thoughts appalled the good women.

Only Felizitas's eyes shone.

'Our Lord knew. He knew when He would die! He knew!'

I looked at the young girl gratefully. Oh, God, could I . . . could I hope . . . could I hope that . . .

'I understand,' I heard her say loudly, but this time she was told to be silent by her elders.

Feigning discomfort after these strange incidents, I spent the rest of the day resting on a divan in one of the other reception rooms downstairs. Indeed I waited until I felt reasonably sure that all the members of the household had retired before I made my own way up to my bedroom.

On tiptoe I walked over the wooden stairs, the creaking boards, the candle in my hand throwing frightening shadows along the walls.

I closed my bedroom door behind me, and loosened my cravat. Inevitably, ineluctably, I was drawn again to the dreaded window. The velvety curtains billowed slightly, the wind moaned with discreet urgency; I looked across the dark, sucking waters of the canal: I saw the gabled roof of the fire-charred building opposite with its dead-eyed black windows; briefly I imagined I heard again the swooping and crying of seagulls . . . black seagulls.

Deeply as I feared to be alone in that room, what else could I do but seek the conciliatory embrace of sleep? How I prayed – and dreaded – that Elyse or dare I admit it, even Felizitas – would, on some innocent pretext, knock upon my door, and enter and stay close to me to help me attain the balm of peace . . .

Abominable thought! Was it for such heinous speculations that my father had sent me to this city to assist him in his affairs? Was this how I would conquer my fears?

I determined to take a sleeping draught and to pray to my mother for grace – when – oh, horror, oh night! – I thought I heard a noise behind me.

I retreated towards the billowing curtains . . .

Would someone now strike me from behind, punishing

me swiftly for my evil, lecherous thoughts . . .?

But – and my eyes widened – it was there – in that alcove – where my bed stood curtained off, that the noise originated. And now there was a quick, slithery movement, too . . .

The glass I had picked up from the table for my sleeping draught fell from my hands, as that morning the cup had fallen from frozen fingers.

And what happened now, suddenly, without further warning was more ghastly, more horrible than anything I could have imagined, even in the gaudiest of my nightmares.

For out of the bed-niche, drawing back the velvet curtains with claw-like hands, now stepped a figure . . . *myself!*

The creature not only looked like me, he was dressed exactly like me, except that he had not removed his cravat. The only difference that my entranced mind could perceive was that while I was quivering and shaking with abominable fear, a fear so powerful as to be physically painful, my double seemed to be superbly at ease and relaxed.

The incredible ghost-like apparition opened his mouth to speak; then, instead, he smiled, and gracefully placed two fingers against his lips.

I, meanwhile, felt impelled to retreat, eventually leaning back against an obstacle, a table. My hand gripped my heart, my eyes closed in anguish, I let out a gasp of terror and disbelief.

'Who are you,' I heard myself groan in a choked voice. 'What do you want?'

Although my double's lips were open to speak, all that his mouth emitted was the word '*want*', which I imagined could well be an echo of my own voice.

In my fevered brain, the seagulls mewed and dived. Black seagulls . . .

Now, as I stood rooted to the spot, the creature pointed at me imperiously.

The entire room seemed to sway; now it really *was* a ship's cabin. Were we tossing on the high seas?

Oh God, I felt so sick suddenly, so desperately sick . . .

I turned, collapsed over the wash-stand and watched helplessly, as my mouth spewed forth the disgusting contents of my stomach.

I could feel my double approaching me from behind, then standing quite still as I collapsed on to a chair.

Obediently I stretched out my hand, my fingers closing around the glass that he was offering me. Greedily I drank the water, then held the glass against my feverish forehead.

'What do you want?' I asked again.

'What do *you* want?' (Was it he speaking – or merely an echo?)

I looked up and drew in my breath. There he stood, throwing back his head, a grimacing smile corrupting the even line of his lips – his fingers pointed once more – at the table? At my plans and drawings that lay upon it?

'The truth,' I whined, turning my face away from the creature. 'I want the truth!'

'The truth,' he echoed calmly. 'I want the truth.'

The taste in my mouth was foul; my face burned; I had begun to cry bitter tears. Obscene nightmare! Would the creature stay in this room with me all night? Was I destined to be pursued by it forever?

'Help me!' I muttered feebly. 'Help me! Or they will fly in!'

The seagulls! The gulls! The black gulls . . .

This time there was no reply.

I felt so weak, that I thought I would sink to the ground and find merciful oblivion in sleep.

Instead I looked up to see the creature close – his eyes boring into me! I suddenly found myself carried aloft as if by some invisible force. Upwards, I was being carried, lifted, *held*! Upwards, ever upwards, until I floated horizontally in the middle of the room, resting there, unaided, in this unnatural position for longer than I thought I could bear.

It was only after I had opened my mouth to utter a scream to seek release, as – indeed – I heard myself yell out in midnight terror, that he, the creature that was me, swiftly but surely bore down on me, seemed to merge with me, and in an unholy, unearthly manner took total and complete possession ...

When I awoke the following morning, I heard church bells, and then – a short distance away – a choir singing that lovely Bach cantata, that I, too had sung, as a choirboy in Norwich, worlds away, at a different time in another universe.

Ich habe genug ...

Was I dead? In heaven? Had it all been a dream?

The agonizing moment that it took me to realize that I was not dead, that I had not spent the night in the womb of a hideous nightmare – for there were ugly signs of a struggle, of my sickness, about the room – that moment was finally shattered by a sharp knock at the door.

'My father has sent me. Will you come to the church? We are already late!'

Felizitas! I smiled. My angel, ready to surrender that wretched innocence of her body to me. Where? In her room? The kitchen? In the incense-laden atmosphere of her precious church? There, among the pews ...

No, of course not. Protestants! Evangelicals! They used no incense, did they?

'I shall be ready,' I piped sweetly, got out of bed, walked nimbly to the window and drew back the curtains to let in the warm, welcoming sunshine.

How happily I prayed, how loudly I sang in that church! How strong and proud and juicy my voice sounded! How unusually musical were the hymns that assailed my ears! Damn my soul, but those Steekebeck women looked good enough to eat, even Frau Steekebeck who, I wagered, had not felt her husband's maleness close to her for many a year!

However, when the family asked me to accompany them to the evening service, I thanked them politely and declined. Once was quite enough. And, I should have guessed it of course, but the impatient Elyse, whose needs were as urgent as my own, elected also to stay in the house! Indeed she insisted on staying in that very room to which I had retired to read . . . (To read! The overripe widow would waste little time before taking the book from my hands!)

I watched her from under half-closed eyelids.

'I think the family may disapprove, Herr Nightingale,' she said quickly, pretending to concentrate on her embroidery.

I said nothing. Let the woman make her demands clear. Why should I help her? I'd give her the service she wanted soon enough!

But she was clearly nervous, dipping her needle in and out of the cloth, wasting precious time in explaining that Grosspapa was Frau Steekebeck's father and that Grossmama was Herr Steekebeck's mother. As if I cared! And as if I didn't know what it was that she wanted to do with those eagerly dipping fingers of hers!

I let her dangle for a few more minutes – the poor benighted creature. Then I was upon her, as *he* had been upon me during the evil night just past, and as I ripped cloth and cursed lustily and kneaded flesh, I cried out in triumph, aware that I was administering for the first time in my life that special pleasure and pain in equal measure! The pain for her, the pleasure for me!

Oh, the baseness of good women, the lechery and frenzy that lie concealed beneath a widow's starched white linen!

That night it was my turn to read the ghost story. I chose a tale from a volume in English by that master of the macabre, E. T. A. Hoffmann. I read beautifully, with a clear voice and measured rhythm.

When I looked up from my agreeable labours, I found Elyse gazing at me with luminous eyes and a sated expression – the cat who had supped of a surfeit of cream. And as my eyes turned to young Felizitas, did I observe an almost imperceptible nod of – could it be recognition, understanding, even encouragement?

The old Steekebecks were still paying me fulsome compliments on my reading, when Felizitas suddenly rose from her chair.

'What nonsense, all of it,' she said truculently, 'I didn't

believe a word. I'm going to bed.'

And with that she flounced out, stopping at the door to stick out her tongue at me – *at me*!

The rest of the family were about to disperse.

I, too, rose, in my usual hesitant way, not quite sure whom to address first, whose hand to shake, and so forth.

All those doubts, of which my ghost had briefly liberated me, seemed to be back, and I bowed my head . . .

But then a curious thing happened. The family had left the room, and only Herr Steekebeck remained, holding a candle, and bowing from the waist, waiting to usher me through the door.

I was about to go meekly, when I was once more seized – as if by the throat. A strange power invaded, infected me, and urged, nay, commanded me to stay.

'Sir,' I addressed my host in a voice which I myself hardly recognized. 'I have received some regrettable news from Norwich.' Waving away a gesture of concern on his part I continued: 'To come to the point at once, we cannot now manufacture the vehicles you require.'

Herr Steekebeck altered his stance visibly. He ceased to be the jovial host; he added two inches to his height to become the senator – moreover the senator confronted by an unexpected difficulty.

'You mean something untoward has occurred in Norwich?' he began stiffly. 'Your father's firm . . . it is in troubled circumstances?'

'It is not, Herr Steekebeck.' I replied. '*You* are.'

'Then would you allow me to point out that it would doubtlessly be more correct were you to discuss matters of commerce at my *Kontor* upstairs, Herr Nightingale – '

' – where, you, sir, are assisted by your own clerks and ledger-keepers to offer you protection?'

Herr Steekebeck made a vague, fluttering gesture with his fingers close to his forehead as if he had not understood me correctly.

'And furthermore,' I followed up, standing close to my exposed 'partner' in business, breathing fumes of righteous indignation into his face, 'I must trouble you, sir, to accommodate us in all future negotiations with that same fee and price for the completed yellow carriages that you see fit to charge the Council of the City of Hamburg!'

Herr Steekebeck, I could see, was summoning up his last reserves of self-control. Was I, he enquired, by any chance accusing him of corrupt practice?

'Indeed, sir,' I replied with a smile. 'Were I not a guest in your house, I would doubtlessly express myself even more forcefully.'

The other man trembled – as well he might, for had I not unmasked the scurvy villain? Then he turned, picked up a glass from the table, and sniffed it punctiliously.

'I see,' he said with a forced smile. 'Tonight is the first time in your life that you have tasted alcohol, correct?'

And with that remark, the coward eluded my deserved reprimands for the moment, and strode out, leaving me in darkness.

And suddenly I was yet again overcome by a retching sickness – bile welling up in my intestines – and my hand clawed my heart in pain. Then I rushed from the room.

Poor Elyse – how she had to suffer that night!

The pleasure for me – the pain for her.

And was this not how she wanted it?

Exhausted by my labours of love, I returned to my room, only to find all my new strength draining from my body, leaving only my dreadful fears intact.

I moved to the window to gasp the night air in large draughts – but black seagulls swooped and lamented about my head, and the house opposite with its dark, dead, charred eyes gaped at me with mocking warnings of doom.

I turned round, only to find – standing under the bottle that contained the meticulously constructed grey ship – that creature who purported to be me, my shadow, my ghost.

He had returned, looking as calm and relaxed as ever.

'Oh, God,' I moaned.

'. . . God . . .' came the echo.

(Was that it, I wondered briefly, had He appeared in my image to punish me for my dreadful wrongdoings? Could He not understand that all my actions so far had only been means to the desired end?)

'Help me,' I groaned, 'I must find it.'

'*Find it!*' He commanded.

'The truth, the date!'

'*The date . . .*'

'The how, the why, the *when* of my death!'

'*Death!*' He asserted imperiously, and blew out the candle, and I was alone – in darkness – with my tormentor, my conqueror.

'It is *that*?' I called out weakly, 'the purpose?'

'*It is that* –' in the impenetrable darkness – '*the purpose!*'

And I screamed and screamed, like a child waking from the most horrendous nightmare imaginable, and now our ghostly dialogue continued in a shrill vibrato double-shriek, that must have brought the other occupants to my door, though it was the middle of the night.

And indeed, as I was to learn soon after, my hostess Frau Steekebeck had been summoned to my door, listening outside to the shrill screams. ('*You promise! The truth! About death! Go on! Go on! Go on!*' repeated doubly, trebly, and accompanied by vile moanings and retchings.) But the poor woman had been too frightened to enter.

She waited until dawn, and entered as I lay, drained of power, on my bed in that ship's cabin of a room – feeling as emptied and lifeless as a poor sailor of a passenger after a stormy night's dreadful sickness.

'Herr Nightingale,' the good woman enquired solicitously, 'last night I heard such strange voices – were you unwell? Why did you not call for a servant?'

'Or for you, eh?' I grinned, knowingly, baring my teeth and cowering back in my alcove.

She hesitated for a moment, then advanced upon me in the grey diffused light of morning.

'But you must tell me, Herr Nightingale, I must ask you: is it in such a fashion that in England one repays the gift of hospitality?'

The woman came even closer. Now she was practically upon me. I clutched the bed curtains in distress.

'Do not come one step nearer, you vile woman,' I hissed at her.

She stood quite still then. Yes, my warning had not been

lost on her. Her eyes were swimming with tears.

'What is my husband's house to you, Herr Nightingale?' she suddenly wailed. 'What have you made of it? What have you made of poor Elyse, what . . .'

I was up on my feet before she could utter another word. My hands had reached out for her. I bowed deeply to kiss those hands, no longer young . . .

I spoke with great reverence, as befitted the good Frau Steekebeck. 'If I have done anything at all to merit such censure, dear Frau Steekebeck,' I said in hushed tones, 'I must humbly solicit your own and your family's pardon and forgiveness . . .'

The poor woman, hardly daring to cast a look in my direction, turned to leave the room, still sobbing unaccountably. But as she closed the door behind her, what did that closing door reveal, but *him* standing in the corner of that dawnlit room, more upright and imperious than I had ever seen him, his lips quivering . . .

With rage?

Oh God, had I offended him?

I gasped, clutching my heart, as my *Doppelgänger* advanced upon me, and I closed my eyes in reverent submission, moaning, as from far away I could hear my black seagulls circling and screaming . . .

It was fish for dinner. Delicious, flaky white plaice.

How I enjoyed chewing that white fish-flesh, then sucking clean the bones. I had not even been aware of the family around the table, too preoccupied with the delicious promptings of my appetite, when Felizitas leaned forward to ask:

'Why – how strange, Herr Nightingale. Did I imagine it, or did you say you did not care for fish?'

'I like nothing better, Fräulein Felizitas,' I said, my mouth still full.

'How odd – I thought I heard you say upon more than one occasion that you could not abide fish of any kind.'

'I love fish, Fräulein Felizitas,' I reassured her, my foot pressing hers under the table, 'as I love life itself.'

Then without pausing to catch my breath I announced

my imminent departure, hugely enjoying the varied reactions, particularly the horrified gasp of poor Elyse.

Only Felizitas remained calm, it seemed, for she suggested without further ado that as a parting gesture she would make up for her neglect of me by showing me the ships in the harbour tomorrow.

'We will do it tonight,' I leered at her. 'When it is dark. I feel more composed in the dark.'

I looked around the table, drinking in the silence, the appalled embarrassment of all the members of the family, as if it were ambrosia itself.

Oh yes, indeed: He may have conquered me. But I had conquered them. And I asked my hostess to instruct the servants to fry another large plaice without delay.

When he appeared to me later that evening, standing behind the bottle containing the ghost ship so that his face seemed to become a living part of the ship, I was not afraid.

'I know now. I understand,' I told him. 'Why you have come. I shall never die . . .'

I held her arm, felt her flesh vibrate under my touch as we walked through swirling mists along the gloomy harbour wall, past lanterned railings, above which rose the desolate masts of anchored ships, the crowns of wintry trees, the roofs of timbered wharves . . .

On we walked, Felizitas and I, close to each other, close to the wall, away from the lights of the city, the clip-clopping of late carriages, away from the members of the Steekebeck family and their faked proprieties.

We spoke little; she kept her chin tucked down, to protect herself against the rising night wind. But when we stopped briefly, it was because she wished to present me – whom she had recognized long ago as her only lord and master – with a secret childhood memory which concerned the Great Fire.

'It was wonderful,' she whispered, pressed close to me. 'Wonderful. I was so little, and the fire raged about us, myself and my father, that is. I was curled up in my father's strong arms, as we watched the flames leaping all along the roofs of the little cottages, higher and higher, making me feel so warm and safe and happy, and all the time the fire was coming closer, the flames swallowing everything, the ships and their masts, the little cottages by the harbour, and my father holding me so tight, oh how I wish . . .'

'You wish . . .?'

'I could see them again, the flames! Look at that decrepit old freighter! Useless and old! How beautifully it would burn! Like dry firewood!'

'We could both watch it burn,' I echoed urgently, 'until only ashes remain . . .'

'Burning and blazing . . . so you want it too . . .?' She opened dream-laden eyes in horror. 'What is it?' she gasped. 'What is happening to you?'

What indeed? For suddenly I felt the blood drain from my face, and my entire frame shook as if someone or something was throttling me, and squeezing the life out of my body.

I limply raised my arms – for there – some distance away, by the harbour wall, stood my double, grinning, pointing, mocking me and my pretensions.

I pushed myself against the wall; my shoulders hunched like a frightened cat; I snarled and wheezed and felt the bile once more rising inside me. Furtively I glanced in the direction of my companion, who, horrified by the alterations in my being, had turned and fled, her footsteps echoing away daintily over the cobblestones.

I was alone with the night and with him. And with the virgin's dreams of raging fires . . .

In the morning, long before the family was up, Elyse crept into my room, where she found me neither asleep nor awake, but still and passive, as in a womb-like limbo.

A ray of early sunshine struck her head, as she knelt down by the chair where I sat, and in which I had gone to sleep, still dressed, some hours ago.

Gratefully, the besotted widow clutched my hand and raised it to her cheek, but let it go, shrinking back from me, as she heard my chuckle.

'You are expecting someone else,' she breathed. 'Oh God, what have you made of me – what have you done to all of us . . . why . . . ?'

'Black seagulls,' I said tonelessly. 'They came first, swooping and diving outside my window. And then *he* came to bring me to life and to reveal the truth.'

'He? Truth?'

She looked at me wide-eyed, squatting on the floor, a strand of hair hanging over her eye, all dignity gone . . .

'Today he will reveal the ultimate truth to me,' I intoned. 'I can sense that it will be today. Because, you see, I must know exactly *when* . . . The hour – the precise moment! Pray with me that he delays no longer . . . For that small sliver of knowledge, you see, I have given him my immortal soul . . .'

'Oh God, oh my God,' I heard her breathe.

'The precise hour, minute, second when death will strike me down,' I continued obliviously. 'All of us. You, me, the old fools, the cheating senator, the foul-loined women . . . the time and nature of all their deaths . . .'

The woman crouching beside me had begun to cry, as cobwebs began to descend over my eyes, over my head, over my entire body. He – invisible now – was abandoning my disgusting body to gulls and spiders, while his voice – inaudible to all but me – was urgently whispering that one further truth would be vouchsafed to me: the exact time and nature of my children's deaths!

I reared up from my chair to elude the thick mesh of cobwebs, which had begun to bind my flesh.

'I have no children – I never will have,' I screeched.

'Oh yes,' the creature on the floor muttered, 'you will have one child.'

'Who are you?' I asked, for I did not greatly care to know a frail and fallen woman.

'The mother of your unborn child, my love,' the creature confided, and left me to do battle with the cobwebs which now bit deeper and deeper into my poor flesh . . .

Invoking my *Doppelgänger*, I called out to him:

'Why – when we are one – are you now seeking to destroy me . . .?'

'*Destroy me,*' came the mocking echo. '*Destroy me!*'

It was one of those sweeping rain-storms, at first languid, then angry, finally destructively enraged, so peculiar to northern climes, that began to blow up that night.

The family Steekebeck, sitting around the dinner table in oppressive and oppressed silence, pretended to ignore the sweeping winds outside, as indeed they had chosen to pretend that the guest in their midst was not a monster.

I chuckled inwardly at their discomfort, their polite desperation, after I had pointed out to them that the so-called omelette they had seen fit to serve me was, indeed, no omelette but a common pancake. (The taste of flour was unmistakable.) Since I had not spared them from their hidden lecheries and larcenies, why should I not also reveal to them their more mundane and petty dishonesties? Was that not after all my purpose in this household? A fresh wind of violent honesty – of honest violence?

Somehow there came to be a nervous overlap in the conversation, with the Steekebecks talking simultaneously of the brewing storm, the stuffed pancake and the Great Fire.

'Tell me, is it not really death you are talking about, you miserable, frightened creatures?' I expostulated.

Oh, how they fluttered and piped, stuttered and gasped. 'Why are you all so afraid of it? Why do you make a secret of it?' I continued, watching the old couple, Gross-mama and Grosspapa, shrink back into their chairs with disbelief and terror. 'Come – it is not vice, it is not un-speakable. The Bible never ceases to speak of it. It is an adventure – it approaches us and we should approach it gratefully. Inevitably we will collide . . . At any moment it may strike us down. Forever!'

'Please,' Elyse whined in supplication, 'my dear friend...'

'Yes,' Frau Steekebeck now shrieked with uncontrolled hysteria. '*Your dear friend*! In my house! Strumpet! Wanton!'

As they all began to flail about, losing all self-control, all their North German stiffness, cursing each other, shouting obscenities, I pretended that nothing was amiss, and continued calmly – in counterpoint with the rising storm – to hold forth:

'Can you not see, all of you, how marvellous it would be, if one had the power to divine with absolute precision – the moment itself . . . *the moment itself* . . . savour it . . . taste it with the tip of one's tongue . . . to determine for everyone in advance – the exact day, the precise hour, not only of one's own demise, but of all others!'

Only Felizitas was listening to me. The others were shouting at me to stop, shouting at each other to make me stop. So I turned to Felizitas.

'Admit it, can you not imagine the power with which it must invest one to know – and I tell you, yes, that I have assumed that power. I can – and shall – vouchsafe to each one of you the exact hour – the precise moment of your deaths!'

'Make him stop, make him cease,' they all wailed, all of them except Felizitas, whose body was quivering, who had thrown back her head, her lips bringing forth the single word 'Ecstasy!'

But nothing would stop me. I had risen, climbed upon my chair, and then upon the table, sweeping all the crockery and cutlery out of the way.

'The love of life, my friends,' I roared at them with unassailable strength, 'is merely – as Hazlitt wrote, "an habitual attachment, not an abstract principle." Surely simply to be cannot suffice? One must strive to discover the truth! For over a month I have watched you – your lies, your pretences and your secrets, your pathetic needs and your terrible fears! Hoping to banish the truth by telling each other stories of ghosts and vampires! While I – I saw death itself, shuddering towards me, persuading me that only a life of action, of danger – yes, of betrayal – can overcome it – the universal dread of death. And so I have acted. And loved and betrayed and exposed you all, making myself fit to embrace everlasting life!'

And then I did it, I pulled a sheet of paper from my inside breast pocket, on which, I proclaimed, was written the dates of their deaths, all their deaths!

Oh, how they yelled in anguish, the dear, stately Steeke-becks, imploring me to stop, calling me a monster, a mad-man, a murderer!

All but Felizitas, who had moved to the window, Felizitas whose eyes shone with an unnatural bright-ness, whose whole face was illuminated by weird dancing lights.

'Mother! Look!' she cried out as if experiencing at that moment the height of physical pleasure. 'The ship! The ship is on fire!'

I jumped from the table and hurried across to the window, catching the heaving, sighing young woman in my open arms.

And it was true.

The ship was in flames! The windjammer by the harbour wall that so resembled the ghostly grey ship in the bottle in my room – it was on fire . . .

The Great Fire had returned! He had brought it back! For you, Felizitas! For us!

While the others wailed and cursed, I had swept Felizitas up in my arms, and rushed her out of the room, out of the house, on, on . . . towards the harbour wall, where the flames were leaping and dancing, higher and higher, warming our faces and bodies . . .

I held her even closer as we watched the great masts of the ships collapse like burning matches.

'Yes, this is as I dreamt it,' she cried, 'all of it – happening again – being held so tightly, so sweetly, while the yellow flames grow, consuming everything . . .!'

She tore herself away from me.

'Let me find it,' she yelled in a demented voice, 'the centre, the golden centre . . .'

Beside me now was he, my mentor and *Doppelgänger*.

'It was her day, you see!' I muttered.

'*You see!*' he echoed mockingly.

And I did! I saw her consumed by the golden centre of the flames, my poor Felizitas, and the golden body, the beauteous face, turning to grey and crumbling ashes before my eyes . . .

And he and I – together – linked arms and danced away;

entwined, ecstatic, along the burning harbour wall . . .

Shortly afterwards, I made my departure from Hamburg and returned – a wiser and more mature man – to Norwich. After a fortnight or so, I decided that it was time to write my hosts the conventional letter of thanks for their hospitality, which was certainly their due. I wrote:

Dear Mr Steekebeck,
    Even in the midst of the lamentable circumstances that have befallen your house, sir, it behoves me, as an English gentleman, to write to you – not merely to thank you for the impeccable hospitality which you and your family vouchsafed to me during my all-too-brief visit to your charming city, but also to offer you my most heartfelt condolence over your dreadful misfortunes. During the few short weeks I was privileged to be your guest, I learned to admire your late daughter's vivaciousness and love of life, as well as the warm, generous character of dear gentle Frau Weissmar. Having grown so fond of them, I can appreciate your appalling double loss: the death of dear Felizitas, and the abandonment of reason by Frau Weissmar after her miscarriage in an institution for the mad. Let me say in conclusion that should it ever occur to you that I was in some small measure responsible for the misunderstandings that led to these tragic events, I herewith offer you my most humble apologies.
Your loyal friend,
Nightingale.
PS. The directors of my father's company note with regret that our yellow conveyances will no longer be required by your city councillors.

Sir Francis rose at the conclusion of Mr Nightingale's tale. His face was flushed with moral outrage.
    'But sir!' he expostulated, 'you are by your own account, sir, a damned murderer!'
    'Me, sir? Am I?'
    'You killed the daughter and you are entirely responsible, sir, for

what happened to the unfortunate widow and your unborn child in that institution!'

'If anyone was to blame,' Mr Nightingale pointed out blandly, 'it was – him.'

'In that case, sir, produce him!'

Mr Nightingale looked surprised, and a little hurt.

'Are you saying that you really cannot see him, gentlemen?' There – beneath that candelabrum he stands, as young and strong as he was that first night he came to proffer his powers to me . . . While I, as you see, have grown old and frail . . .'

The members saw nothing. Nobody stood beneath that candelabrum. No ghost. No creature. No Doppelgänger.

'Mr Nightingale,' the Chairman announced, after the committee of members had held their deliberations. 'In the judgement of all of us, you have failed to satisfy us. Your story, though bizarre enough, is patently untrue. This – er – Doppelgänger, were he to exist . . .'

'But there he stands.' Mr Nightingale's pointing finger quivered in the air. 'He smiles.'

'We conclude, sir, that the creature is a figment of your diseased imagination and invoked solely to justify your criminal conduct!'

The Chairman nodded curtly to the Club servants who instantly took the struggling, screaming, frail old fellow away, to dispose of him in the manner laid down in the merciless regulations of the Club of the Damned.

ROBERT MULLER

GALL
or
GHOST OF VENICE

adapted by ROSEMARY TIMPERLEY

The members were gathered before the open fire in the drawing-room awaiting their story-teller of the evening.

'Gentlemen!' *The Chairman raised his hand, commanding silence. All became quiet.*

'Tonight we are unusually fortunate,' *he began.* 'It is not often that we may welcome into our midst a true celebrity, an illustrious member of one of the professions. Men of notoriety, yes, of infamy even, but tonight's guest is a truly illustrious member of one of the professions. Respect, gentlemen, respect! Mr Adrian Gall can be described as one of the truly great actors of this century. Yet more than that, he was the principal of that famous company of actors which travelled far and wide, not merely in this country but abroad, to present the works of William Shakespeare.'

A shadow lurked unnoticed in the doorway: the outline of a wide-brimmed black hat and flowing cloak could be discerned: A mysterious figure, imposing, dignified. Faceless.

'My goodness,' *the Chairman continued,* 'did I say was the principal? Is then the actor's renown so ephemeral a thing that after a mere decade of retirement, one already talks of his work as if he were dead? True, one remembers certain unsavoury rumours concerning the great man's rather sudden retirement – '

'I am here!' *A sepulchral voice startled them all.*

The members turned their faces in the direction of the doorway.

'Yes, I am here,' *repeated the voice,* 'so pay attention to me. Hear the story of Adrian Gall, then judge me afterwards. Dream my tale of endless horror with me, and then decide if mine is not the most appalling story ever to be told in this room.'

And he laughed, a cackle of agony and irony, in which there was not a glimmer of hope. The fire in the big fireplace seemed to crackle with anticipation. The listeners held their breath.

For Adrian Gail had begun his story.

Though – as most of you will know – my home is in England – this, my story – or as much of it as matters – took place in a foreign city, a timeless city, the name of which I often forget – which is curious, since that city's contours are more real to me than any episode or relationship from my own life. In my mind's eye, then, the city has the *feeling* of that Venice where my wife, myself and my company of players celebrated our greatest triumphs. Yet it is *not* Venice. It *cannot* be Venice. For during my nocturnal hauntings of its streets and alleys, I can never find the Piazza San Marco, nor the Teatro La Fenice, nor any of the other landmarks I have known and loved. Certainly, it is a city built on water, a city of haunted squares, dingy alleys and moonstruck bridges, renaissance arches, dark vaults, and subterranean passages, of crumbling masonry and endless rows of once-perfect columns, all – it appears to me – withering away with time's merciless sentence. Though it is here, in this forever-dying city, that the recent events with which I shall shortly acquaint you, occurred, I must confess that those events seem to belong to quite another epoch – indeed to a life other than my own . . .

But I must begin at the beginning.

And I choose to begin my story in the year 1875 on a damp and unfriendly night, much like this one.

My wife Charlotte and I were asleep in the bedroom of the modest but charming country house which we have occupied since our retirement, when I awoke once more in terror. Once again I had been held in the throes of that recurrent nightmare which tormented me to breaking-point. It was as vivid as life itself.

I awoke in a rage, crying out: 'God! They've done it again! Robbed me! Taken it all from me! Thieves! Scum! I shall be revenged on them – I'll confront them. They've taken everything, every penny in the purse, the purse I've cherished since you gave it to me on our wedding day. They've robbed me of all I possess.'

Poor Charlotte. She'd been through this often before, seen me so often frantic with fury and dreams of persecution. She got out of her own bed and came to try and soothe me. 'Hush, it's only that old dream, my darling.'

But the dream was totally real to me. I was awake, yet not awake. The dream lived on.

'Can't you recall?' I insisted, trembling all over. 'They took everything from me when we were playing at the Fenice Theatre, in Venice. We were giving *Macbeth*. The Prefect of Police was out in front, in a box, with his family, and while they were applauding us, thieves and robbers were occupying our dressing-room, rifling through our belongings.'

'It did not happen,' Charlotte insisted, as soothing as always. 'There were no thieves, Adrian. You lost no purse. Nothing was taken.'

'They took everything from me,' I yelled at her. 'Why will you deny it?'

'I must deny it, or we'll both lose our sanity. This terrible rage of yours over an imaginary loss – '

'Imaginary! I have grounds for my rage. But now I know what I must do. This cannot go on. I must go back – to lay the ghost – *to retrieve my valuables* – '

'They took nothing!' she cried again, sobbing.

Stupid woman. She didn't understand. She meant well, but she had become useless to me. And I closed my eyes, and my mind began to concentrate on the details of my journey to Venice, which could no longer be postponed.

To this city, then, I returned, was impelled to return, alone, to seek out an old acquaintance, the Prefect of Police, and to lodge with him once and for all, an official complaint about the loss of my valuables, my belongings, indeed that aforementioned purse stolen from me during one of my performances in the city. That purse which my enraged dreams had exhorted me to regain – because it seemed to me that it was of life itself that I had been robbed.

As soon as I arrived in the city, I sent a message to the Prefect of Police and told him to meet me at a well-known, disreputable café by one of the side canals. There under shadowy arcades, solitary among whores and pimps, I awaited the Prefect. One of the prostitutes had the audacity to approach me. *Me!* Adrian Gall!

'My name is Stella,' she began.

But I thanked her and tossed her a coin to get rid of her. She instantly went on to an eager old man at another table.

I could not help myself. I had to turn my head to watch her, puzzled. Did she seem familiar to me? Had she made overtures to me at some other time, was she one of the hundreds of women I had known briefly but intimately over the years? And why should I imagine that she looked like my Charlotte's best friend, Regina, once herself an actress?

The Prefect of Police arrived at last, a courtly grey-beard, who greeted me over-effusively and ordered wine.

'Ah, Signor Gall, never will I forget you and the gracious Signora. The richness of the poetry. The music of your voices. *The Winter's Tale*, the magnificent *Macbeth*.'

I tried to stem the flow, insisting that I had not returned to the city to hear compliments, but the Prefect was not to be curtailed.

'Especially your *Macbeth*! And your wonderful wife's Lady Macbeth. And those terrible witches. That atmosphere of violence and ghostly terror – ' And he began to recite one of Macbeth's speeches, beginning in over-correct English and then continuing without modulation in melodious Italian.

'The stage, sir, lost an ornament when you determined to make your career in the police force,' I said finally.

He must have detected my irony, for his eyes narrowed and he suddenly asked: 'How is the Signora? I trust that she is fully recovered.'

'Recovered?' I echoed sharply.

'From that dreadful accident. That is how we first met, you and I, do you not recall, Signor Gall? After that unfortunate performance – the fall – the accident!'

'Signore,' I interrupted him. 'I haven't – to be frank – asked you to meet me here to discuss minor incidents or past performances. My wife and I have retired from the stage. You must know why I have made this long, tiring journey!'

'Indeed I do not know. Nor can I divine why you have chosen to meet me in this unpleasant and disreputable café . . .'

'I am here to investigate a crime.'

'A crime? Of what nature?'

'A crime that was done to my person, here, in this city, as you well remember.'

He shook his head. 'No. I am completely mystified by all you say.'

That angered, indeed wounded me. Why was he pretending? 'No doubt, sir, you prefer the file on that particular incident to be closed for ever,' I challenged him.

'But what incident, Signor Gall?'

'You know full well what incident, sir!'

At that moment the champagne arrived. The Prefect insisted on paying for it. 'In this city I am bound to be the host,' he said, and I observed a new, steely quality in his eyes.

As we sipped the wine I calmed down somewhat. Then the Prefect said, 'Now my dear old friend, let us return to this – er – incident of yours.'

'You must recall it, surely! While we performed *Macbeth*, thieves entered my dressing-room and robbed me of – Oh, God! – of everything!'

Suddenly, at the very time when I wanted to be firm, I was in tears. Humiliating tears. I tried to hide them with my hands.

'Forgive me,' I muttered, 'a certain weakness . . . I was once famous for shedding "real" tears . . .'

'Dear friend, you are not well,' murmured the Prefect. 'Come, let me take you back to your hotel. It is late and the company here is hardly suitable.'

'Yes. Perhaps you're right. Forgive me. The champagne was excellent – I thank you, and beg you to excuse my appalling manners.'

'We shall drink another bottle on a future occasion,' he cooed, 'when next we meet again – ' And suddenly recognizing that the old goat was humouring me, my humility turned to fury. I sprang to my feet.

'Oh, yes, Signore, we shall most certainly meet again,' I shouted at him. 'I have not travelled hundreds of miles to be fobbed off by the insincere ramblings of a pusillanimous petty official, who has clearly decided in advance to deny the crimes that were undoubtedly carried out in his name!'

For a second, I though the Prefect was going to strike me, then he decided on a mildness of manner employed by those who converse with the mentally sick. 'If you will tell me the name of your hotel, Signor Gall, I will have one of my officers take you there in a gondola.'

'I don't need your solicitude,' I snapped, 'and I advise you to investigate my complaint forthwith – or you shall hear from the British Consul. I demand restitution of my property. Do you hear! I demand it!'

The Prefect bowed elaborately, tipped the waiter, and left.

Seconds – minutes? – hours? – later, I found myself sitting alone in that deserted waterside café. Midnight struck. A coarse night wind blew, rustling papers under my marble-topped table. I was filled with dread. Was this the city I had longed for? This desolate city of the dead?

I looked at the empty tables around me. And now I noticed that one, only one, was occupied. A bent figure crouched there, a dreadful, witch-like old woman, a beggar, a crone, a thing of rags and tatters. Slowly she turned her head to look at me.

Charlotte!

The evil crone – this angel of death – had my wife's eyes!

Horrified, I covered my eyes. When I slowly let my quivering hands fall again, I saw that the table was empty.

I sat on for a while, in fearful solitude, and thought of Charlotte. That creature had reminded me of my great sorrow. I had not been able to make love to my wife since the night of the robbery. She now left me cold. We slept in separate beds. I – the great lover of his time, the conqueror of a hundred women – could no longer relish her whom he loved most.

At last I trailed back over the bridges and past the canals, along dark alleys with sinister doorways, until I reached the attic room in the hotel where I was staying. I tried to sleep in the narrow bed, but remained restless and tormented. I got up and stared out of the window. Somewhere in the distance a mandolin played. The world outside was silver with moonlight. Beautiful. Yet fearful.

'Oh, Charlotte,' I wept, 'is it all a dream? Shall I wake up in your arms? Can we never be our old selves again?' I went down on my knees. 'Charlotte, forgive me if my heart seems closed to you – there has been a robbery, you see – they took things from me – forgive me – '

And so – because of the intransigence of an inefficient and insincere police official, I found myself forced to haunt the nocturnal alleys and accusing arcades of this city – knowing that only through my own efforts – only through my own strength – would I be able to settle the score, and retrieve that of which I had been robbed – unfairly, unfathomably, in my prime . . . But if it could not be won back by kind words, polite requests or admonitions – very well: they who had thus undone me would have to be *compelled* to return to me what was rightfully mine.

And thus I – who had acted so many great parts written by the great masters, now performed a part I had written for myself – that of a monstrous phantom – dressed in cloak, ostrich-feather hat and skull-mask on which was painted the skeleton head of a revengeful ghost. And this phantom of the midnight hour walked along the canals and alleys of the city they call Venice to terrify alike the guilty and the innocent – until at last the truth would be revealed to me – the true story of the loss of my belongings, my valuables . . .!

And men and women learned to flee the phantom of vengeance, including the nauseous Stella, who reminded me not only of some half-forgotten flame of the past, but also of my ruined present self, and who seemed to be forever cowering in doorways, watching the phantom's progress.

You have only to imagine human acts for them to become possible, then likely, then inevitable. I was drifting on and on in a world of fantasy and nightmare. None of this could be happening, I told myself, and yet it was. How I wished I had never returned to Venice; how I wished I could be spirited back to my dear wife's side. Yet I had begun to realize that there could be no return, and I sensed that Charlotte knew it too.

One night as I wandered again, but this time without wearing my mask or feathers, I saw Stella again – this time with another girl. Stella glanced at me briefly, without interest, for I had not frightened her this time. But the other girl turned to look at me, and her eyes widened in recognition. Her lips shaped my name: 'Adrian Gall.'

Memory came edging back. It couldn't be, of course – it couldn't possibly be – not possibly – not even in the furthest recesses of imagination – and yet –

I cried out the name: '*Leonora!*'

Then she vanished, as if she had never been. But it *had* been – Leonora, whom in some bizarre way I associated with my loss. Was it indeed *she* herself whom I imagined I had lost? So many years ago, in that same Venetian arcade, I remembered her, so unbearably, so desolately young. Had she not pursued me then with hero-worship and love, from the streets of London, from the theatres, where she claimed she never missed a single performance of mine? Had she not pursued me even to Venice? For what? To applaud me? To catch a glimpse of my shadow sailing past in a gondola? For a glimpse of mine and Charlotte's entwined shadows . . . For no more than that? No? Had there perhaps been more – a promise? Possibly only a promise extracted rather than willingly offered. And had Leonora – now apparently herself one of those wretched arcade prostitutes – had she not then been something altogether different? One of *us* – possibly even a member of my company?

I plagued and teased my memory – without avail.

The following night I sought out the Prefect of Police again. Over a deserted bridge, the ghostly Ponte delle Turchete, I stopped him in his tracks to demand: 'Have you done as I instructed you? Have you investigated my complaint?'

'Indeed I have, Signore,' he said smoothly. 'And I am delighted to tell you that no object or objects were reported stolen from your dressing-room at the Teatro La Fenice those many years ago. Your triumph was undiluted, except, of course, for that regrettable incident of the fall.'

'Ah, the fall . . .' I stared at him. 'The fall . . .!'

'You must remember. We discussed it the other evening. When the Signora fell upon the stage.'

I could recall nothing of the kind.

'During her wonderful sleep-walking scene,' he went on. 'Naturally it brought your season to a premature end – '

'What about that young girl – lady?' I asked abruptly. 'A young lady?'

'You know her as well as I do, probably better. Her name was Leonora.' Ah! – I was suddenly remembering. 'Yes, she wanted me to engage her, did she not? She wished to play small parts, then longer parts; finally she sought to usurp my wife's place – '

'Dear friend,' said the Prefect, 'I would not ever presume to invade such intimate spheres of your life . . .'

'You lie!' I said, grasping at the straws of memory that now eluded me again to drive me frantic. 'You have robbed and betrayed me and now you even wish me to doubt my own reason.'

'Sir,' said the other, 'it is best that we part, lest our much-valued relationship should be damaged beyond repair. I wish you good night.' Cold and angry, he strutted away.

It was then that I saw her. She had been watching and listening, and looking at me with such love. Then she came and knelt down at my feet, took my hand and kissed it. And my hand quivered in the night air as if it had been touched by fire or ice.

I found myself thinking of that lost purse again. Its contents scavenged, stolen.

But her hand remained in mine, as I wandered with Leonora through the alleyways of that strange Venice which was not Venice. Over bridges we walked, past dank canals. Gargoyles stared down at us. Water lapped against ancient decomposing, sinking palaces . . .

At last we found ourselves at a café table. Yes – *that* table, that café. I was bewildered, enchanted. In a dream! Yet tightly wrapped, secure, in that dream.

'I can't understand,' I whispered to her. 'How can this be? *Are* you Leonora? It cannot be you.'

'Cannot?' she said, so softly.

'Cannot. Since all those years ago, you *died* – '

'Died?' echoed Leonora, with a touch of mockery.

'Even if my memory has deserted me – well, you look no older than you did then – not a day older – '

She smiled, ruefully, I thought.

Before she could speak, there was Stella again, to disturb me with her face so like another old flame – *or was it that friend of Charlotte's?* – and I thought: Does she want me, as she had wanted me long ago? But, to my relief, the whore took no further notice of me, or of Leonora, and went to join another old man at his table.

Once more I concentrated my thoughts and energies upon the lovely, long-lost creature sitting opposite me. 'You do not deny it – you *are* Leonora?' I breathed.

And she calmly rejoined: 'Indeed I am.'

'You are – ' I said in wonderment. 'You are . . .'

'As you are still the great Adrian Gall.'

'But then how can this be? Why are you – '

'Why am I here – with you?'

'Yes, in this café, among these women?'

She said: 'I am certainly not *among* them, my dear.'

My dear, my dear. How sweet it sounded. How good to be loved again . . . I reached for her hand.

'Things are not always what they seem,' she went on. 'Except for one thing. I love you. Still.'

I held her hand tightly, fearing it might burn me. Yet I was shivering.

'And you live here? Alone? In this city?'

'I am free to roam wherever I please. As free as you appear to be.'

Free? Yes, for suddenly I became aware that now at last I had freed myself from Charlotte.

'Yes,' I said. 'I see it now. It must have been you I came back to . . . to recover – you whom they took away from me – Oh, my dearest Leonora – ' And I gripped that hand of ice and fire even more tightly and kissed it.

A tiny smile played about her lips. 'Then we'll meet again tomorrow,' she said in a matter-of-fact voice. 'Wherever you are, I shall find you, beloved. Have no fear.'

And then she was gone.

I sat, deserted and desolate, afraid of death, but more afraid of life.

Stella, with the face I now finally recognized as that of my wife's best friend Regina, a former member of my company, with whom I had once long ago played at love, had strolled across to me. 'Old fool!' she snapped. 'Have you finished muttering to yourself? Now – ' Her voice softened professionally. 'Do you want a woman for a warm hour – for the night?'

I was tempted. I was so cold and afraid. But I was also repelled by this creature of the night, who seemed to belong to the past, a past I had now abandoned. I crept away as if haunted by a ghost, a ghost of old lusts. I heard Stella's mocking laugh and hastened away into the shadows of the dying city.

'*Leonora . . . Leonora . . .*'

What had been the most extraordinary encounter of my life was to become merely the first of many such meetings . . . indeed a never-ending embrace as sweetly satisfying as anything I had ever known. Sweet yet uncloying . . . without past or future . . . I felt reborn, as if new blood were surging through my veins. Leonora's passion drove out all my anxieties. Cured of my fears I now felt as young as my adorable mistress. For lover and mistress we were once more, Leonora and I, and our kisses obligingly melted away all the dread and guilt, the unaccountable rages upon waking, the compulsion to regain lost objects which mad dreams had exhorted me to find.

We lived the most extraordinary unearthly existence, Leonora and I. We spoke to no one, wished only to behold one another, simply lived from one encounter to the next. Leonora's love had invested us with an uncanny strength. When we were together we needed neither food nor drink; yet no wish, no task, no discipline was beyond instantaneous fulfilment. In long-forgotten caves and vaults that only she seemed to know, we held our timeless trysts, confident that nothing and no one could ever disturb the idyll. Here in our womb-like darkness, we celebrated life without remorse or apprehension, life without thought for others, life without memory . . . indeed – her love was so potent that it seemed to have extinguished all traces of the past in my brain, so that after a while I neither knew nor cared what had become of my family, or precisely how Leonora and I had met and parted all those years ago, or how long this love, sweet and timeless, could endure.

But neither in my intoxicated, dream-like state, nor in the nightmares that had preceded it and, alas, were to succeed it, could I have imagined the tragic and grotesque events that were so soon to restore dreaded reality and to end and mock my illusions.

One night we were together in a subterranean vault. I was leaning against a wall which was leprous with fungus. Leonora sat at my feet, while to the 'orchestral' background of dripping and flowing water, I was reciting Shakespearean verse, speeches from my old parts which had brought me fame, and which Leonora had taught me to speak in the Italian tongue.

As I declaimed, she laughed and clapped her hands. Then the foreign words deserted me; I reverted to English, and then back to Italian and suddenly, although the lines were fearful and tragic, we both collapsed with callous laughter. We were about to embrace, when the silence around us was cruelly broken. Revellers in carnival costume burst into the cave. They were crudely, grotesquely masked. They leaped and danced drunkenly and exchanged unimaginably coarse jokes. Were they so drunk that they couldn't see Leonora, I wondered, as I shrank back against the wall, repelled, half-afraid. One of the women touched me. She ripped off her mask and I was face to face with the detestable Stella – or was it Charlotte's friend Regina?

'Well!' she jeered drunkenly. 'It's you, the lonely Englishman, he who mutters to himself.' She turned to the others. 'Come away from here. He'll bequeath his disease to us, this one. Look, he's almost dead already. He's the gravestone upon his own fresh grave, the lonely greybeard who prefers to love alone.'

They all roared with cruel laughter and danced away. The festive music they had brought with them faded away. Only the dripping water continued its dirge.

'My love,' murmured Leonora, 'if you, too, could be rid of them for ever – '

'Rid of them? Of whom?'

'Those who think of themselves as men and women.'

'I can't understand. What are you trying to tell me, my love?'

'Don't brood on it. Let us remember that all life is a joke and what comes after it is funnier still.'

I looked at her then as if I had just seen her lovely face for the first time.

'Tell me,' I asked her, 'am I sleeping my life away? It seems I can no longer distinguish what is life and what is dream.'

'Then I have succeeded.' She was softly triumphant.

'I think I shall wake up at any moment now to find that I'm still an ambitious young travelling actor, merely *dreaming* of playing Macbeth one day, *dreaming* of success, and money, and love.'

'Let me teach you another play in Italian,' she murmured consolingly. 'Let me distract your mind – shall I be Rosalind? Viola?'

'No.' I was shivering with anguish. 'I have to know, Leonora! *Why didn't she see you?*'

Her eyes filled with tears.

'Why didn't Stella see you?' I demanded again. 'Why didn't any of them see you? They were drunk, I know, but not blind. And why do we seek out these strange places where, it seems, only I can see you?'

'Because,' she answered gently, 'I would frighten them, if they could see me.'

'Why?'

'Would not you, my dear lover, be terrified to see one who has been dead for so long?'

Dead . . . dead . . . dead echoed the dripping water.

'It was here, you see, in this city, those many years ago, that I did it,' Leonora continued. 'When I imagined that you, whom I worshipped and adored, had repulsed me. It was then that I swam out into the moonlit lagoon until the waters closed over my head, and I sank down, down into the dark. Oh, yes, my love – *you are my murderer.*'

My beloved was a ghost. I suppose I had guessed it all along but refused to consider it, because of the ecstasy of our love. Now, lost in a limbo between life and death, I slowly drew my dark cloak around me. Then – as if to

186

show that I too now wished to belong to her strange race – I placed the skull-mask over my face. Leonora held out her arms to me, but I turned away. I could not yet be entirely of her kind.

'I shall do it then,' I said to myself. 'Do what must still be done.'

As I hurried away, I looked back once at the watery vault. It was empty. There was no one.

Once more I slunk back to that crumbling bridge to seek out the damned Prefect of Police. 'Scum!' I flung at him as he emerged from a dark archway. 'Murderer!'

The fellow, though clearly startled by the Mask of Death, seemed to recognize my voice, and pretended to be amused.

'Signor Gall, I see you are rehearsing a new part? Then may I –'

'You may let me spit on you, thief, until you return that which you have taken from me.' The voice sounded mad to my own ears, but the Prefect remained infuriatingly calm.

'We both know I took nothing, sir. We both know that what you lost in this city was merely your own –'

'Don't say it!' I yelled at him, tearing the mask off my face. 'Don't speak this lie or you force me to kill you!'

'Listen,' said the other. 'You must listen. The threads of your memory have become tragically tangled. Think back, Signore, to that night when the young actress who loved you drowned herself. That same night, with your mind still clouded by your terrible conflict of being torn between two women, you set up that obstacle on the stage so that your wife would fall –'

'No! Slander! Falsehood! All of it!'

'You must hear the truth at last,' the Prefect went on steadily. 'You were then as you are now, in a condition of such mindless rage that you no longer knew what you were doing. It all happened so long ago, Signor Gall. Why do you not try to forgive yourself, as we, who understand, have forgiven you since?'

'You whore's son!' I cried, left totally bereft in my blind rage, 'You scum of the diseased canals! *You* dare accuse me of murder?'

'Have I not merely confirmed your fears, my friend?'

'Lies! All lies!' I struck him hard across the face. He staggered back – a little surprised, no more. Then he shrugged his shoulders and drew his pistol from his belt: 'You leave me no option, Signore.'

'No option? First you rob and slander me, and now you wish to kill me to eradicate all evidence of your evil.' I threw myself violently at the man. We fought and struggled together, swaying from one side of the bridge to the other. Beneath our shadows, the dark lethal water awaited one of us. Distantly I perceived that Leonora was watching. At last there was an anguished scream, and a body splashed into the water and the cries of a drowning man died away. For a shuddering moment, I beheld that ragged old crone again, toothless and withered but with Charlotte's face – unmistakably Charlotte's face. And then for a while a great blackness overwhelmed me and bore me away.

A long time later, I was again walking along the alleys and canals of Venice, confident that the good Prefect – oh God, why had I killed him? For what reason? — had by now expired in the foul waters, and that his bloated body would not be recovered until morning. I stopped and turned. And once more I sought protection and refuge in the love of my ghostly mistress. And that night I could find no alteration at all in the nature of the caresses with which she sought to overwhelm me . . .

Only my own person had undergone an unmistakable physiological change. The light of my love for Leonora shone undimmed, my renewed powers were undiminished. Yet all my bodily needs had suddenly – ceased. Even as dawn turned into day I felt neither hunger nor thirst, nor did I appear to need sleep. I seemed to be agreeably drugged, my mind at peace, and my body weightless. And though my person seemed to be absent from events, it appeared to be capable of controlling them. All I wanted was to lie close to my Leonora – to burrow with my ghostly love into an endless dream . . .

Yet as night now followed night without any perceptible interval of daylight, I appeared to be ineluctably drawn back to that horrible bridge, the Ponte delle Turchete, where – in defence of my person, gentlemen – I had dispatched the villainous Prefect of Police to his death.

As my ghostly love and I leant over the railings of the bridge, my gaze boring into the murky waters of that canal that contained the evidence of my heinous crime, I suddenly became aware of a third reflection in the water.

It was the Prefect of Police! He looked grave and thoughtful, as he strolled across the bridge, pausing only briefly to make a note in his notebook. Ignoring us both completely, he sauntered on.

I seized Leonora's shoulder. 'You saw? But – I killed him! I drowned him! You saw it!'

She smiled her over-sweet mysterious smile. 'Come, my love.' She took my hand and led me across the bridge, and I followed meekly, as if I were a little child.

Soon we were seated at our usual table at the café. Around us hurried the prostitutes, their clients and protectors in endless traffic. The carnival revellers were back, lewdly mocking each other, dancing obscenely, denying death and damnation. But they took no notice of us. And even as they brushed against me I felt nothing.

'Tell me,' I pleaded. 'I must know . . . just one more thing.'

'*Seek to know no more,*' Leonora said, quoting from . . . from *Macbeth*.

'*I will be satisfied,*' I quoted back defiantly. '*Deny me this and an eternal curse fall on you. Let me know –* '

I paused, as I could not remember the lines that followed.

'It goes: *Ay, sir, all this is so, but why stands Macbeth thus amazedly?*'

'I had forgotten, yet you remember.'

'Remember!' Her voice sounded sharper than I had ever heard it, strangely familiar, almost human. 'Remember it was I who played that dreary First Witch in *Macbeth* all those months – the only part she, your good wife, would allow me.'

'Yes, yes, I remember now. But I did promise you – '

'You promised me much!' she said bitterly.

'Leonora,' I stuttered, a silly, lost, middle-aged man, imprisoned in a banal emotional muddle, 'you always did know that I . . . that I loved you, but now – dearest, I simply cannot go on like this, drifting between – between wife and mistress – between Lady Macbeth and First Witch – between . . .'

'. . . A woman and a ghost?' she mocked.

'My dearest,' I begged. 'I implore you. Be kind to me. Try to understand. I must flee. Don't you see? I can no longer stay in this city. I'm in such terrible danger. The police – '

'Poor man. But why precisely must you "flee"?' Her voice was again edged with sharpness, with evil. 'Do you still imagine you killed the Prefect of Police? Is that it?'

'Of course it is. You saw me do it.'

'Did I? Then look over there.' And she pointed to a man sitting at a nearby table, in the midst of the revellers, clearly enjoying himself. And Stella, the whore, was caressing him. It was the Prefect himself.

'Why do you look so horrified?' Leonora asked harshly. 'You saw him before, did you not? On the Ponte delle Turchete!'

'I did — think I saw – it – '

'What's "it"? His spirit? His ghost? Say it!'

'No – why do you torture me so, my love?'

'But there he is! Touch him. He's as real as any mortal, and as mortal as any living man.'

A wave of relief flooded over me. 'So it was a dream! I didn't kill him after all!'

'Poor fool, of course not,' she said, her eyes widening as she added: '*He* killed *you*.' Briefly she smiled with the simple joy of victory, the smile of the small-part actress who had finally obtained the leading role. Then she became my angel again, my heavenly companion. 'And now,' she said, 'now we can be together for ever. And ever. Alone. Together. Forever. Isn't that what love is?'

The celebrating crowd had suddenly vanished. A gust of fresh night wind blew across the terrace of the empty café. But then I saw that a shape had formed itself at a remote table. There she sat again, the old crone, toothlessly grinning and watching. The Angel of Death. With Charlotte's face . . .

We crept away from the table, Leonora and I. Already,

gradually, we were turning into an old couple. Old ghosts . . . We wandered about the City of Death, tired and defeated, like beggars of the night. We crawled into the old vaults that were rejected by the living, and groped our way along the ground like dying rats. Yet we were not dying, and knew we could never die, having become eternal wanderers in an endless night.

My dear wife long ago gave up all hope of my return, though sometimes, even now, I often feel observed. Even as a ghost, I feel watched, spied upon, by someone who could be, might be, one of *us* . . .

Can you imagine what it must feel like to live eternally, invisibly, without purpose, without form, without desire? No, gentlemen, you cannot imagine! For it is to try to discover such feelings that you come here, is it not? Do you not seek the ultimate horror in this Club of the Damned! The frisson of something worse than death, worse even than the fear of death . . .!

In the drawing-room of the House on the River, there was a deep silence. The members seemed stunned.

But although his tale was told, it seemed that Adrian Gall had more to say.

'Listen,' he said.

A smell had crept into the room. A smell of stagnant water and fungoid growths, of excrement and decay, of rotting flesh and deadly sweat. A fearful, sickening smell.

'Listen,' said the voice again. 'I hope that you are satisfied — but how I despise you, with your gloating faces — you who relish the sufferings of others while living life at second-hand yourselves. I expect even your dreams are second-hand. Leonora, my hateful beloved and I — we despise you. We laugh at you. We, the undead, have only this kind of laughter on which to feed. You think you are immune from hell, because you relish stories of its horrors with twisted lasciviousness! But can you not smell us, can you not sense our dreadful presence in the very air about you?'

The voice ceased suddenly; there was a sudden interruption. A lackey had crept into the room to whisper into the Chairman's ear, and to hand him a letter which had just been delivered. The

Chairman ripped it open, and the lackey held a candelabrum aloft so that he could read the writing.

'I shall read this note to you, gentlemen,' said the Chairman. It says: "Mr Adrian Gall regrets that for reasons of his indisposition he is forced to cancel his engagement with you tonight. He begs the members of your worthy establishment to excuse and forgive his — absence".'

The man's face turned ashen. The letter fluttered from his hand.

'Absence?' he repeated. 'Absence???'

All eyes turned to where Adrian Gall had been standing only a moment ago. They found themselves staring at empty space. And then the laughter began. It did not come from the members' lips, but crawled out from the stench and mist around them. It was the mocking laughter of the undead, damning all those present whose mad presumption had permitted them to call their unholy group the Club of the Damned.